TOURNAMENT OF SHADOWS

Pauline E Dungate started her career writing playlets to entertain her siblings with a cut-out puppet theatre. Later, and like many potential writers, she and a group of friends created new scenarios for favourite TV characters. When she went to Aston in Birmingham University to read for a Combined Honours Degree in Chemistry and Geology, she showed a friend one of her stories and was directed to the newly formed Aston SF Group. That introduced her to conventions and other people that read SF and wanted to write it. Her first published story appeared in *Imagine* magazine in 1984. Since then she has had nearly 40 other stories published as well as poetry.

In 201 she co-edited *Something Remains* with Peter Coleborn, a tribute volume to Joel Lane.

As Pauline Morgan, she has penned a very large number of reviews for SFCrowsnest, the British Fantasy Society, the Birmingham SF Group, and is responsible for a number of articles in American academic publications.

She lives in Birmingham with husband Chris Morgan. In the summer she is often found counting butterflies for Butterfly Conservation, or in the garden.

TOURNAMENT OF SHADOWS

PAULINE E DUNGATE

Published by
The Alchemy Press, Staffordshire, UK
www.alchemypress.co.uk

CONTENTS

ACKNOWLEDGMENTS

Fandom has played a large part in the development of my writing and without the Aston SF Group and then the Birmingham SF Group I would never have met the people who encouraged me to keep writing. I am immensely grateful to Lisanne Norman, Joel Lane, Peter Coleborn and Theresa Derwin who have believed in my writing. I am also glad that the Milford Writers Conference exists to help point out the flaws in my work.

Most of all, though, I am very pleased with my choice of husband, Chris Morgan, who continues to encourage and help find my typos and doesn't object when I spend hours alone in my study. Thank you all, and especially Chris.

INTRODUCTION

This collection by Pauline E Dungate covers genres from horror to poetry to fantasy, and features stories situated in the author's hometown of Birmingham, to the edge of the Andes, the Namibian desert, India and beyond. Pauline's range is geographically wide and her thematic focus, too, is expansive, dealing with the vagaries of human psychology – need, desire, hatred and revenge – as much as it does the supernatural.

Her sense of place is detailed and evocative, whether she's writing about Birmingham's mean streets ("In the Tunnels" and "The Magic Roundabout" among others), or the South Coast around Shoreham ("Night Hunter" and "Plant Hunter"), or the twilight, flooded city of Venice ("Angelo's Bar"), or one of the many other global locations in which her writing is set (she is, I know, a seasoned traveller). But perhaps Pauline's work best reflects the multi-cultural nature of modern Birmingham, a city which has a strong history of the fantastic in literature, to which this collection is a worthy addition.

There is a distinctively noir sensibility in many of these stories: a number of them cannot be said to end well, for the author does not flinch from gritty supernaturality and its terrifying consequences. Her settings are often downbeat and her characters frequently make the wrong choices, sometimes against their own volition, such as Lucy in "Skylight", but Pauline is not afraid of the unsympathetic protagonist.

Yet the reader does not rejoice when these characters falter: redemption is always a possibility. When reading a number of these tales, I was struck by the possibility that the story could have been told from other perspectives, such as in "Nina". In this Birmingham/Indian arranged-marriage tale, the point of view could easily and more sympathetically have been that of Nina herself, but Pauline has made a bolder choice, one which is characteristic of her work. But there are protagonists whom we might embrace, too, such as the empathetic Cameron in the haunting "Red Slave", with its historical background of slavery amid the salt pans and oppression by the Dutch.

The shapeshifter stories, some of which feature recurring characters, are lighter in tone than the earlier horror, but the sense of place and character tension remain strong. This is a collection in which humans are prey as much as they are also hunters, and not only other humans, either. In "Away With the Fairies", it is not made clear to the reader quite where the danger to the cave rescue team might lie, opening up a number of disturbing possibilities, and in several of these stories the ending is left to the reader's imagination – although you would need to be singularly optimistic to envisage a wholly positive outcome.

The poetry included in this collection also shares features with the fiction: "Devolution" is a take on Saturday night in the city centre, and Birmingham's history features strongly in "Birmingham Mythic". But there's an admirably concise ghost story in poetic form here, too, as well as the moving titular poem which rounds of this collection, "A Tournament of Shadows", and which visits the World Wars and their impact on the city.

Harrowing, haunting and strange, Pauline's new collection stands out as a testament both to place and to imagination. It will make you think long after you've finished reading.

— Liz Williams

IN THE TUNNELS

The platform of Birmingham's Moor Street Station was crowded. Late shoppers and office workers stood crushed together, waiting for the Leamington train. Bernie, who wanted the one that followed, stood out of the way near the mouth of the tunnel. It fascinated him, this dark cavern that ran under the city and disgorged trains at regular intervals. He had walked through it once, just before they reopened the rail link between Moor Street and Snow Hill, the station at its far end, but there had been too many people on that special trek for him to be fully able to appreciate its echoing magnificence.

Just a minute or so before the train arrived there was a disturbance. Shouting distracted Bernie from his contemplation of underground places. As he turned he saw a ripple of movement and a child-sized figure belting along the platform towards him, weaving and barging between commuters. Vaguely recognising the cries of "stop thief!", Bernie prepared to make a grab for the boy. The child slowed, grinned at him, and leapt onto the rails.

"Ilyas!" Bernie would have plunged after him if someone hadn't grabbed him from behind.

The figure disappeared into the tunnel moments before the lights of the train became visible round the curve in the track. He tensed, waiting for the impact. But the carriages drew quietly into the station. Doors banged open as passengers scrambled for seats, emptying the platform of all but those waiting for the Stratford train, a small knot of people halfway along.

"D'ya know the kid, sir?" the porter who had

restrained him asked Bernie.

"Yes… No… It couldn't have been," he stuttered.

"But yer got a good look?"

"Yes, but…"

"An' yer'd know 'im agin."

"I think so."

"Could yer come an' 'ave a word with the station manager, then?"

Bernie glanced at the clock. The yellow numbers flicked over to show 17:39, one minute to his train. His mother would hardly notice if he was late for tea. She never did. "If you think I can help," he said.

There was a policeman in the station manager's office when they finally showed him in. A tearful woman was being led out as he entered.

"Now, young man, the constable would like you to answer a few questions, if you don't mind."

Bernie nodded and gave his name and address.

"Do you know the bag-snatcher?" the policeman asked.

"No. He just looked a bit like someone I knew at school."

"What was his name?"

"Ilyas. I can't remember his other name. He was in my class, that's all."

"This lad was about twelve," the manager said.

That's why it couldn't be him, Bernie thought. He wouldn't recognise most of the kids from school, just the few he saw sometimes down the market, like Javad, who'd nick things off the stall if he wasn't watching, or Shazad, who had a club foot. In six years, Ilyas was sure to have grown a bit, and changed.

The phone rang partway through the interview. The manager listened, nodding his head from time to time.

When he cradled the receiver he spoke to the constable. "He hasn't come out at Snow Hill yet. And none of the drivers have seen anyone on the track."

The policeman wrote it down in his notebook.

Finally they let Bernie go, just in time to catch the 18:40, the manager saying, "Thank you so much for your help, young man."

It was dark and raining when the train pulled out of the station. Bernie sat staring at his reflection in the window, seeing the round grinning face of Ilyas as he passed under the bridges that muted the sound of the carriage wheels. Whoever the boy was, he couldn't have disappeared.

~~~

Bernie found himself searching crowds for familiar faces, especially those pushing their way through the market towards the subway leading to the station. He found it easy to superimpose features on his customers at the fruit stall. Once he was sure he caught sight of the small dark-haired figure of Ilyas disappearing behind an unloading lorry. When the boy re-emerged he could see clearly that it wasn't. But from the back...

"Stop daydreaming, lad. We've got customers," his boss told him.

Bernie blinked and stared down at the change he was clasping tightly. He grinned nervously and handed it to the old lady who counted the coins carefully before stowing them in her purse.

"Where's me oranges?" she said.

Bernie passed her the bag, thankful that no-one could see his blushes.

"I don't know what's got into you recently, lad," his boss said later when they were clearing away. "You've been a pretty good worker up till now. Don't spoil it."

Bernie gave himself a mental shake and resolved to concentrate.

At the station, Bernie took to standing as close to the tunnel entrance as he could. He remembered the station master's words about the boy not coming out at the other end. There were caverns under Birmingham, he had heard. Vast concrete hangers where they had stored supplies in the war. Perhaps there was a way in through the tunnel, but he couldn't remember seeing any side branches on the day he had walked through.

~~~

Bernie decided that he had to go through the tunnel again. Instead of heading for Moor Street as he usually did, he set off across town, deliberately choosing a round-about route to take him through as many underpasses as possible. He liked the enclosed spaces and wished there were fewer people around. He wanted to hear his own footsteps rebound from the walls.

There was a busker in the one leading to the mainline station, a bald elderly violinist whose squeaky music followed him as he passed. He walked through Old Square. They were just locking the basement doors to Lewis's. He could see the security man of the department store through the heavy plate glass as he slid the bolts into place. Then down the ramp and past the toilets.

He hadn't realised there were so many small men in the city centre. There was another of them leaning on a broom in the entrance to the gents; he looked like a gnome.

Bernie glanced at his watch and began to hurry. He didn't want to miss the train.

The trip was a little disappointing. He managed to get a seat at the front so that he could see through the driver's cab and out onto the track, but it was difficult to watch both sides at once. There were lights strung all along the tunnel, and although he could see the shadows of archways set into the walls he missed any dark opening leading away.

~~~

Under Colmore Circus, he saw Ilyas again. Bernie had taken to staying later and later in the market area, taking the most circuitous route he could devise to the station, and lingering in the empty subways. Some were shabby and rubbish-filled and stank of urine. Others had murals painted on them or incised in the tiles. He was surprised how little graffiti was added to those pictures, the street artists seeming to confine their efforts to the railway, scarring the walls along the lines with their spray-on paint.

Sometimes the subway would open out into an oasis of green. The walls of the Horsefair had a delicate mosaic depicting the old market, and plants grew unmolested in the centre. Bernie had almost forgotten his search for Ilyas in his growing delight with the variety of underground passages. Then he saw him. The small figure had his back to him as he crossed the open space under the traffic island. Ilyas disappeared behind a supporting pillar. Bernie hurried after him.

"Ilyas!" he called.

The boy stopped and turned. Ilyas was exactly as he had been six years before, when they had both walked out of school for the last time. They had never been friends, and Bernie remembered him most for his broken front teeth and the fact that he only ever seemed to wear Wellies to school.

"It is Ilyas, isn't it?" Bernie said.

Ilyas grinned.

"It's me. Bernie Robinson. From school."

"Hi," Ilyas said.

"What are you doing these days?" It was an inane question but Bernie couldn't think of anything else to say. He couldn't very well ask if he'd been stealing handbags.

Ilyas shrugged. "Working for my uncle."

"I've got a job in the market," Bernie said. "Selling fruit."

"That's nice. See you around." And Ilyas disappeared into the shadows so quickly that Bernie hardly saw him go. Bernie started after him, reluctant to lose him after all this time; but the doorway he thought Ilyas had gone through was a locked service duct. Bernie looked round expecting to see Ilyas hurrying up one of the ramps. There was a movement to his left that quickly stilled when he turned that way, and an echo which might have been laughter or the tail end of a whistled tune. The only person in sight was an old tramp that Bernie was now used to seeing around town. He believed he slept on the steps outside the Nat West bank.

~~~

People didn't disappear into walls. Only ghosts did that and Bernie didn't believe in ghosts. Ilyas was real. The more he thought about it, the more he was convinced that there was a way underground. Probably several ways.

If graffiti artists could get onto the railway line, Bernie reasoned, then so could he. He bought himself the most powerful torch he could find, with a pocketful of spare batteries, and caught the last bus into town, choosing Saturday night for his exploration after the trains had ceased to run on the branch line.

The subways, now totally deserted, resounded to the echoes of his feet. Bernie was torn between increasing the resonance of the sounds by stamping his feet, and keeping quiet as he was about to break the law.

The station was locked up as expected but next to the old part was a rutted car-parking lot surrounded by a high chain-link fence. He glanced around quickly before sauntering in through the gate. He had expected to have to climb the swaying fence but it lay trampled in the dirt by other feet. He crossed boldly. To his left the old part of the station was secured from intruders, the fencing topped with vicious twists of barbed wire.

Bernie stepped over the rusting rails and walked round, past the sign which warned NO PASSENGERS BEYOND THIS POINT, until he stood between the rails looking into the maw of the tunnel.

It was lightless, a solid wall of dark facing him. Beckoning. His heart thudded with excitement, and fear. Bernie took two steps inside, then another two. The sound of the gravel beneath his feet was loud but muffled, as though the black air tried to erase his presence while the curved walls wanted to advertise it. He felt everything was being focused on him.

He looked back and was reassured by the paler arch that marked the cavernous mouth, an orange-tinted grey fed by the lights of the city above. Bernie switched on his torch and began to walk slowly, swinging the beam from side to side, scanning the soot-coloured brickwork for doorways, anything that would suggest a way further underground. A rat, startled by the light, scuttled along the wainscot and vanished into a recess. Bernie ran his hands over the brickwork, hunting for an opening. Nothing.

He went on. At one point he switched off the torch and just stood. The darkness was total. Out of sight of either tunnel mouth it enfolded him gently. Far above he could hear the occasional rumble of passing cars. There was the odd tick of metal and mortar contracting. Bernie shivered.

It was cooler than he had expected. It was supposed to get warmer, the further you went underground.

He found it almost by accident. A streamer of paper had caught on the cable that was strung between the lamps. It stirred, as if on a breeze, as the torch beam flashed past it. Bernie looked upwards, expecting to see some shaft burrowing from the roof to the surface and creating an eddy. There was none. Neither was there a discernible wind through the tunnel itself. He stood still, wondering if his own movements had caused the fluttering. But, no – the strip still jigged about in the torchlight.

Bernie crouched next to it, feeling for the air stream. He traced it to a crack at the base of the wall in another of the alcoves. He pushed tentatively. The brickwork seemed solid until he tapped it. It had a hollow ring. There was no catch he could see. He pushed harder, in all the places and directions he could think of.

He grinned in the darkness as a panel slipped suddenly sideways. He shone the torch through the opening. It was a service passage running parallel with the tunnel and connected by a short linking corridor, five paces long. Cables and pipes stretched in both directions, but there was room for a small man to move carefully between them.

He jumped as the door slid and snicked back into place. He felt a momentary rise of panic as his beam caught the blank, closed wall. A quick check showed how easy it was to open again.

Bernie turned right, hopefully towards Snow Hill. It was damp here, condensation forming and dripping from the ducts to form intermittent puddles. Some pipes gurgled with the passage of water through them.

There was a grill in the wall a little way along that

concertinaed like the doors of old-fashioned lifts. Peering through, Bernie could see steps spiralling down. The passage was tiled in pale blue. It reminded him of the steps leading down to the lower levels of some of London's Underground stations. He'd spent a week's holiday there two years ago haunting the network and wishing he could follow the trains that burrowed into the earth like giant worms.

The gate was held by a rusted padlock. Bernie stared longingly into the inviting gloom before searching for something to break it with. The penknife he always carried was too flimsy, the blade bending as he twisted it in the catch. He needed a more sturdy length of metal, like a screwdriver. He cast around for something suitable without much hope. The piece of wood he found snapped the moment he applied force.

Bernie tugged viciously at the padlock in his frustration. The loop snapped. It lay in the palm of his hand for a few moments before he realised what had happened. Then he carefully put it in his pocket. Passing through the gate he pulled it almost closed behind him, satisfied that he could get out easily.

His footsteps echoed, bouncing and reflecting from the curving walls, continuing after he stopped. It was almost as if there were someone before and behind him.

There was someone behind him. Another pair of shoes keeping time with him. But not quite. The click of the heels was slightly different to the slap of his trainers.

"Who's there?" Bernie called. The cry stretched. Amplified by the stairs, it was returned to him altered: "hoos sair".

Bernie dithered, knowing he was trespassing. As long as he remained still, so did the other. He tried tiptoeing down, then flashing the torch suddenly behind him, miscalculated and bashed it against the wall. The light flickered.

"You don't scare me," he whispered into the darkness.

"Scairee," it came back.

The torch went out, the bulb broken.

"Scairee," the echo repeated.

Bernie froze. Being underground wasn't quite so much fun anymore.

He started to creep back up the steps, fingers of one hand touching the tiles, the other holding the torch up as a club.

He encountered no-one.

He stumbled on the top step and sprawled across the floor hitting his head on the gate. He hauled himself to his feet and pulled at the grid. It didn't move. He tugged again. And heard laughing. He thought it was just the gurgle in the pipes above him, but it continued. Chuckling at first, then louder. A demented sound. Bernie shook and rattled the gate.

"Let me out," he shouted.

"Ow, ow, ow," came the reply from behind him.

He clasped his hands over his ears to shut out the sounds.

He could wait, he thought, wait until morning. Until someone came.

But perhaps no-one ever came.

He brushed a tickle from his cheek. It was wet. A tear. He wiped his face on his sleeve. Men didn't cry. And there must be another way. Besides, whoever it was had been behind him.

Without light, Bernie picked his way down the stairs again, feeling for every step with his toes before committing himself. It made his legs ache. But there were no echoes.

As he descended he became aware that he could see. Not clearly. Just the dim outline of his outstretched hand. There were lights below. People.

Bernie stopped. People had locked him in. His throat was dry, his head sore and he could smell his own sweat. He edged round the last bend.

It wasn't much of a light. A pale glowing in the distance, its source blocked by a dark shadow. Bernie sank down, his back to the wall, shivering. He was in a cavern, he realised, the roof held up by massive columns.

The wartime caverns. Now empty. What was it he'd read in the newspaper? If the idea was to convert them into a huge bus depot then there must be another way out. And the light must be a bonfire lit by vagrants. They would know.

Bernie bent his head to rest on his knees. To calm down. To still the fear. He would walk across to them. Warm himself, ask the way. It was nothing to get fretted about.

He moved forward before he saw them. Grey figures stooping over a pile of burning sticks. One picked up a brand, straightened. He was no taller than a twelve-year-old boy. None of them were. Slowly they all reached for the flaming torches. The flames illuminated just their faces. They were round and wrinkled and ugly. Like goblins.

One smiled. His teeth were small and sharp and pointed. Bernie spun round. They were behind him too. He panicked.

He screamed. He ran, heedless of the fact that he couldn't see.

He hit a pillar with his shoulder. He held his arms out before him and ran into another.

~~~

"Bernie, Bernie." Someone was shaking his shoulder.

"The alarm's not gone off," he muttered, trying to pull the blankets over his head. There weren't any. He was cold.

"Bernie."

His head throbbed. His shoulder ached and there was pain in one of his wrists. He knew his eyes were open but he couldn't see.

"It's Ilyas, Bernie. Do you remember me?"

"I can't see you," Bernie said.

"What are you doing here?" Ilyas asked again. There was a babble of unintelligible voices around him.

"Exploring," Bernie said.

One of the other people spoke to him. He couldn't understand. Ilyas answered in his own tongue, then in English. "I've told them we were at school together. That they cannot have you."

"What do you mean?" The feeling of panic was coming back, seeping through the pain of his hurts. He remembered the leering faces, the pointed, eager teeth.

"You must go," Ilyas said. "Can you stand?"

"I'm locked in. Someone locked the gate." He heard himself whining.

"I'll show you the way." Ilyas put his arm under Bernie's shoulder and helped him to his feet. Bernie swayed, disorientated. He felt invisible walls pressing in on him and the weight of Birmingham descending slowly to crush him. He whimpered.

The voice in the darkness spoke again, sharply, insistently. Ilyas again replied and began to lead Bernie forward. He felt hands pawing him, long nails touching his face. Ilyas spoke and they withdrew. Bernie could hear their feet shuffling after them and somewhere the squeaky sound of a violin began to play. It was a dirge.

They splashed into water which became deeper, soaking his trainers and numbing his legs inside wet trousers. The sound changed as though they were entering a narrow, enclosed space.

"This is the river Rea," Ilyas said. "It runs underground here, down through Digbeth."

"What're you doing here?" Bernie asked partly to drown the scuffles of their followers. He felt slightly safer now. The air around was warmer, though it smelt a little of sewage.

"I live here. My people always have. We steal from above when we have to, and eat what comes down to us."

"But we were at school together."

"Times change. We have to adapt."

Progress was slow. Bernie staggered when he tried to walk unaided. He blundered into the tunnel wall. Pain shot up his arm from the damaged wrist. He leant heavily on Ilyas, though it was uncomfortable due to the other's lack of stature. There were splashings and squealings from the water.

"Just rats," Ilyas said, "squabbling over food."

Bernie shuddered. He would feel happier if he could see the animals. Something soft brushed by him. Far behind he thought he heard howling, the kind that could emanate from human throats.

Then Bernie could see. The end of the tunnel was a small orange-grey circle in the distance. It looked much too tiny for him to get through. The shaft they were traversing began to narrow. Old brick was replaced by smooth concrete. The water, concentrated into the compressed space was deeper, swirled faster, tugging at his legs.

"You will have to crawl," Ilyas said. "There was no time to fetch the raft."

He tried, but his wrist gave way, throwing him into the water. He screamed with pain and swallowed foul tasting liquid. He surfaced spluttering and sobbing.

"I can't," he said.

"You must. I can't keep them away for ever. There's a grid at the end but it lifts up easy. I used to come this way to school most days."

Bernie dragged himself through the tube. Cold and soaked, he kept watching the patch of light.

Ilyas started back the other way whispering a hasty, "Goodbye."

~~~

Bernie peered through bars set about nine inches apart. Beyond them the river ran between steep banks, above which were silhouetted buildings outlined by sodium lights. The fringes of the water were studded with the debris of city life. He could hear the noise of an occasional car.

A piece of chicken wire stretched across the bottom of the bars, catching paper, twigs and gnawed bones as the river flowed out of the culvert. The gate itself was recently repaired and held in place by shiny, new bolts. By reaching through, he could just reach them. He had drawn one when he heard the snuffling behind him, and a whispering. He stretched for the other. Refusing to glance behind, he stared out at freedom, and at the four men who were walking towards him.

A streetlamp created a brighter pool of light, illuminating the round wizened faces and the pointed teeth.

A MOTHER'S LOVE

I watched the news today. No sound came to me through the toughened glass of the TV Rental shop, but I knew what they were talking about. It grieved me, casting a shadow on my present happiness because I knew what that mother was going through. It had happened to me once. Losing a child can seem like the end of the world.

I don't have much – there is just me and the baby. I follow the news by picking up discarded papers from park benches and scavenge around the markets for food. It's surprising what drops from the stalls during the day, but they say a vegetarian diet is good for you. I hope so. It is important I keep healthy, for her sake.

My first baby was taken away from me even before she had a chance to live. The saddest thing was that I wasn't even able to hold her. It was because I didn't have a boyfriend then. At least, that's what my mother said. All babies must have fathers. But we're getting on all right without one at the moment. I don't really see what fathers are for – they can't feed the baby and I would have got on better without mine.

At the start I didn't know what was happening to me. The curse has always been irregular. When it didn't come I shrugged. It would be back in a month or so and meantime there was no mess, no gripping bellyache and no furtive washing of underwear because I didn't want my mum to see the stains. It didn't worry me when I got sick or didn't want to eat. But when she kicked, I knew there was a miracle inside me. It was my secret. I began to dream of how it would be when she was in my arms.

Then my dad found out. It was one of those nights when Mum was took bad. I'd seen the signs of a spell coming on as she'd left the empty bottles behind the sofa for me to clear away. In better times, she manages to put them out for the dustman herself. She'd passed out downstairs so I'd gone up early. It was a hot night so I lay with just a sheet over me, thinking about the baby and stroking my belly. It was beginning to swell nicely but under my normal shapeless jumpers and T-shirts no-one had noticed.

I heard Dad come in. He'd been at the Perry Barr stadium. He always goes there Thursday nights. He and Uncle George have got shares in a greyhound. It's called Plastic Paddy and it wins sometimes. He must have lost that night cos he was shouting at Mum. I knew she wouldn't answer. Once she's gone nothing can stir her till morning. So he gave it up as a bad job and came after me. He's done it before, lots of times. I don't mind and usually he's quite gentle. This time, though, he must have noticed something because when he'd finished he put his hand on the baby. She kicked him.

He didn't say a word, just pulled his belt from its loops and hit me. The first blow landed across my belly. I curled up small to protect her. My back and shoulders were sore afterwards and I cried. Last time he belted me cos I'd taken a fiver from Mum's purse, but this time I couldn't understand what I'd done. I thought he would've been pleased.

No-one spoke to me for five days, but I heard the whisperings.

"It's got to go," Mum told me.

At first I didn't see what she meant. I carried on nibbling the piece of dry toast that was all I could manage for breakfast, and shrugged.

"We've made all the arrangements."

"What arrangements?"

Dad came into the kitchen then. "Are you ready?" he said. "We mustn't be late."

"For what?" I asked.

"I've made the appointment. Come on."

He did give me a minute to collect my purse and change my shoes, but he was fretting all the while. He was even worse as we waited at the bus-stop, keeping a hand on my elbow and peering anxiously round the shelter for the first sight of a bus turning the distant corner.

He took me to an ordinary terraced house in Kings Heath. It had a neat pocket of front garden and a door painted in royal blue. The net curtains at the windows looked clean and bright. Definitely a smarter house than the one we lived in.

"Why are we here?" I asked as Dad rang the bell.

"To get things sorted," he said.

The lady who answered the door could have been any one of the older teachers from school. She was that kind. Neat like the house, her short hair permed and coloured. Dad ushered me inside and the lady led us up the stairs to what I suppose was the back bedroom. It had a reclining chair in it, like the ones at the dentists, and a vanity unit in the corner. The lady gave me a cup of something to drink.

"What is it?" I asked.

"Just something to make you relax."

"I don't want it. Why are we here, Dad?"

"Don't make a fuss, girl," he said. "Drink up."

His voice had that edge to it that meant that if I didn't obey I'd feel his belt next. The liquid was sweet and bitter at the same time and there was brandy in it. I don't drink much but I do like a brandy when I can get someone to buy one for me. This mixture made me feel woozy. The lady guided me to the chair. Dad stood behind me, holding my shoulders. She hiked my skirt up round my waist and pulled down my knickers.

"What're you doing?" I asked. I could hear my words slurring and my limbs felt heavy.

She didn't answer me but said to Dad, "It's big. You should have come sooner."

Dad just growled, "Get on with it."

I was too lethargic to move. I don't really know what she did. I only felt the sharp pain and the cramps that went on and on. I tried to scream but couldn't. And when it was over, my baby was dead. I could forgive my dad a lot of things but not that. I bled for a week and when the ache in my empty womb had gone, I left. I had no-where to go and I've never been back. They can't make me. Especially now I have this little darling. I feel so sorry for that mother who has had her baby stolen. I think, It could have been me.

When she first came, she cried a lot. So I wrapped her well and rocked her. I put her to my breast and she sucked so hard she made my nipples sore. Her little face would screw up in sleep; it's impossible not to love her. I don't understand how some people can be so cruel to babies. I won't risk them taking her away from me.

We live in a dilapidated house in Ladywood, one of a terrace that has been boarded up for months. I suppose they will eventually knock them down but for the moment they do as shelter for the likes of me. I keep clear of the end house. It is a hangout for junkies and glue-sniffers. Next door are a couple of winos, harmless to anyone but themselves. The old woman fell downstairs yesterday and only the dozens of cardigans she wears saved her from injury.

I had to come here. I couldn't stay in the hostel. Not with a baby. They would've taken her away and I couldn't have that. And I didn't want to sleep on the streets. I did that when I left home. It was the most miserable time I ever spent. The first night I slept under a bench in Cannon Hill Park. The smell of piss and dogshit made me feel ill and if I hadn't been so hungry I would've thrown up.

The second night I shivered in a shop doorway in the city centre. I'd tried the steps outside the NatWest Bank down Dale End first but a smelly old tramp moved me on. It was his spot, he said. I was less tolerant then and focused my resentment on him. I waited until he was snoring then crept up and kicked his head in. My Doc Martins crunched satisfyingly into his face. If my mum and dad had been there instead of him I would have enjoyed it even better. It was their fault I was cold and hungry with no-where to go.

When you're desperate, you learn to survive. Too many people put their bags down while they're distracted by a shop-assistant selling perfume. It easy to snag something as you brush past, specially in a crowded store. Some actually leave their purses on top of their shopping. You'd think they'd know better. The trick, then, is not to leave the shop with the purse. Cash is virtually untraceable. And in the crowds of the Bull Ring it's even easier. In the jostle between the stalls, they don't notice as you lift the food they've just bought, and vanish. And I soon found the flops where the homeless doss. Old buildings mostly, derelict and dangerous but offering more cover than a doorway or a bus-shelter.

I lived like that for about three months before I got caught shoplifting in Marks & Spencers food hall. They found me a social worker and a place in a hostel. The hostel was fine, the social worker was shitty, a wet blanket who insisted I call him Tony. He kept trying to get me to admit that my situation was caused by childhood trauma – his words, not mine. I think he wanted me to say that my father had raped me and my mother was an alcoholic. True, but I wasn't going to tell him that. I feigned indifference to his questions. He did teach me, though, how to claim benefit. Not that that's much good to me at the moment. If I go to sign on they'll insist on knowing where I'm living and take my baby away. It's part of the terms of my probation that I live in the hostel and I've broken that. I got twelve months, suspended, for the shoplifting, and a probation officer. She's supposed to meet me once a week but she's too busy with worse cases than me. The most I got was a message at the hostel, saying to ring her so she could say we'd had contact. I couldn't be bothered, so it might be some time before she realises I'm gone. The people who run the hostel haven't the time to care.

Once I knew I was going to have a baby, I saved as much from my benefit as I could and made a little extra on the streets, begging and suchlike. I knew I'd need money for things like nappies but I didn't like the idea of selling my body. I did it a few times when I was really desperate but I don't like it. A quick screw in a shop doorway isn't my idea of fun and I wouldn't want my baby to grow up thinking I was that kind of person.

As I stood watching the silent screens, I thought about what to call my baby. I hadn't given her a name yet. I liked Natasha. It's what I'd planned to call the one they took away. But seeing that poor mother, I wondered if Lucille would be better, after the missing baby. I turned away, tasting the name on my tongue, seeing how it would sound. Lucille. It didn't seem quite right, almost as if I were stealing someone else's joy. Lucy, perhaps. I must get back to her. I don't like leaving her alone but there are times when I can't take her with me. She is a very good baby. She doesn't make much noise and she sleeps a lot.

~~~

Those two boys have spoilt everything. I just hope no-one thinks to look in here, so we can go home as soon as it's dark.

Lucy is such a lovely baby. There is no way they can make me give her up now, though they'll try to take her away. They won't see how well I can care for her, only the damp, cold squat we live in and the fact that it has no water or electricity. They can't see that a mother's love is the most important thing a baby can have, and all mine is for Lucy.

I know babies cry a lot and Lucy did, to begin with. She was always hungry, crying, feeding and sleeping – an endless cycle of. She was only quiet when she was at my breast or sleeping. Often when I put her down she would wake and call for my attention. It was almost as if she was afraid I would abandon her. She couldn't know I'd never do that. Those first few days, the only way I could sleep was to cuddle her. I'd hold her so her bare skin was warm against mine and wrap a blanket around both of us. It was a good thing I'd got in loads of food because I couldn't risk going far from her.

After a while she settled. She'd sleep for longer periods and between times, lie quietly. I'm sure she followed me with those big blue eyes of hers. She'd dream sometimes. I would hear her whimper in her sleep, the same way a dog does when it's dreaming of chasing rabbits. What babies dream of? Once she settled I could leave her a while. I didn't like to but I couldn't take her with me. It's difficult to move quickly when you are carrying a bundle and I couldn't afford to get caught again. For her sake.

All went fine. Then I made a mistake. Two in fact. To begin with Lucy smelt wonderful – like milk and sunshine. But it's difficult to wash nappies with no running water. I do my best to keep her clean and sweet smelling but after about three weeks I realised I had a problem. The flies noticed first. They would run over her little face, quite unharmed. She'd blink them away or cry when they tickled too much but she got used to them. I'd come back and find a dozen of the vile things settled on her cheeks. However much I shooed them off, they were ready to alight the moment I turned away.

When I came home and found a rat nibbling her toes I knew I had to do something. I decided to take her to the mother and baby room in the toilets by the station. I'd washed the nappies out there before and thought I could bathe her in one of the sinks. The first mistake was taking her out.

The second was stopping in the churchyard. Not the one round the cathedral in the city centre but the one at the top of Warstone Lane, where the catacombs are. It's deserted most of the time except for the odd drunk or glue-sniffer, and it was a long walk from the squat to the station. Lucy was heavier than I realised. It was a hot day so I stopped to rest. I sat back against a headstone and unwrapped Lucy's shawl a little thinking the fresh air and sunshine would be good for her. It was one of her sleeping times. She was quiet and the only real sounds were from the distant traffic. It's strange how entering a cemetery seems to muffle outside noise. Even the chirrup of sparrows was muted.

I must've dozed.

I remember jerking awake at the sound of giggles. There were two boys there, in T-shirts and torn jeans. One held a stick broken from a nearby tree. He was reaching out with it to prod Lucy, the end already hooked under her blanket. The other noticed me looking at them and nudged his friend.

He grinned. "What you got, lady?" he said, as if he couldn't see Lucy's beautiful sleeping face.

"Smells awful," said his friend. "Like a dead dog."

The boy jerked the end of the stick, flicking the blanket from Lucy. A mass of disturbed flies exploded around us.

"Bastard!" I yelled and grabbed Lucy to me.

"Jesus Christ," the boy said. "It *is* a dead dog."

The other child threw up, the vomit spattering my shoes and Lucy's blanket.

I scrambled to my feet and began to run, clutching Lucy to me. She belched but didn't otherwise protest.

There's a crumbling gatehouse at one end of the cemetery. It's surrounded by scaffolding and a battered fence put there initially to keep out the unwary. Hugging Lucy to my breast with one arm I scrambled over the broken chain link, glancing back to see if I was being followed. I tripped on fallen masonry and heard the thud of Lucy's head hitting the ground. She didn't even whimper. I sprawled across her. I felt her little body deflate beneath mine like a broken balloon.

I got up carefully and carried her inside the building. I don't think anyone saw us come in but we cannot stay here for ever. Tomorrow is Monday and if they haven't found us by then, the workmen rebuilding this place will be back. In the meantime, I will use what is left of the daylight shining through the window to try and put what remains of Lucy's decayed intestines back inside her sweet body.

THE MAGIC ROUNDABOUT

The three of us would walk Jenny's dog in the park most evenings. Some people, like my Mum, would say, "Don't you see enough of each other at school?" They don't understand the difference. During the day, there are always other influences, pulling us in other directions. In the park, with just the dog and the grass to listen in, we could tell each other things we didn't want anyone else to overhear.

We had our own reasons too. Jenny wanted time to herself before being absorbed back into the seething maelstrom of four siblings in a terraced house. As an only child, I wanted the levity of my peers before being the third responsible adult in our household. Nimmi escaped briefly from parents who both pushed her to do well, though for slightly different reasons. Our walks were the safety valve for the pressure they put on her.

Rex was perpetually inquisitive and would make friendly overtures to anything. The moment he was let off the lead he would hare off to investigate any non-grass object in sight. Several times last summer he had disturbed courting couples by placing a damp nose where it wasn't wanted. Occasionally his enthusiasm would get him into trouble – like this time.

Highbury is a large park with areas of formal bedding, clumps of bushes, a small playground and lots of open space. Rex saw a couple of interesting people in the distance and raced towards them. Their dog met him halfway. To look at him, you wouldn't think that Rex was the offspring of a Supreme Champion. Instead, he looks rather like an off-white, badly shorn sheep. All Bedlingtons do. This other dog, a bandy-legged Jack Russell, either saw him as a rival or as a large rat. Either way, the Jack Russell didn't even pause for the ritual bottom sniffing but went straight for Rex's ears. Rex squealed.

Jenny broke into a run. Nimmi and I jogged after, neither of us expecting to get there before there was slaughter. The third dog streaked out of nowhere. The grey flash bowled over the Jack Russell, which howled. Rex fled, leaping into Jenny's arms and spraying her with blood from the torn ear. The lurcher got the terrier by the scruff and shook it. It went limp as a dead rabbit and whimpered.

"Call off your dog!" The owners of the Jack Russell lumbered across the field, gasping rather than shouting.

Jenny shrugged helplessly. There was nothing she could do.

I just heard the edge of a high-pitched whistle. The lurcher froze, ears pricked.

"Leave!" The dog obeyed the shout. The terrier remained lifeless where it fell for a moment before haring off into the distance, tail between its legs.

The lurcher responded to a call to heel as its owner approached. The elderly man limped towards the group, using a hiker's thumb-stick to speed his pace. His beard and the long winter coat that flapped at his calves gave him the air of a story-book wizard. The terrier's owners squared up to him.

"Your dog's fucking dangerous," the younger, less breathless one said.

"It ought to be put down," the other wheezed.

"At least my dog obeys commands," the old man said.

I stepped forwards to stand by him. "Perhaps you

better find your dog before he causes an accident – or attacks someone else."

They looked at us, then down at the lurcher which bared its teeth in a silent snarl.

"You just watch it, then," the older one said.

"And keep that rat on a lead," the other shouted at Jenny.

Both of them turned away, though they glanced back at us occasionally as they headed off in the direction the Jack Russell had taken.

The old man stepped towards Jenny and Rex. The dog whimpered and was visibly quivering in her arms. He stroked Rex's head and gently touched the savaged ear. Remarkably, Rex seemed to calm and licked the old man's hand.

"I should get him to a vet," he said. "That wound will need stitching."

"What if they're waiting for us?" Nimmi asked.

The old man smiled. I noticed how young and bright his eyes were in contrast to the wrinkled, weather-brown of his face. "I will walk with you to the main road," he said. "Dulac and I will guard you."

I was just thinking that Dulac was an odd name for a dog when he half-turned towards me. "We found each other at Earlswood Lakes," he said. "Someone had thrown the puppies in the water and he had just managed to swim ashore."

"It's French," I said wondering if I had imagined that he had just read my mind.

He nodded acknowledging the spoken and unspoken responses.

~~~

Jenny couldn't talk of anything but the old man for the next two days. "He saved Rex's life," she told anyone who would listen.

"His dog did," Nimmi said. "Dulac was the real champion."

"We should buy him something,"

"Like what?" I asked. "We don't even know where he lives."

"A cake," Jenny said unimaginatively.

"Dog biscuits," Nimmi said.

Soap was my contribution. I suspected that if he wasn't actually a tramp, he spent a lot of his life outdoors and somehow I couldn't share their enthusiasm. I thought it had been a lucky coincidence that he happened to be in the park at that time, and that we should forget the incident.

"How will we find him to give him these presents?" I asked again. It wasn't that I didn't want to thank him for his help, more I that I didn't want to get involved.

"He'll be there," Jenny said. I could hear uncertainty in her conviction.

"We'll find him," Nimmi said, "I know we will."

I believed her.

~~~

Not far from Highbury Park is one of those large roundabouts that mark the junctions of the Ring Road with the major trunk roads that radiate from Birmingham's city centre. Traditionally, the traffic islands are bright with flowers, the council renewing them each season to welcome visitors. The larger ones are planted with mature trees and shrubs.

Once Rex's ear had healed enough for us to resume our evening walks, we took, by common consensus, the longer route to the park. We kept a wary eye open for men with Jack Russells. We'd walked past the roundabout loads of times before but, since it was invariably submerged in swirls of angry traffic, we'd ignored it.

This evening, over the traffic noise, we heard barking. Fortunately, Rex was still on his leash or we would have lost him under the wheels of a bus as he strained to reach Dulac. The lurcher stood poised as if to rush towards us through the flow of vehicles.

"He'll get hurt," Jenny said, obviously afraid for his safety.

"He's got more sense," I said. Most dogs would have gleefully launched themselves into the traffic, regardless of the havoc they would precipitate. I suspected that the old man was around somewhere and his unseen presence was restraining the lurcher's innate foolishness.

The moment there was a lull in the traffic, Jenny, Nimmi and Rex made a dash for the island. I followed with a little more caution.

Dulac and Rex made a fuss of each other, yapping (on Rex's part), sniffing (both of them) and licking (Dulac). I am glad human etiquette is simpler. The fret Jenny made over the lurcher went largely unregarded by the dog. Nimmi noticed the old man first. He was sitting on a park-type bench, watching us. Nimmi moved towards him. I tagged along.

"Welcome, ladies," he said.

"This a weird place to..." I couldn't think how to finish the sentence. Surely, only a nutter would choose to sit on a traffic island surrounded by noise and fumes, regardless of the fact that it was over-large for a roundabout.

"Why do you live here?" Nimmi asked. I noticed then that a shelter was slung between the bushes, perfectly camouflaged within the clump of evergreen shrubs.

"Here I have the freedom to do as I wish," he said.

"But don't the council object?" I asked.

He smiled. "They might if they noticed. How many

times have you walked or driven by? Have you ever seen my home before?"

"What about the parks people?" Nimmi said. "When they cut the grass."

"I am the parks people. What better job for someone who can't stand being cooped up inside?"

I looked more carefully. The island was a perfect circle. Lampposts warded the cardinal points. I suspected no-one would see the place unless he wanted them to. So why were we there? Why had he let down the guards to allow three teenage girls and a Bedlington terrier in? I also wondered why or what he was hiding.

"Can we take Dulac for a walk?" Jenny said.

"Of course."

Nimmi looked dubious. "Does he have a lead?"

"He doesn't need one." The old man called Dulac over. He knelt down and whispered to him. "Go with them," he said aloud to the dog. "Guard them well."

Jenny giggled, Nimmi frowned as if working something out, and I felt cold fingers walking up my spine. A warning, perhaps, that this old man would break up our trinity.

In the beginning it was innocent enough. We would stop by the roundabout and pick up the dog before we went into the park. Jenny, always the most athletic of the three of us, would race off with Dulac, chasing sticks. Rex, more timid since his encounter with the Jack Russell, tended to stay close to Nimmi and me. Often Jenny would bring a gift for the lurcher; dog biscuits, a chew, a tin of food. I asked the old man once if he minded.

"Dulac goes where he will," he replied. "He chooses his own fate."

We seldom talked to the old man; he never told us his name – we never asked.

~~~

Summer passed. Our GCSE results came and we all found ourselves embarking on A-Level courses. Jenny and I both did English and History, but whereas I chose Sociology (I had ideas of becoming a social worker), Jenny did Biology with Nimmi. Nimmi's parents had visions of her becoming a doctor so she had no choice but to go for all the sciences.

It was that interest that led her to ask the old man if he ever suffered from colds. This was a time when all of us, including many of our classmates, were sniffling from the latest infection to sweep through the school after a particularly chilly Christmas.

"I use herbs," he said.

"Got anything for flu?" Jenny asked. She was shivering in the orange lamplight and probably should have stayed in bed.

"Feverfew is good for bringing down a temperature," he said.

"I don't suppose you've got any?" She sneezed into an already soggy Kleenex.

The old man dragged a tin trunk from his shelter. When he opened it, it was full of layers of dried plants in plastic bags, all neatly labelled. He passed one to Jenny. "The leaves are better fresh but use this like tea – infuse a spoonful in a pint of boiling water. Drink half a cup every three hours."

"It won't poison me, will it?" she asked.

"No, but it may taste a little bitter. You can add honey if you want."

Nimmi was delving into the trunk as if she had found a chest of jewels. "I've never heard of most of these plants," she said. "What are they all for? Are they all used as tisanes?"

"It varies from plant to plant. And what you want to use it for."

Nimmi's eyes were bright. "Will you teach me?" she asked.

The old man hesitated, then shrugged. "If you wish."

"Magic!"

I now had a problem. I could either go with Jenny and the dogs, or I could stay and chaperone Nimmi. I knew Nimmi's parents would not want her left alone with any man, however harmless he might be. They were enlightened Sikhs, but not that enlightened. I was not sure that they would approve of her learning herbalism either. That was quack medicine and she was going to be a real doctor.

Nimmi tried to include me, making me part of a conspiracy against our elders but I couldn't get involved in herb lore. I wasn't interested. I felt that overnight I had become the outsider. Dulac had replaced me in Jenny's affections, as the magic of dead plants had in Nimmi's. I suppose I was jealous – of a dog and an old man.

I began to make excuses – too much homework, other things to do. I don't suppose Jenny or Nimmi believed me for one moment, but they accepted it as friends do, or people who are so wrapped up in their new interests that they haven't even noticed you aren't around anymore. The trouble was, we had always been such an exclusive group that I hadn't really got any other friends. A couple of boys asked me on dates and I went out of boredom. I wasn't really interested, which showed as the relationships didn't last.

The guy I fancied didn't seem interested in me. Mordecai Reddy was a sort of cousin. He was about five years older than me and only interested in cricket. Even though he lived about a mile away we only met occasionally, at family gatherings. Obviously I wanted to impress him, so when we found ourselves as the youngest people at Uncle Gareth's twenty-fifth wedding anniversary party I told him all about the old man and the dogs. I thought he seemed really interested but it could have just been that my story was marginally better than all the other things going on in the room. I don't know what I expected to achieve, perhaps the downloading of some of the angst that had built up after my friends had deserted me. I hardly expected Mord to go and tell the tale to the members of the Warwickshire Cricket Club's Youth Team. Even if it had occurred to me, you can't blame me for forgetting that Nimmi's brother was a member of the squad.

First thing I knew about it was two days later when Nimmi started shouting at me in the loo at school, then bursting into tears and locking herself into a cubicle.

"What did I do?" I asked Jenny.

"Piss off, bitch." Jenny swore at me. I was too stunned to react. This was supposed to be my best friend, yet she looked and sounded as if she hated me.

"Did I say something?" I asked.

"You've said plenty." She was almost snarling. I thought for a moment she might actually hit me. "I never thought you would do such a nasty, spiteful thing."

"I don't know what you mean." I was ready to stamp my foot in frustration. I genuinely hadn't a clue what she was on about.

"Just fuck off. And don't speak to us ever again."

In my next lesson, English, Jenny pointedly sat as far from me as she could get.

"What's up with her?" Blanche asked as Jenny snubbed her as well.

"I haven't the faintest idea," I said.

"Bet she's jealous," Kai said.

"Of what?"

"Nimmi. I heard she was getting married."

I felt something cold and hard settle in my stomach. "Who told you that?" I asked.

"My brother. It's all over his college."

"What did you hear?"

Kai shrugged. "That she's leaving at the end of term and will finish her studies in London."

I got a sudden feeling that if the rumour was true, for some reason Jenny and Nimmi were blaming me. I didn't know why but even her family wouldn't arrange a marriage that fast unless they thought they had cause.

~~~

When Nimmi disappeared, her brother came looking for me. I told him I hadn't spoken to her for weeks. I sent him to talk to Jenny, and I went to see the old man.

The roundabout looked exactly as it always did from the other side of the traffic flow – green and deserted, yet once I crossed over and passed through the circle of lamplight it all changed. There was a hint of smoke, though I knew the only heating he allowed was a small Calor Gas camping stove. The air prickled with static. The dog wasn't there but he sat on the bench almost as if he was waiting for me.

"Is Nimmi here?" I asked.

He shook his head.

"Do you know where she is? Her family are looking for her."

"So they can trap her into a marriage she doesn't want," he said. "They won't find her. She has already chosen her freedom."

"You don't understand," I said.

He smiled sadly. "I will miss her magic," he said.

"Magic doesn't exist," I told him.

"You are wrong. Your magic is with words. You can destroy with them. I had hoped that this time round you would use them wisely."

I didn't understand. I thought that either he was hiding Nimmi or he had helped her run away. I did know that everything had changed.

They found Nimmi's body the next day. Two fishermen hauled her out of the water at Earlswood. The newspaper headlines called her "The Lady in the Lake". The old man was convicted of killing her. The evidence was all circumstantial.

~~~

That was ten years ago. Everyone knows that a life sentence doesn't mean you rot in jail until you are dead. Not in this country. They parole you to make room for more dangerous criminals. As a probation officer I had to help them back into society.

I showed my pass to the guard as I entered the prison. He scrutinised it carefully.

"Faye Morgan. You're the new probation officer," he said. Some people always state the obvious.

I had recognised the name the moment I was assigned the case. He didn't recognise me. Ten years behind bars had destroyed him. They were letting him out because they had no facilities for a man who had been diagnosed with Alzheimer's. All I could do was to arrange accommodation for him in a home. I knew, though, that it had been the loss of freedom that had caused his decline.

Between us, Nimmi and I had buried him alive.

NINA

This morning I got married. I was apprehensive; who wouldn't be? Now, I am shit scared. You see, despite the fact that I was born in Birmingham, England, our family still follows some of the traditions of Indian culture, like arranged marriages. I wasn't even consulted. It was all sorted out between the heads of families.

At first, when father told me my bride was to be Nina Chandha, I didn't think too much of it. In fact I was quite pleased as I thought I remembered her from school. She was two years below me in my sister Mita's, class and reasonably pretty.

Then Mita started teasing.

"Hope you like girls with spirit," she said. "You've got a right one there."

"What do you mean?"

"Nina likes her own way." She clammed up then, Mita did, and no amount of cajoling on my part could get anything more than giggles out of her. Which just went to prove what I always thought: sisters are a creation of Kali sent to plague and annoy brothers. Not that I believe in all that gods and demons stuff, though it does make an exciting tale.

~~~

Bali's sister, Jasveer, was a little more forthcoming. Balvinder and I go back a long way despite him being Sikh - we both started junior school on the same day. Bali wouldn't be wed for three or four years yet - his people liked to marry their daughters to mature men. Besides, the scars from the beating he took almost a year ago still showed. Still, he was pleased for me though he didn't really remember Nina either.

Jasveer did.

She was sitting at the big table in the kitchen of Bali's, supposedly doing her homework. She had declared that she was going to do better than Bali in her exams. Not difficult, since Bali only just passed in Technology and Art. Bali and I sat at the other end of the table, sipping lager. His mother would tut-tut about it but his dad was more progressive. "We're in England now," he would say before going off to join his Irish workmates from the factory for a few beers.

We stayed in because Bali didn't want to be seen drinking through a straw – his jaw was still wired in places. That was another reason why his dad let me bring alcohol into their house. "Only the kitchen, mind," he would say. He reckoned Bali had suffered enough and deserved a few pleasures. Others would say Bali got what he deserved.

As I was telling Bali about my proposed nuptials I could see Jasveer's ears prick up. Like young men do, we started discussing the wedding night. All innuendo, of course, and mostly for Jasveer's benefit. We pretended to ignore her, but I could see she was getting agitated.

"You're both fools," she eventually burst out.

"Little girls shouldn't listen to men's talk," I said, grinning.

Jasveer darkened and began to pile her books up. "It won't be like that, you'll see," she said. "Especially with Nina."

"What will it be like?" Bali croaked through his smashed larynx.

Jasveer looked straight at me. "Nina said she would kill any man who laid a finger on her."

Bali and I laughed – at least I did. Bali spluttered but it was the same thing. How many times had we heard that line? It was straight out of an old movie and every girl says it at some time or another.

"If you think it's so funny go and talk to Anita Maini. She used to be Nina's best friend," Jasveer said.

~~~

Anita's not the kind of girl you take much notice of. At least, not when you are young and randy. She's plain and sensible, not a tease like my sister. Her uncle's got a supermarket down Ladypool Road and she works there Saturdays at the check-out. The shop seemed to be full of fat women lugging overflowing baskets and dragging protesting three-year-olds. The aisles were filled with boxes of dog food or washing powder, seemingly deliberately placed to trip you up.

I squeezed through the entrance and immediately realised that I'd have no chance of speaking to Anita unless I bought something, and joined the meandering queue for her till. I could have got the packet of crisps and can of coke in a fraction of the time at the newsagent's next door. More than once I was tempted to leave as Anita rang up yet another basket of rice, chapati flour and bags of lentils. But I wanted to know more about the girl my father had arranged for me to marry.

Eventually it was my turn. Anita glanced up at me, surprised when I placed just the two items in front of her.

"I want to talk to you," I said.

She ignored me and rang up the bill. "Fifty-two pee please."

"I'm going to marry Nina Chandha," I said.

Anita held out her hand and I placed a pound coin in her palm. "Please," I said.

She slid the cash drawer closed and passed me the

change. "Meet me in the park. By the swings. One-thirty."

I feared she might not turn up but hung around anyway. She was prompt. She had a six-year-old boy in tow, who ran off towards the playground the moment she released his hand.

"I've got an hour for lunch," Anita said. "What do you want to know?"

I shrugged. "Anything. I just don't like the idea of marrying someone I know nothing about."

"Don't, then."

"Don't what?"

"Marry. Get out of it. Get a white girl pregnant. Run away from home."

It sounded a little drastic. "Why?" I asked.

Anita watched her brother – or cousin – climb to the top of the slide twice before she answered. "I just get an itchy feeling between the shoulder blades when she's around. That's why I don't see much of her these days." Anita sighed. "It's probably my imagination, and I've no business questioning what your family have arranged."

"But?"

Anita was sixteen but she sounded like the kind of matriarch who quietly watches and absorbs information and then pronounces hidden truths. The kind of grandmother one respects and is a little in awe of. "You know Nina's father killed himself?" she said.

I nodded. I'd heard something of it about three years ago. That's why my father had negotiated my marriage with her uncle.

"Nina saw him do it."

That stopped me. There'd been rumours that Nina had found the body. I recalled that now and wondered what kind of effect that would have on someone, but to actually be there.

"Can you tell me about it?" Suddenly I felt different. A week ago I'd have laughed at Anita, or made crass comments. Instead, a coldness settled in my stomach and I was afraid. I remembered a story being read to us in junior school about a curious girl who opened a box and let out a lot of horrible demons. It was like that, only Anita was the box and I didn't think I would like what was inside. I would have been relieved if she had refused.

"I have to tell someone," Anita said. She took a deep breath and plunged into the story. "People always assumed Nina and I were best friends. It was more a case of our families being neighbours. We used to share secrets. We knew that Nina's older sister, Saira, was seeing a Muslim boy. We even helped them deceive both families. For a time. Eventually a relative of Maboob, the boyfriend, saw them holding hands in the street and told his father."

It was a common problem, trying to follow the rules of our parents but wishing for the freedom our English classmates had to pick and choose friends. It was a bit easier for boys than for girls.

"We were upstairs in Nina's room when Maboob's father came round." Anita said. "We could hear every word they said. Saira was called a whore and a slut; Maboob was an evil seducer. Each father blamed the other for their child's behaviour. I was surprised they didn't actually come to blows. Fortunately, Saira was out at the time doing some shopping for an elderly aunt, or I don't know what would have happened. The atmosphere was explosive. When Mr Ali left, Nina and I tried to think of ways that we could warn Saira. If she could have stayed at the aunt's house overnight her father might have calmed down. Just as we agreed that I should go looking for her, she returned. Nina leant out of the upstairs window trying to signal her away, not daring to call out, but Saira didn't understand. Her father saw her standing bemused on the path. He dragged Saira into the house by her hair. Then he took his belt to her. Nina and I crouched at the top of the stairs, watching."

I saw Anita shiver as she remembered. I knew that kind of thing happened. I don't think that my father would ever treat either of my sisters like that. At least, I hope not.

"Afterward," Anita said, "Nina told me that she would never let him do that to Saira again. She meant it, though I didn't see how she could stop him. He was within his rights – as he saw them, as our community would see them. Saira had brought shame on his family and he had punished her. He also kept her confined to the house. Okay, she went to school but he took her to the gate and was waiting to escort her home afterwards. When he was home she had to be in the same room as him. I think he had arranged a marriage for her, in India. Saira refused to go."

"So he beat her again?" I said.

"Not quite. I was at Nina's house when it started. Nina's mother was out visiting, as were her two younger brothers. I followed Nina down to the back sitting-room. 'I won't do it, Father,' I heard Saira say. She sounded scared. 'You can't make me.' Nina pulled me after her into the doorway. At the far end of the room a heavy brass curtain rail ran across an archway into the kitchen. Nina's father had fixed a length of washing line to it. The other end was tied into a loop. This, he held out to Saira. 'You said you would rather die than marry a decent boy.' he said.

"Nina stepped into the room. She told Saira to go to her aunt's house. Nina was nearly three younger than her sister yet Saira obeyed her. She walked out of the room, down the passage and through the front door, slamming it closed behind her. Her father never said a word. Nina was watching him as he stood silently with the noose in his hands. She told him to put it over his own head, to see what it felt like. I expected him to lash out, to berate Nina, maybe even take his belt to her. But no. Calmly, he put the noose around his neck, just as Nina bid.

"Nina must have remembered me, then, because she told me to go home. And I went. I've never been back there."

I asked Anita, "Do you really think he killed himself because Nina said so?"

"I don't know. It was in the newspapers next day. Nina's father had hanged himself. Nina had found the body. She was off school for the next few months, staying with relatives, being counselled. I hardly saw her after that, except at school, and I always felt uncomfortable when she looked at me. I don't know what happened after I left that night. I don't think I want to know."

Anita called her brother from the playground. As she went to walk away she turned back. "If you can, Anil Patel," she said, "find someone else to marry."

~~~

I didn't think too much of Anita's tale. She was only a kid at the time Nina's dad killed himself and probably misremembered much of what happened. If anything, I felt sorry for Nina. It must be horrible to find any kind of dead body, but to find your own father swinging at the end of a rope must be extra awful.

When I got home later in the afternoon I found my dad waiting for me in an agitated state.

"Hurry up and change," he told me. "We are supposed to be meeting your intended in half an hour."

"You should've told me earlier," I shouted, racing up the stairs.

"You're never in," he called back.

"Last night." I generally get on well with my dad. Especially now I'm working he treats me more like an equal. It's only in this matter of marriage that he still expects me to defer to his wishes. I was glad though that I'd be given the chance to get to know Nina a little before the wedding actually took place. I might even be able to take her out on proper dates. I looked forward to that.

This meeting was extremely proper. It was in her uncle's house as he was now her guardian. She sat on an uncomfortable, straight-backed chair on one side of the room. I did the same on the other side. Her mother and aunt filled the sofa between us while the men, my father and her uncle, faced each other from over-stuffed armchairs. Conversation was sparse and polite. Nina's mother poured tea which Nina, with properly downcast eyes, carried to the guests and then offered round a plate of sweet biscuits before resuming her seat.

The desultory chatter between the adults gave me a chance to study Nina. She wore a long well-fitting tunic and trousers, in a dark-chocolate brown material, embroidered at the hem and ankles with gold thread. It might sound dull but it wasn't. It was exactly right for Nina. Her black hair was loose and covered by a gauzy scarf in the same colour as the rest of her clothes. She wasn't quite as pretty as I thought I remembered, and if anything her nose was a bit large, but she had strong pale-skinned features and incredibly long eyelashes. I could see her watching me through them. I sensed she was behaving impeccably for the benefit of the adults, just as I was. She wore plenty of gold jewellery as well – large hooped earrings, ankle chains, and an armful of bangles which clinked together as she sipped her tea. My father could have chosen a lot worse for me.

Nina had obviously been primed as to what to do. After about half an hour she collected up the cups and plates.

"Why don't you carry the tray through to the kitchen, Anil," Nina's mother said to me. "It will help Nina."

We were being given time together.

Nina didn't speak to me but ran hot water straight into the sink to begin the task of washing-up. Her movements were economical and tense, whether from being alone with me or from some other reason I don't know, but she seemed different.

"It wasn't my idea," I said, feeling someone had to break the silence.

"You didn't have to agree to it," Nina said.

"It's my father who arranged things. And your uncle."

"Do you always do what your father says?"

"No. But he probably knows better than me in this matter."

"You've changed since you were at school, then," Nina said. "Or was it all just for show?"

"What do you mean?"

"The crudity. The swearing at the teachers, the groping in the corridors. You probably don't realise how foul we thought you were, you and your friend Bali."

"That was more than two years ago. I'm different now."

"Are you? You revolted me then, you still do. I may have to marry you, Anil Patel, but you will never touch me. Do you understand that? Never!"

The look she gave me was withering. For a moment she looked sixty, not sixteen, and the only things I could think of were that her eyebrows met in the middle, and what it would be like to kiss her.

When my dad and I left, Nina stood next to her uncle on the doorstep, demure once again. As we turned out of the gate I glanced at her. She was staring at me with loathing and I remembered I had seen her look like that once before, only then it had been Bali she was watching, not me. It shook me so much that I walked home in a kind of daze. If it hadn't been for my dad grabbing me as I stepped off the pavement I would have gone right under a bus.

~~~

I admit it. Bali and I were pretty obnoxious at school. We weren't the only ones. Part of the problem was that neither of our families expected us to have girlfriends – nice girls don't go with boys – but our peers did. A lot of our school mates were discovering sex so didn't have to boast about it. We just pretended. We would swagger along the corridor wearing the tightest pants you can get away with, bulging at the crotch. Or lean past a girl to get an eraser and accidentally-on-purpose brush her tits with an arm. Bali got an elbow in the guts one time when he tried standing behind the maths teacher and looking down her cleavage. But that's basically all we did. We fantasised. And the opportunities for being crude diminish when you leave school. For a start, you're worked too hard to want to. My bakery job gets me up at five in the morning and there aren't many girls in the garage where Bali works.

I suppose our male egos were a bit frustrated, which was why, about a year ago, we had decided to crash the school disco. The usual rule is that if you don't actually go to the school, you must be the partner of someone who does. It's not difficult to arrange.

Bali and I hung around the entrance watching various

groups going in. Black girls are usually the best bet. They've got a greater sense of daring, less respect for petty rules.

We recognised a couple in the group we picked, though Georgina and Evette had filled out considerably since we last saw them, when they were skinny third-years.

Bali took the lead. "Hi, Georgie. Remember me? Balvinder Singh.

"Who don't?" Georgina might be on the plump side but she has a wicked smile. She used it on Bali. "You jus' passin'?"

Bali draped an arm about her shoulders. "Thought you might like to go to a disco."

"An' thought I might jus' take you with me? How you gonna make it worth my while, boy?"

Bali pulled a bottle out of his pocket. It looked like lemonade. "Vodka?" he said.

Georgina unscrewed the top, took a swig and grimaced. "Okay," she said passing the bottle to Evette. It went round the group.

"That gets you in, Bali," Evette said, eying me. "What about your friend?"

I held my jacket open exposing the bottle in my inner pocket. "White rum," I said.

Evette slipped her arm about my waist. "Wicked," she said. "Shall we go?"

The girls didn't expect us to stay with them all evening. That wasn't part of the deal, though we might well have gone back to them towards the end if our luck was bad. By then they would've been too drunk to care since they either had their own booze in their handbags or had stashed it in the loo cisterns during the day.

Bali and I prowled. It was mostly dark in the hall. The

lights had been covered with coloured paper and the lightshow spat occasional streaks of red and blue across the dancers. The music was so loud you could scarcely hear yourself speak.

I was actually getting quite friendly with this one girl, Harminder, her name was, when I noticed Bali was having a bit of trouble. If he'd had any sense he'd've backed off. Bali's girl was pinned between a table and the wall. He was leaning close to her; I suspect he was touching her as well. She didn't like it. She had gone tense. He hadn't noticed. That's the signal to back off. He wasn't. She was staring at a group a short distance away. Nina was with them but it wasn't her I noticed. It was the blokes with them. All three were older and bigger than we were and I didn't like the way they were eyeing up Bali.

I made an excuse to Harminder and took Bali's arm. "I think we ought to spread ourselves about a bit more," I said, indicating the watching blokes.

For a moment I thought Bali would ignore me but then he tore himself away with a wave and a wink. "See you later, doll," he said.

All I wanted to do was to keep clear of those three. I don't court trouble as a rule. I know what I can get away with, but I know some guys can get very nasty if they think you are interfering with one of theirs, especially in our community. These gave me an itchy feeling.

We didn't hang around until the disco ended. It was getting boring.

It happened fast. We were less than a hundred yards from the school gates. Someone cannoned into me from behind. I sprawled, hands grazing the pavement. I was yanked up and slammed into a tree. My head cracked against it. My vision swirled. A boot caught me under the ribs. I couldn't breathe.

Screaming assailed my ears.

My sight cleared a little.

They had Bali down. They were kicking hell out of him. All three of them. Nina's friends.

Bali had his arms about his head. The boots went in, anyway. Leather against bone crunches. Bali stopped screaming.

Then they walked away.

A shadow came between Bali and the streetlight. I looked up. Nina stood a few feet away, her arm linked with that of the girl Bali had been feeling up. Nina was staring at Bali. Her expression was one of hatred and loathing. A killing look. She turned and they disappeared.

Clutching my stomach, I crawled over to Bali. I thought he was dead. His face was unrecognisable. There was blood everywhere.

Why he didn't die, no-one knows. His skull was fractured in two places, his left cheekbone shattered, his nose destroyed and his jaw had been kicked loose from his skull.

The look Nina gave him that night was just like the one she gave me as I left her house after our first official meeting. I don't believe in the evil eye. It's just a load of superstitious nonsense, but that's what it made me think of. I tried not to let it worry me, but it was hard. Over the next few weeks I was thrust into Nina's company on several occasions. We almost avoided speaking to each other. I did try. After all, this was supposed to be the woman I would spend the rest of my life with, and I thought it would be useful if we started out liking each other a little bit.

"Forget it," Nina said when I asked her what kind of music she liked.

"You are not the first Nina's been betrothed to," Bali's sister said one evening when I was complaining to Bali about the way she always put down my efforts.

"What happened to the other guy?" I asked, as casually as I could.

"He was arrested for stealing cars," Jasveer said gleefully. "He was let off with a caution but her uncle said they didn't want that sort in the family."

I wondered briefly what I could get nicked for. I would probably upset my mother more than anyone else. That wouldn't be fair. I resigned myself to following my father's wishes.

Two nights before the ceremony was supposed to take place I tackled my sister Mita again. She was stitching gold braid to the sari she intended to wear.

"What was Nina like in school?" I asked.

She must have realised how nervous I was. "Why do you want to know?" she asked.

"I've been hearing all sorts of rumours. And Nina doesn't seem to like me much."

"What kind of rumours?"

I told her what Anita and Jasveer said, and how Nina had been around when Bali was hurt.

Mita made a show of tying of her thread and bit through the cotton. "She always gets her own way," she said. "Nina rarely did her homework. She got away with it with most teachers – for some reason they never pressed her. But Miss Gordon insisted. She seemed to be immune from whatever guile Nina had. So Nina copied the chemistry homework from one of us. No-one ever refused her twice."

"Were you scared of her?"

"Not really. You just got an uncomfortable feeling when she looked at you. Things would go wrong.

Nothing you could ever pin on her. Silly accidents."

"Did she ever do anything to you?"

"Nina never did anything. But I did fall in the river on a geography field trip the day after I refused to let her borrow my pen. Jasveer cut herself badly in chemistry when a beaker broke, the same day she refused to tell Nina the answer to a maths question. Coincidence probably, but coincidences happens when Nina's around."

"I don't think I want to marry her," I said.

"Don't worry," Mita said. "After the first night, she won't be able to do anything to you."

"How can you be so sure?"

Mita laughed. "Why are witches always unmarried? Why are unicorns attracted to virgins? They want to steal their power."

"I don't believe in witches – or unicorns," I said doubtfully.

"No?" Mita looked pointedly at my crotch and giggled before gathering up the cloth of her sari and heading out of the room.

~~~

Somehow, I got through the marriage ceremony. I can only presume that Nina was as nervous as I was. I don't think we looked at each other the whole time. The wedding celebrations were held in the dining room of the school we both used to attend. It felt peculiar going back there legitimately. Eventually we were escorted, separately, back to my house. Someone had removed most of my possessions from my bedroom, moved in a double bed, and hung decoration from the ceiling. I arrived first.

I heard them on the stairs, a shrillness of female voices. Then the door was pushed open and Nina came in, along with a cloud of flower petals. I felt extremely nervous. Unsure what to do. Nina, however, closed the door and looked at me. She had the same expression of loathing on her face that I had seen before.

"Shall we get it over with?" she said.

"What?"

"Let's finish this farce, hit me."

I didn't think I had heard her right.

She took a step closer, "Hit me," she said again.

"I don't hit women," I said feebly.

"Yes you do. Especially women who refuse to have your filthy hands pawing all over them,"

My mind was stunned by bewilderment, but I felt my fingers balling themselves into a fist. I tried to relax them. I deliberately attempted to stretch out my fingers. They were frozen.

"I am refusing to submit to my husband," Nina said. "I need to be punished. Hit me."

I did. I couldn't help it. My arm just raised itself to eye level and straightened sharply. The shock jarred up my arm as my fist struck her face. I felt sick. I couldn't believe what I had done.

Nina took an involuntary step back, recovered her poise and smiled. She unwound her scarf from her hair and knotted one end into a loop.

"Tie the other end to the light fixture," she said.

"Why?"

"Because I cannot reach."

In a haze, I climbed onto the bed. The mattress flexed under my feet. Her request seemed very reasonable.

"Now put your head in the loop," she said.

"Why should I?" I tried desperately to break out of the spell she seemed to have cast over me.

"Because you are ashamed. You don't hit women,

remember? You feel you have to atone for your wickedness."

She was right. I had to do something to wipe out the shame. A feeble voice at the back of my mind suggested that this was a bit drastic. "I'll do whatever you want," I said. I was getting scared now.

She smiled. "Yes, you will," she said. "You will set me free."

"Yes. I will set you free. I'll annul the marriage."

"You will set me free by dying. Put it over your head."

I couldn't stop my hands from lifting the cloth and settling the noose around my neck. I wanted to ask her why, but my mouth wouldn't work. I could feel my body trembling.

"If I am single my uncle will try again to marry me off. As a widow, I can do what I want and no-one can stop me." As she turned to the door, I could already see the bruise forming on her cheek. "Goodbye," she said.

~~~

I hear her running down the stairs. The sitting room door opens, and I briefly hear the sound of laughter. As it closes I have this overwhelming compulsion to leap from the bed. I must wipe out my shame.

THE SCENT OF ELDER FLOWERS

Jennifer Lewis gripped her daughter's hand tightly and wiped away a stray tear as the dry soil rattled on the lid of the tiny coffin. It covered and crushed the single red rose that Evan Lewis had tossed into the grave.

"Mummy, you're hurting me." Melanie wriggled in Jennifer's grasp.

"Sorry, darling." The response was automatic but as she glanced at the eight-year old's pale face she felt the grief squeezing her chest and tightening the iron band behind her eyes. She was scarcely conscious of the hands which reached out to offer sympathy as she turned from the gash in the turf that echoed the pain-filled cavity lodged just under her ribs.

The door of the black car was opened by the solemn faced chauffeur from the funeral home. As Jennifer helped Melanie into the back seat she paused and looked back towards the grave. Evan stood watching the sexton shovel earth into the hole, repairing the wounded ground. Despite the warmth of the day he was hunched into an overcoat, his hands thrust into the pockets.

"Wait here, Melanie," Jennifer said. She walked back across the uneven grass and touched Evan's sleeve. "Come home with us," she said.

He looked at her sadly. "You know I can't," he said. "They would take Melanie away."

"Evan, I need you."

He put his arms around her and hugged her close. Jennifer wondered why everything had gone wrong.

~~~

Jennifer hadn't realised how dark and viscous the mire was until the brewery had sent Evan Lewis to oversee the accounts of The Rowan Branch. She had worked in the lounge bar during the two years since her husband died under the wheels of his tractor. Evan had shown her that there was still some happiness owing to her.

"Ye'll regret it," her mother-in-law had said when Jennifer broke the news that she was marrying again. "The town's no place for folk like us."

Jennifer knew it would work out, especially after she saw the house they were to live in. It was a long narrow house, a relic from the time before the city, when the area covered by Birmingham contained scattered villages isolated by fields. The part-timbered house with its lath-and-plaster walls and uneven floor was a ghost of former times, sandwiched between a block of flats and a pair of Victorian semis.

It was the elder tree by the back door that made her absolutely certain she had to live there.

"It will have to come out," Evan said, surveying the angular branches and the knotted trunk. It had grown there for a very long time.

"No. You mustn't." Jennifer linked her arm in his.

"It straggles across the doorway and blocks the light from the kitchen window."

"Do what you like to the rest of the garden but don't touch the elder tree."

Evan glanced at her indulgently. "Is this one of your country superstitions?"

Jennifer smiled shyly, unsure of admitting something that Evan obviously thought was foolishness. "Elder is supposed to protect those who live in the house."

"Can I at least trim it back a little?"

"Well … only if you ask permission."

"Whose? Yours?"

"The witch's, of course. Every elder has a witch living in it and you must apologise before you cut anything off her tree."

Evan hooted with laughter. "You're teasing me," he said.

"I don't make fun of the things you believe in." Jennifer released his arm and walked into the kitchen through the open door.

"Okay, okay." Evan hurried after her. "I won't touch the tree." He put his arms about her waist. "We could make elder-flower champagne."

Jennifer wrinkled her nose. "Better to wait until autumn and make elder-berry wine. The flowers smell awful. They'd stink the place out."

"If you say so. What about the rest of the house? Do you like it?"

"I love it." She paused a moment. "I only hope Melanie does too."

"I'm sure she will."

Melanie didn't. The little girl was quiet and restive, often sullen in her replies when Evan spoke to her. Twice, Jennifer was called to her new school because Melanie had thrown a screaming tantrum over something trivial. She would become clingy and weepy the moment Jennifer arrived, saying she hated it there and she wanted to go home.

Jennifer tried to give her as much time as she could, feeling that part of the child's resentment was aimed at Evan for taking her mother's attention from her. It became more difficult, and easier, after Michael was born.

Michael was a quiet, co-operative baby but his needs took up a lot of her time, time she felt she should be sharing with Melanie. She tried to involve her daughter as much as she could, talking of the baby as "theirs", letting her help bathe and dress him. It seemed to work. She seemed more settled and happier though Jennifer wondered if Melanie was becoming a little too possessive of her brother. Several times when she had thought both of them to be asleep she had looked in to see Melanie standing by Michael's cot, just staring at him.

One incident, almost trivial, stood out in her memory. Evan was holding the baby on his lap, moving a brightly coloured ball before his face. Michael gurgled with pleasure. Jennifer thought how contented they both looked. She glanced at Melanie. The girl had put down the crayons she was using and was watching father and son. Her hands were clenched tightly at her sides and her whole body was rigid. Hatred contorted her face. Then Melanie shuddered, smiled and calmly continued with her colouring. Jennifer tucked the image away.

~~~

Jennifer was shaken awake. She was normally a light sleeper but Michael had been fretful all day. He had a slight temperature and she suspected he had caught the cold that had been bothering the rest of them during the past week. Melanie had been off school for two days at the start of the week with it, and she promised herself she would take Michael to the doctor in the morning if he was no better. Today she was too tired.

"Mummy, Mummy." Melanie's whisper held a hint of urgency and something else.

"What is it, darling? What time is it?"

"Mummy, Michael's gone a funny colour."

Jennifer heard Evan grunt as she kicked him in her scramble out of bed. She grabbed her dressing gown, barking her shin on the vanity stool in her haste. Melanie fled before her.

The baby struggled for breath, saliva drooling from his mouth. His limbs twitched convulsively. Jennifer snatched him into her arms.

"Melanie, wake daddy. No ... no ... go and dial 999. Get an ambulance." Jennifer couldn't think. It felt as though Michael was fighting her. She didn't know what to do. Suddenly his body went rigid and she almost dropped him. For a moment she thought he had stopped breathing. Slowly his limbs relaxed. His breaths came harshly and his skin burned.

"The doctor's coming, mummy," Melanie said. Her face was very pale in the artificial light of the bedroom.

"What's going on?" Evan said from the landing.

"Michael's sick," Jennifer said.

Evan pulled the quilt from the cot and took the baby from her, wrapping Michael in it. "Get dressed," he said. He must have seen her reluctance to let him go. "You will want to go to the hospital with him. We'll be downstairs."

The doorbell chimed. Melanie ushered in the young doctor who had seen Jennifer through her pregnancy.

"Didn't you ring the ambulance," Jennifer said.

Melanie shook her head. "They won't send one without a doctor's sayso, 'less it's an accident. Miss James told us that at school when Sandra fell out of the tree."

"She is correct," Dr Khan said. "She did exactly the right thing." He opened his bag and extracted a stethoscope. His thermometer case peeped from his top pocket.

"Tell me exactly what happened," he said, kneeling beside Jennifer and listening to Michael's chest.

His examination and Jennifer's description over, Dr Khan said, "We will take him straight to the hospital. We will go in my car."

"What's wrong with him?" Jennifer asked, holding

tight onto the seed of panic that threatened to unfold in her gut.

"I cannot be sure. Tests will tell us."

"But is it serious?"

"I always take convulsions in babies seriously. Shall we go?"

Jennifer glanced at Evan. "Will you be all right? You and Melanie."

Evan nodded, resting one hand on the girl's shoulder. Melanie shrugged it off and grimaced.

Jennifer remembered little of the journey. Except that the roads were empty and dark – like her soul – and all the lights were red, warning her. Bright lights greeted them on arrival at the hospital, with an undercurrent of quiet efficiency. Michael was taken from her. Someone took her elbow and led her into a waiting room, the sterile walls lined with semi-comfortable chairs. A plastic cup of hot sweet coffee was thrust into her hand.

"What's happening? Where's my baby?" she asked but she was alone. There was no-one in the corridor and she had no idea where they had taken him.

Shivering uncontrollably, she sat on the edge of one of the chairs clutching the cup for warmth, not drinking. She hated sugar in coffee. Time stretched.

She looked up when the door snicked open. Dr Khan was there. And another in a white coat. Dr Khan took the now cold cup from her hands and held them. "Your baby is very sick," he said.

Jennifer looked from one to the other. "Can I go to him?"

"In a little while," the other doctor said.

"What's wrong with him?" It was a question she didn't want to ask. She was afraid of the answer.

"We are treating him for meningitis."

Jennifer stood up quickly, snatching her hands from Dr Khan's grasp. "Don't you *know* what's wrong?" she asked.

"He has some of the symptoms but until the results come back from the lab we cannot be certain," the other doctor said.

He was maddeningly calm. Jennifer wanted to shake him, make him give her some real answers. "Can I see him now?"

He glanced at the clock on the wall behind Jennifer's head. "Certainly."

She was led along lino-floored corridors, disorientated by the turns. She vaguely remembered putting her arms into a white coat, tying a covering over her hair. Michael lay in the kind of incubator normally reserved for premature babies. He looked much smaller, frailer than his eight months. A tube disappeared up his nose, another was taped to his arm. Wires led from a pad stuck to his chest. The lower part of his trunk was covered with an ugly, purplish rash.

"He's going to die," she said.

"We will do all we can," the doctor said.

A nurse looked up from the monitor and gave her a quick smile.

Jennifer sat watching her son, waiting for some sign of change. Any sign. She hardly noticed when Evan arrived and put his arms around her.

"I took Melanie to school," he said. "She wanted to go."

She heard the words but they didn't register. "Come and get some sleep," Evan said.

Jennifer shook her head, certain Michael would die if she left him.

"I'll watch him," Evan said.

She allowed a nurse to lead her to a tiny cubicle. She took the drink and the pills without understanding, and slept. She felt guilty afterwards, that she had abandoned Michael, that she had deserted Melanie. But Evan was there, reassuring her. He could cope at home. He would come back later. All she had to do was to stay with Michael.

Thirty-six hours later the baby was dead. They let her hold him one more time before they took his body away. For a post-mortem, they said.

Evan took her home.

The afternoon was unfairly bright and warm. Bees hummed about the sweet-smelling may blossom in the hedge. The elder's white umbels nodded a welcome as she opened the back door. And stepped into desolation. The normal homely sounds were missing, and her shoes were loud on the red-clay tiles. The air chilled, raising goosebumps on her arms. She felt unwelcome for the first time in this house, and wondered if it was the sedative that was making things seem blurred.

"I'll make some tea, love," Evan said.

Dazed, Jennifer wandered upstairs into the children's darkened room. The sun flooded in as she pulled back the curtains, spotlighting Michael's cot. Automatically she straightened the sheets, brushing tiny browned flowers from under the pillow. She stood for a moment listening to the emptiness, then heard Evan clattering around in the kitchen. The sounds seemed to be the only real thing in the place.

Evan was rinsing out the jar Melanie had used for putting wildflowers in. Granny flowers she called them because they grew in the fields where her grandparents lived. It reminded her what was missing.

"Shouldn't we be collecting Melanie from school?" she

said, frowning at her inability to think clearly. It was unusual to forget her daughter.

Evan started, the jar smashing against the tap. Shattering.

"It's Saturday," he said, not turning round.

"Where is she then?" Jennifer could think of no-one in the neighbourhood who might look after her. She hadn't made many friends.

Evan faced her then. Leaning against the sink he looked close to tears. "They've put her in a home."

"For God's sake, why? Meningitis isn't contagious."

"At school, yesterday, she told her teacher I'd been touching her."

"What do you mean, touching her? We all touch each other."

"I... I've been accused of interfering with her, sexually. So they took her away."

He looked so unhappy that Jennifer crossed the room and put her arms about him, hugging him tight. "I didn't do anything, Jenny," he said miserably. "Honest, I didn't."

"What are we going to do?" she said.

"I'll move out. Tomorrow."

"You can't. Where will you live?"

"A bed and breakfast place," Evan said. "They won't let you have Melanie back if I'm still here. I asked."

"How long?"

"Until they decide whether to prosecute. Until after the trial."

The house seemed to crowd in on her. She felt cold.

~~~

It was four dreadful days before they let Melanie come home, she remembered. Four days of phone calls, visits, prying interviews and loneliness. She had never been alone before – there had always been someone: her parents, Melanie's father, Melanie... She considered going back to her in-laws, or at least sending Melanie there, but she could not face being parted from her again. She often woke in the night thinking she heard Michael crying, or Evan's footsteps in the hall, even when the girl was safely back in her own bed. Then Jennifer would go and watch her daughter sleeping, afraid she might disappear. She would scan her closely, seeking signs of illness, relieved when Melanie remained healthy.

Melanie never mentioned Evan, or Michael.

She met Evan only once, at the inquest on the Friday after Michael's death. Jennifer sat in the court clinging to his hand during the short presentation. Natural causes, the coroner said, and they were free to go. Evan took her for a cup of coffee but she hardly touched it and they hardly spoke.

"I'll have to go," she said finally. "I must collect Melanie."

The gloom followed her. It stayed, hovering over her in the intervening days before the funeral. Now that was over, but the depression hadn't lifted from the house. It seemed to deaden everything – sound, emotions, movement. Even Melanie seemed to feel it. "Can we go home yet?" Melanie asked as she tucked her into bed.

"We are home, darling," Jennifer told her.

~~~

Jennifer held the bottle in the palm of her hand. She could just make out the pills through the brown plastic. It would be so easy, she thought, to take them all. Dr Khan had prescribed them for her, in case she couldn't sleep. So far she had done without, though the temptation was great. They might bring tranquillity to her dreams, keeping out the reproachful faces of Michael and Evan and Melanie, accusatory at night as they never were by daylight. She knew it was her own guilt haunting her. She should have taken the baby to the doctor's earlier and never left Melanie with Evan, or married him, or…

She put the bottle firmly on the bedside cabinet and turned out the light. She closed her eyes against the shadows that gathered in the crooked corners of the room. Once they had been friendly. Now, alone in the wide bed, she felt menaced, watched, though she knew there was nothing there. They seemed to whisper too, yet her mind told her it was only the purr of cars passing along the main road outside. One seemed to come straight for her, shouting incomprehensibly. Jennifer clamped her hands over her ears and forced herself to relax. Perhaps she had better take one of the pills after all.

Sounds from downstairs awakened her. She had locked the back door, she was sure, but not bolted it. Evan usually did that. In the country it wasn't necessary. She never put the chain on the front door either. Evan said she was too trusting.

Jennifer slid out of bed and unhooked her dressing gown from the door. There was nothing at hand she could use as a weapon. Perhaps downstairs. In the kitchen. Perhaps there was no intruder. But she dared not hide. Not with Melanie asleep in the next room.

She tip-toed down the stairs, listening hard for a repeat of the noise that had awakened her. The kitchen door was ajar and she slipped inside. Moonlight brightened the square of window, and elder branches tapped on it, at once both reassuring and unnerving. "Protect me, little witch," she whispered.

The dresser drawer slid open easily. Jennifer picked out the carving knife and slipped the leather sheath from the sharp blade. The warmth of the wood in her hand gave her courage. She stepped into the hall and reached for the switch.

Evan stood by the front door, blinking in the sudden light.

"What are you doing here?" Jennifer whispered.

"You said you needed me." He looked cold and tired.

She put the knife carefully on the telephone table opposite the front door and hugged him to her. "I do," she said, "Really I do."

Evan stroked her hair. "I sat outside in the car for an hour before I dared come in," he said.

"Come to bed," Jennifer said.

"I mustn't stay."

"You can leave before Melanie wakes. Please, Evan. You can't just go away now you're here."

"Okay." He removed his shoes and placed them carefully on the mat.

Her need was for more than just his presence, she realised, as he softly closed the bedroom door. Without speaking she helped him undress. He left her nightdress in a crumpled heap on the floor.

They made love in quiet desperation, each trying to assuage their grief in the other's body. Afterwards Jennifer held him as he wept, her own despondency lifting a little, trying to forget that he would soon leave her again.

Morning brought the desperation back. Evan's side of the bed was cold and unrumpled as though he had never been there. She didn't remember his departure, nor putting her nightdress on again. The pills from the bottle were spilled over the bedside cabinet. Carefully Jennifer replaced them, screwing the child-proof cap on tight, thinking that she ought to lock them in the bathroom cabinet lest Melanie get hold of them.

That reminded her. She should talk to her daughter about her accusations. Jennifer couldn't believe that Evan would ever harm the girl but they always said you should believe children, that they didn't lie. She would make Melanie her favourite breakfast – scrambled eggs and marmite fingers – and then they would discuss the matter.

Jennifer dressed quickly. She heard Melanie in her room as she passed the door, crooning to her dolls. It was later than she thought. The kitchen was bright with the sun that slanted in from behind the block of flats, glancing off the brick-built garage that Evan never used; it was hardly wide enough to take his car and usually only their cycles and the lawnmower were kept there.

She worked quickly, concentrating on her task, knowing that the pain of grief would eventually ease. It had last time, when Melanie's father died, though meeting Evan had helped. She placed the plates on the table and crossed to the door.

"Breakfast's ready, Melanie," she called.

Jennifer took the empty pan to the sink, filling it with water. As she glanced outside she noticed that her bicycle was propped against the wall. Melanie's tricycle stood in the centre of the cobbled area between house and garage. She heard Melanie enter the kitchen behind her. "You haven't been outside this morning, have you, darling?" she asked.

"No, mummy."

"Well, someone's left your tricycle out."

She waited until Melanie had taken her first mouthful before stepping out through the unlocked back door. The spring sun was warm on her face. Bees hummed from elder to hedgerow flower. A car engine thrummed in the garage. The incongruous sound stopped her. Coldness gripped her stomach.

Jennifer glanced behind, seeing Melanie's dark head bowed over her plate. As if aware of her gaze the girl looked up and smiled. Jennifer shuddered. She forced herself to walk across the patio area.

Placing her palm on the wooden door she felt the vibration of the vehicle within. She tugged at the handle. Reluctantly the door opened just as the engine died. Exhaust fumes billowed out around her, choking, stifling.

She didn't have to look to know that Evan's body was slumped in the front seat.

~~~

Jennifer sat on the telephone seat in the hall. The police had gone. And Dr Khan. He had been kind. She could stay with his wife if she wanted. It would be no trouble. Jennifer had shaken her head. She shouldn't be alone, he said. But she had Melanie. Was there somewhere she could go, relatives she could stay with, he asked. Yes, yes, Melanie's grandparents.

And she would go. The old lady had been right: the city wasn't for her, and Melanie would prefer the open fields. Jennifer would be glad to leave the house. It had welcomed her as a friend and then betrayed her. It oppressed her now with its narrow passages and dark oak beams – like a trap she couldn't free herself from.

She looked up at the sound of footsteps. Melanie stood framed in the kitchen doorway, one hand behind her back.

"Can we go home now?" Melanie asked. "To Granny's?"

The words stirred a memory. "Yes, darling." Jennifer held out her arms for her daughter.

Melanie took a few steps towards her and smiled. "Would you like a present?" she asked.

Jennifer wasn't in the mood for playing games but the child had been through so much. It wouldn't hurt to respond to her lovingly. Whatever her own grief, Melanie had to come first. She nodded.

Slowly, with evident delight, Melanie brought a bunch of flowers from behind her back. Hedgerow blooms. Long stemmed buttercups, yellow cat's ear, bright ragwort, and in the centre a stalk of creamy may blossom.

The hall seemed to darken around her. The walls closed in. All she could see were the pale flowers. Superimposed was the image of the jar on the dresser she had seen but not noticed the day she had come home from the hospital. And Evan furtively rinsing the jar. And her hand sweeping the browned elder flowers from Michael's cot.

Jennifer's fingers closed on the shaped, wooden knife handle, still on the telephone table.

"They're gone now, Mummy," Melanie said. She grinned. "We can go home."

Jennifer launched herself at the flowers.

The silver blade plunged into Melanie's smiling face.

SKY LIGHT

Lucy opened her eyes. The room was dark save for the glint of silver at the edge of the skylight. Panes of glass sloped upwards reflecting the glimmer of mercurial streetlamps. She felt nothing.

At the edge of awareness were the bare splinter-riddled boards. If she reached out, she knew her fingers would touch the roughness. Though her naked back pressed against the wood, she recognised only the comfort of lying still, limbs sleep-numbed. Sensory-deprived ears heard nothing but the creaking beams that barely held the house erect.

She was waiting.

She knew he was close.

The light in the street dimmed, casting shadow across the skylight, enveloping Lucy deeper into the darkness. Then it went out. At first the retinal image remained with her, painting the window frames across her sight. The image faded, finally eclipsed by the presence of the moon. Hunter's Moon. His moon. It glowed full behind thin cloud cover.

He was coming now. She sensed him as minute changes in the air – not sound or vibration, or different temperatures; something subtler. Her lips parted and she smiled, the tip of her tongue tasting the salt beading on her upper lip. She opened her thighs, feeling the juices moisten her labia; the fine hairs of her body shivered erect.

He was here. The hunter.

She felt his insubstantial touch as he entered and

engulfed her. She gave him warmth. He gave her his carefully hoarded seed.

Above the house the clouds began to drift away. Pinpricks of stars glinted on the glass of the skylight.

~~~

Lucy roused, shivering. She groped around for the clothes she had discarded in the room's corner. She bet that none of her friends would have stayed so long alone in the upper room.

Somewhere she had left her phone. She felt around, blind despite the moonlight that now shone strongly, limning the attic in patterns of black and grey. Her fingers brushed the slim case. It skidded away from her. She reached for it, grabbed hold of it tightly before it could escape. The light from the screen scattered shadows then created more the moment she thumbed it on. The numbers showed 3.15. It was later than she thought. She hoped the others were still waiting below. They had her torch. She'd wanted to bring it with her but Marvi said she would cheat, the girl forgetting that phones could be torches, too.

The stairs creaked as Lucy picked her way down, holding the phone high so that the ghostly light touched the steps below her, treading always into the circle of light that preceded her. The whole house seemed to sigh as she reached the bottom, dust motes rising, then settling from banister to floor. She padded across the narrow hall, following the footmarks she had made earlier, and opened the door to the front room. It was stiff and heavy. The last stub of a candle flickered and died with the movement of air. A sweet smell of smoke reached her. Only it and the debris marked the fact that someone had been there. Chip papers still exuded the faint aroma of vinegar, and a beer can dripped the last dregs onto the already rotting floorboards. Her friends had gone.

Lucy didn't fancy the idea of walking through the streets alone at this hour. It was a good mile-and-a-half home.

"Bastards," she said and the house echoed the sentiment by groaning – as if someone walked across the floor overhead.

~~~

It had started as a dare. Earlier that day, Lucy and the rest of the group of six bored school leavers had found themselves walking past the empty house. It was one of a row of tall Victorian terraces, derelict and awaiting demolition to make way for new offices, or a car park or something equally useless. Only one house showed any signs of habitation, an old man who had refused to move out when his neighbours had left, relocated to newly refurbished council flats, just like the one where Lucy lived with her mother and sister.

Darren leapt atop the low, crumbling wall that surrounded the end house and walked precariously along it, arms outstretched. A dislodged brick tottered and slid into the tangle of bramble and ryegrass that replaced a once-neat garden.

"Which one were the murder done in?" Marvi asked.

"Wasn't no murder," Tonia said. "The old biddy topped herself."

"No, the bloke. The tramp," Marvi said.

"I know the one you mean," Vinder said. "But it wasn't a murder."

Harvinder had spent his first fourteen years in the south-east and always sounded a bit posh, but his father was the newsagent on The Green and picked up all the gossip.

"What happened then?" Darren asked. He was picking

bits of weathered brick from the wall and lobbing them at the house. There was little he could damage as all the windows were boarded and those missiles that struck disintegrated into spurts of red dust.

"He was just an old man that nobody cared about. He fell down the stairs and lay there for three months before he was found."

"Boring," Stephen said, joining his brother in his target practice, at which point Darren stopped. He always did that when Stephen copied him. They were twins but as unlike as siblings could be. Darren was dark haired and swarthy with a footballer's build while the fairer Stephen was stick-thin and a head taller than his brother. Darren only tolerated him hanging around because his dad said he should look out for him.

"Let's go round the back," Marvi said. "There'll be a way in."

"Will there be blood?" Tonia asked.

"Don't be silly," Vinder told her. "He died of a broken neck."

"Oh."

Lucy sighed to herself. She didn't like the idea of breaking into an old house, especially one where someone might have died. She didn't really belong in this group, feeling she was only tolerated because Nathan thought she was his girl. Lucy actually rather fancied Darren, which was why she hung around even though Nathan wasn't with them – his parents had taken him off to the Canaries for two weeks, the result of a prize they had won in a *Birmingham Mail* competition.

~~~

They couldn't get into the end house – the boards were too tightly secured – but Darren, assisted by Stephen, managed to wrench those of the middle house free. The windows beneath were grimy and broken.

"What can you see?" Tonia asked, trying to push the boys out of the way.

"Spooky," said Stephen.

Darren shrugged. "It's just an empty room. A bit mucky."

"Can we get in?" Marvi asked.

"Yeah." Darren elbowed the rest of the glass away. "Who's coming?" he said, pulling himself through.

Marvi hitched up her skirt and struggled across the windowsill. Lucy looked away hastily from the fascination of Marvi's exposed thighs. She hoped she would never get that fat. The others followed Marvi, even Lucy when Vinder gave her a helping hand. She didn't want to be left alone in the garden. At least inside, they were out of sight.

"There's nothing here," Tonia said after a quick inspection of the other ground floor rooms. Not that they could see much, the meagre light filtering through cracks in the boards showed up very little except dust and shadows. Darren thumbed on his phone and the screen gave his face an eerie glow. He held it up, chasing a scuttley thing into a corner. Lucy hoped it wasn't a rat. Stephen copied Darren who sighed, even though the others followed suit.

"Imagine it," Vinder said. "At night. With the ghost of the tramp stalking through the rooms."

"Stumbling more like," Marvi said.

"Perhaps it wasn't this house," Tonia said.

"Who cares?" Vinder said

"It's a great idea," Darren said. "We come back here after dark. With candles. What do you think?"

"Yeah, great." Both Marvi and Tonia grinned with glee at the prospect. Lucy cringed inwardly.

"Spooky," Stephen said.

"Okay. Meet back here. Ten o'clock. I'll bring some cans. Vinder can you get some stuff? The girls can bring the candles."

~~~

It would have been easy for Lucy to just stay away, but word would have got back to Nathan if she didn't show. And she didn't want to look scared in front of Darren. Besides, she told herself, there were no such things as ghosts.

"Thought you weren't coming," Tonia said when Lucy scrambled into the dark house.

"Told you I would." She'd brought a torch which brightened the gloom of the disused kitchen. Her stomach was taut with fear – not of the house but of being caught in a stranger's garden, or even that she would be the only one to turn up. She followed Tonia through into the bare front room where Marvi and Vinder were already waiting.

"Are we all here now?" Tonia said.

"Darren's getting some chips and the beer," Vinder said. He struck a match and began to light the candles Marvi had brought, instructing the girls where to set them down, warning them to be careful. They didn't want to set the place alight.

"Stephen's got the beer," Darren said, dumping the chip packets in the centre of the circle of light.

"Did you have to bring him?" Marvi asked.

Darren shrugged as if the question needed no answering.

Lucy wedged her torch into a crack between the window frame and the nailed-on board. Most of the original glass was missing. Vinder laid out the packets of Rizla's that he'd pilfered from his father's shop while

Darren dismembered a packet of ten, heaping the tobacco onto a cleanish tissue. Vinder crumbled some of the resin he'd brought onto the heap.

"How'd you know how much to add?" Tonia asked.

Vinder grinned, his expression slightly demonic in the shifting candlelight. "Guesswork."

Darren mixed the ingredients with his fingers before laying it out along the prepared papers. The two boys rolled up, one each, and lit them from the candles. The flame sizzled halfway up Darren's, dropping ash.

"It's too thin," Marvi said.

"You have a go, then."

"Okay."

Vinder sucked on his spliff before releasing a cloud of smoke.

"Have you done this before?" Tonia asked.

"A few times." He handed it to Tonia who breathed in too quickly and started coughing. Vinder took it from her quickly and held it out to Lucy who shook her head.

"Go on," he said. "You can't get addicted."

She saw Darren watching her. Hesitantly, she put it to her lips and cautiously sucked. The taste of the smoke instantly filled her mouth. She didn't like it much. She wondered what it was supposed to do, if she was meant to feel any different. Quickly, she passed it to Marvi who made a great play of inhaling, pretending she had done this loads of times before. It was easier to pretend, Lucy thought, as the joint came round to her again.

They shared out the chips, dipping them in a communal pot of curry sauce, and passed round cans of beer and coke, Lucy never knowing which she was getting until she tasted it. Marvi started giggling. The air was getting cloudy with smoke and Tonia was batting at it as if she could catch it. The weird one was Steven. He sat watching each in turn like a cat deciding which of a selection of mice he would play with first. But then he was always a bit weird. Lucy began to think she might make up an excuse and go home as the house was a mile or so from the Green where they usually hung out, and she had quite a bit further to go than that.

"I've got an idea," Darren said. "Vinder. Give me six of your matches."

Vinder handed them over. Darren broke one in half and arranged them in his hand so that they all appeared the same length. "Here's what we do," he said. "First, we decide on a dare. Then we all pick a match. The short one gets the dare. Okay?"

There were nods from all round the circle. Lucy thought it sounded childish, but, whatever.

"What will it be?" Tonia asked, stretching extravagantly.

"You choose."

She thought for a moment. "Go all the way up to the top of the house alone."

When there were no dissenters Darren held out the matches. Lucy tried not to let her hand shake when it came to her turn to choose. Vinder picked the short one.

"Right," he said. "Am I allowed a torch?"

Tonia nodded.

"How will we know if you've really been there?" Marvi asked.

"Tell us the colour of the wallpaper," Tonia said

"Right. Then you can go and check if you so wish."

Stepping with exaggerated care around the candles, Vinder disappeared into the shadows. They could hear his footsteps on the bare boards of the passage, then the groan of brittle wood as he began his ascent of the stairs. Silence fell as his steps faded with distance. It seemed ages before Vinder reappeared.

"Two attic rooms. No wallpaper but the walls are painted a mucky brown," he said.

"I didn't hear you coming down," Tonia said.

"I crept. Like a ghost."

"Spiders," Stephen said.

"Oh, don't." Marvi shivered.

"What's the next dare then?" Darren asked. "It's your turn to choose."

"All right. Go into the kitchen and stay there for fifteen minutes without any light."

Marvi got the short match. "How do I know when the time's up?" she said. Lucy thought she sounded about to sulk, as if she didn't really like this game anymore.

"We'll come and tell you," Darren said.

"I'll go with her, to take away the light," Vinder said.

"Good idea. Off you go, Marvi."

Vinder hadn't returned two minutes before Marvi screamed. They heard her blundering along the corridor.

Tonia and Darren headed out to see what the matter was.

"There were spiders," Marvi wailed. "Lots of them. They were crawling all over." Tonia tittered. "Were they pink?"

"And blue and green with red eyes."

"How could you see them if it was dark?" Vinder asked.

"They glowed." Her voice rose into a wail.

"You'd never have thought of them if Steven had said nothing," Darren told her. He sounded disgusted with her cowardice.

"Tarantulas," Steven said.

"You don't think they were, do you?" Marvi's voice quavered.

"Don't be daft," Darren said. "Let's do it again. I choose this time."

They waited in silence until Darren spoke. "Go up to the attic. Take off all your clothes and lie on the floor for ten minutes."

"It'll be cold," Tonia said.

"So what. That's what dares are all about."

Lucy hesitated about choosing her match. Somehow, she knew that whichever she picked, it would be the short one. It was. She thought about telling them to forget it and go home, but she could do better than Marvi. She wasn't afraid of spiders and Darren hadn't mentioned darkness. She snatched at the torch before she could change her mind but Marvi got to it first. She stuck it under her buttocks and said, "You'll cheat."

"Darren didn't say anything about it being dark," Lucy heard the whine in her voice.

"I had to go dark," Marvi said.

"And you couldn't hack it."

"And you can?"

"Yeah." Lucy sped up the stairs as fast as she could. "And don't anyone follow me," she yelled as she went. "I'll hear you."

Like all the rooms, the attic was bare of furniture but the window, a large sloping skylight, was unboarded and unbroken. A full moon provided enough illumination to see by. Lucy turned off the phone she had used to light her way and, shivering slightly, complied with the parameters of the dare.

~~~

Now, those so-called friends had abandoned her. Lucy walked home, tremulous and seething. She rehearsed in her head the things she would like to say to them but probably wouldn't. Then she considered trying to avoid them but Nathan would want to know why. They would tell Nathan. Everybody told Nathan everything. Everybody was a little scared of Nathan, even Darren. Certainly Lucy was, even though he was always nice to her. He didn't hit her or anything. Not like Darren did when Marvi annoyed him. But Marvi was fat and stupid anyway. Darren only went with her because she'd drop her knickers in a flash. Nathan has asked Lucy to but she'd said no. Nathan said it didn't matter. He'd wait, though she was sure he'd humped Marvi when Darren wasn't around. Lucy recognised that smug look Marvi got sometimes, especially when she and Darren went off together in the park.

~~~

Despite her reservations, Lucy went to meet Nathan's friends at their usual haunt, the triangle of brown turd-covered grass locally called The Green. Its only merits were that a chippie, a pub, an off-licence and a bus shelter were no more than a hundred paces apart, and there were seats. Admittedly, the benches tended to be littered with OAPs during the day but they usually toddled off when the others started making lewd comments. Lucy kept quiet though she thought it rather unfair, and some of the things said just for effect made her squirm.

This morning, she was determined to get her say in first. If anyone saw her as she approached they were deliberately ignoring her.

"Bastards," she said once she got within five paces. Not as loud as she would have liked but enough for them to hear. "Why'd you leave me in that house?"

Darren turned to face her slowly, an attempt at disdain on his face. "We went up to look for you," he said, "but you weren't there."

"Thought you'd chicken shitted," Tonia said.

"Sneaked past us and run away."

"I suppose you sent Simple Simon up," Lucy said. She couldn't help the contempt creeping into her voice.

"I went," Vinder said. "When you didn't come back. The attic was empty."

Marvi's sneer was clear. "Couldn't cut it could you?"

"I did a bloody sight better than you did," Lucy said. "I didn't scream about spiders after ten seconds." She turned to Vinder. "Did you look in both attics?"

"Of course. Which one were you in, Lucy?"

She was beginning to run out of bravado in the face of their hostility. "The one with the skylight."

"There wasn't one," Vinder said. She thought she could hear a snigger in his voice. "And all those houses only have one attic room."

"You said there were two when you went up there for your dare. Proves you didn't bloody well go up." Lucy turned on her heel and walked away. They were laughing at her. She felt close to crying. Not only had Nathan's friends deserted her but they were calling her a liar as well. She'd go home and sulk there, she decided. Nathan would soon sort them out when he came back.

~~~

Stephen smoothed a patch of rumpled bedspread and tipped the counters from the small leather bag that he'd found one time on a rubbish heap and put in his pocket. Last summer he had rediscovered it under his bed and thought it ideal to keep the counters in. He named them as they lay in the hollow surrounded by the hillocks of cloth.

The white one was Lucy. The black one was a little thicker than the rest so that was Marvi. Darren was the yellow one. Stephen touched each with his finger as he moved them around into a new pattern. The green counter, Tonia, he put to one side, then moved the blue, Harvinder, to touch it. Nathan's red, he lay besides Lucy's white, with his own, the purple to the other side of the white. Stephen smiled. That would be a nice place to be. Next to Lucy. He tried to make the two counters touch but the unevenness of the bedspread kept a gap between them. No, being there might not be the best place.

His last counter was orange. He had seen the moon that colour once so that one he named Moon. He used it to flick the others. He pressed its edge to that of the purple counter. It leapt upwards, somersaulted three times and came down in an empty space. Stephen flicked it again. This time it overlapped Tonia's green.

He turned it over between his fingers. Leaning over, Stephen pulled a shoebox from under the bed. He emptied it onto the floor and extracted a bottle of Tippex from the heap. It was something else he had found amongst the rubbish. Most of his treasures were acquired from what others had thrown out. The stuff inside the Tippex bottle was mostly dried up so he spat in it and gave it a good shake. It was just liquid enough for him to paint a candle on the reverse of the green counter. At least, it looked a bit like a candle. He wasn't much good at drawing. He waved it around in the air to make it dry, then dropped it back into the bag and followed it with the others. He heard his mother calling for the third time from downstairs and pushed the bag under his pillow before going down to supper.

~~~

Lucy began to feel unwell soon after she started her first job, three weeks later. It was because she was so tired, she thought – on her feet in the florist's all day, then sleeping badly at night. Dreams bothered her. She often dreamed of babies and being pregnant just before her period started. These were different. They were about sex, but she was seeing things from the man's point of view. Usually she woke sweating and she began to wonder if she was secretly a lesbian. After all, she still refused to have sex with Nathan when all the other girls she knew claimed to have lost their virginity years before they left school.

After a particularly bad dream, she lay back against her pillows and stared out of the bedroom window. The curtains were drawn back to allow the moonlight in. Occasionally, the moonglow dimmed as a cloud scudded across its face heralding more rain. When she could see it clearly the moon looked fullish. She couldn't quite be sure as part was hidden behind one of the tower blocks that crenulated the skyline. Through the thin plasterboard walls she could hear the old man next door snoring, and from the flat below came the muffled sounds of late-night television.

Dreams, she had heard, meant things. If she could recall the details maybe she could look up their meaning and stop them. They always started the same way. She was walking. Across The Green, usually, though it seemed much bigger. She felt different, too. Taller, and her breasts didn't bounce against her thin jumper though she knew she wasn't wearing a bra. And there was a tightness about her crotch. There was a pleasurable sensation of her pants rubbing against her as she moved. She was looking for sex. She knew that.

Dream Lucy saw someone she thought she recognised – a girl with long dark hair and an over-pale complexion. They spoke but Lucy couldn't remember what they said. Then they were walking past the derelict terrace. Lucy and the girl climbed through the window.

"I'll show you where I was," Lucy said.

"I didn't say I didn't believe you," her companion said.

"Liar." Lucy reached out and touched the other girl's breasts.

She flinched away. "I don't think I want to go up there."

"But you must. Then you can tell the others the truth."

They climbed. The stairs, as often happened in dreams, seemed more plentiful than before, but the room was still at the top, dusty and bare, with the skylight allowing the bright moonlight access.

"Okay. Now I've seen, let's go," the girl said.

"No." Lucy restrained her easily by grasping her arm. "Take your clothes off."

"Why?"

"I had to."

"Don't be daft. You've proved your point."

"You'll do it like I did." Lucy said. "We'll do it together."

Lucy reached out and tore off the girl's clothes. She was strong tonight. Bold. She felt her genitalia swelling with excitement as she exposed breasts, belly and pubic hair.

"Stop it! Stop it!" The girl's fists beat on her chest but Lucy felt nothing, only a rising passion. Her own clothes seemed to fall away.

The girl screamed. Lucy wrestled her to the floor. One hand gripped both her wrists, the other plunged between her victim's legs, feeling for the hole she knew was there, seeking moisture with her fingers. Lucy grinned and bit the nipple that rose, pale and tempting, beside her face. Then she was riding the girl, like a man would, thrusting into her, finding pleasure in it until the intensity burst.

Lucy sat back and looked down at her slim, male body.

~~~

Nathan wasn't supposed to visit Lucy at work, not unless he intended to buy something. She didn't want to risk losing the first job she'd ever had. Neither did Nathan. With money in her pocket, she could take him places. He claimed to be doing a college course but she doubted he turned up for many lectures, his parents being expected to support him.

She tried to shoo him out quickly when he came in the following day. "Text me," she said.

He stared around as if he'd never seen the place before. He looked distracted, as if unaware of where he was. He stopped Lucy before she could say anything more. "Tonia was raped last night. I thought you ought to know," he said.

Lucy felt as if she had been suddenly knifed in the gut.

"Where?" The word came out strangled.

"Marvi said they found her in the park. She isn't talking sense."

Lucy swallowed, remembering. Tonia was like the girl in her dream. "I did it," she said. "At least, I dreamt I did." She didn't like Tonia sometimes, but she'd never wish that on her.

"Dreams don't hurt people. And you don't have the right equipment."

"I did last night."

"Don't be daft, Lucy. Look... When I was on holiday I dreamed I was fucking you. We were thousands of miles apart so I couldn't have, could I? Dreams aren't real."

"I suppose not." She knew he spoke the truth but she felt reluctant to be convinced.

"See you tonight," he said. "Perhaps they'll have caught him by then."

~~~

The derelict house became a kind of sanctuary. There was no indication that it was haunted at all.

"It's safer than wandering around the park at night," Darren had said. "We can smoke and drink in peace."

Nathan agreed but rarely took Lucy there. She said she preferred to go to brighter places, especially now she could afford it. Besides, having a den was childish. Yet one night she found herself standing in the doorway of the attic room. An old stained mattress had been dragged up from the local tip. Marvi, lying half-naked, snored loudly, her pendulous breasts rising and falling in time to her stertorous breathing. Her skirt was rucked up exposing obese thighs. Darren lay beside her, staring up at the skylight. He was completely naked. His eyes narrowed as Lucy's shadow fell across his face.

"Who are you?" Darren asked, turning his head to look at her.

"Don't you know?" Lucy admired his lean musculature. The moonlight pearled his skin turning the slight hint of brownness to pale velvet. She knelt beside him.

"It seems a shame," she said, running her hands across the smooth chest, "to waste all this."

"We don't have to." He lifted the silk of the robe she wore for this occasion and gripped her crotch. She ignored the fact that she didn't own anything this luxurious. His fingers probed at the moisture that formed between her legs.

Lucy cupped his balls in her palm, thumb and finger encircling and tightening around his erection. "You want me," she said.

Without asking or any further preamble, she slid him into her. She kept him pinned to the mattress and used him for her pleasure. He groaned in his own ecstasy as

Marvi continued to sleep beside him. His seed filled and warmed her.

"You can get off now," Darren said.

Lucy shook her head. She raked her fingers down his sternum. Blood beaded beneath her nails.

"What are you doing?" Darren said, wriggling and finding himself trapped. Her muscles gripped his penis tight within her. She grinned.

There was a knife in her hand. She carved lines across his ribs to his navel. Leaning back, she slashed herself free of him. Darren screamed.

Lucy stood slowly, gazing at the bloody mess that had been Darren's pride.

Marvi slept on.

~~~

Stephen lay awake. He turned on his side and stared at Darren's bed. It was empty again. He didn't like it when Darren wasn't here at night. There had been lots of nights recently when he hadn't come home until very, very late. Then he'd have a strange smell on him. Not the funny cigarette smell, more like that scent girls had after PE and before they showered. It wasn't quite like that though.

Unable to sleep, he reached under his pillow and pulled out the little bag of counters. He turned on the table lamp before tipping them onto the bed. The green and white ones were stuck together and he had to prise them apart. The Tippex hadn't been quite dry when he'd put them away last.

He laid them out in an arc. His purple one faced them. He used the orange Moon to flick it. It landed on the yellow one – Darren. He changed them over and flicked the yellow with the orange. He felt a crunch. When he picked it up, it had a notch in it.

~~~

Lucy awoke slick with sweat. Her crotch itched and she scratched, her fingers coming away sticky with menstrual blood. She lay a while, working up the energy to go and shower. It was her free day. She had decided to go shopping that morning before an appointment at the hairdressers. She was taking Nathan to the cinema to celebrate his birthday and wanted to look nice. At some point over the last couple of months she had discovered that she really liked him. He wasn't cruel and spiteful like the others – he was even kind to Stephen when he intruded in their conversations. Besides, the group was breaking up. Tonia had totally withdrawn from everything and rarely left her house. On the one occasion Lucy had seen her and tried to offer sympathy, Tonia screamed and tried to attack her. Marvi, she considered to be a fat bicycle; and she had gone off Darren, beginning to see his pranks as childish and somehow she couldn't forgive him for going with Marvi.

Lucy was about to board the bus into town when she spotted Marvi galumphing towards her, calling her name. Despite her dislike for the other girl, Lucy stopped. Marvi never ran – she wobbled too much. She looked distressed and not just from her exertions.

"What do you want, Marvi?" Lucy said, barely keeping the irritation from her voice. The bus doors closed and it began to pull away from the stop leaving her standing on the pavement.

"You've got to help me."

"Why?"

"Something's happened to Darren." She screwed her face up and sniffed. Two tears oozed down her fat cheeks.

"He's probably just being a bastard as usual."

Marvi shook her head wildly. "I think he's dead."

"You're just being silly, Marvi."

"Not this time. Please come. I don't know what to do."

"Where?"

"The old house."

"Why me? You've never wanted my help before."

"Come on." Marvi grasped Lucy's arm. She fingers dug bruisingly into her flesh.

~~~

Lucy was becoming wary of this house. It appeared innocuous enough but it was figuring too large in her dreams. From the back garden she looked at the walls, seeing the flaking brickwork, green-stained by rising damp. A dormer window protruded from the sloping, sagging red-tile roof. The back door was fixed so that although it still looked boarded and secure it could be opened enough to let them in. Marvi squeezed through the gap.

Darren lay at the foot of the stairs. Marvi had put his jacket over him to hide some of his nakedness.

"What happened?" Lucy asked.

"I don't know," Marvi wailed. "We was asleep upstairs. When I woke up, he was gone. Then I found him here."

Lucy knelt beside the body trying to remember what she had been told about pulses. There was one in the neck, she thought. She touched Darren's throat. The flesh was cool but not cold. She thought she could feel something fluttering against her fingertips but wasn't sure.

"Have you called an ambulance?" Lucy asked.

"We're not supposed to be here," Marvi said. "They'll ask questions."

"You could have called me, or Nathan. Texted."

"You'd've ignored me. I know you don't like me." Marvi sniffed, her bosom heaving as a prelude to crying.

"What do you expect me to do?"

"Get him out of here. Take him home. Anything."

"Don't be stupid. If his neck's broken we could paralyse or kill him if we moved him."

Marvi stood staring at her. She was shivering like a jelly.

"Go and get his clothes," Lucy said. She fished around in her bag for her phone. "I'll call an ambulance. You go and call Nathan and tell him to come here. I'll stay with Darren."

"Can't you phone Nathan?"

"Not if I'm talking to the medics."

Lucy sat cross-legged in the dim, dusty hall. Marvi had scuttled off. She wasn't sure if the other girl really cared for Darren or whether she was more concerned about not getting involved. Lucy's own feelings were ambivalent. While tired of Darren's childish cruelties she hadn't really wanted him to get hurt. After her dream of the previous night she felt somehow responsible. Her gaze wandered to the stairs. Dark patches marked some of the treads, almost like newly spilled drops of water soaked into the dry wood. She wondered how long they had been there.

"Hello! Anybody there?"

Lucy rose as she heard voices outside the front of the house.

"Round the back," she called, hoping that they heard her. She pushed open the back door as far as she could to let light and the two ambulance men in.

"What happened here, love?" the taller of them said.

"I ... I don't know." Lucy stammered, suddenly wishing she was a long way from there and cursed Marvi for getting her into this mess and herself for allowing it. She was too soft, too easily led.

"I didn't find him," Lucy tried to explain. "A friend did and she called me."

"Where is she now?"

"She went home. She's scared of spiders." It seemed a lame excuse but it was all she could think of.

"Did you move him, love?" the man asked.

She shook her head. "We were told in school not to."

The second, shorter man was kneeling beside Darren now, feeling for his pulse, checking his breathing. At the periphery of her vision she saw him turn the body over, heard his sharp intake of breath. She saw the mask of drying blood that covered Darren's trunk. Her mind superimposed the dream image over his form. A giant fist clenched at her stomach. A wave of dizziness rose from her feet to her head making her stagger. She rushed outside and gasped in lungfuls of fresh diesel-tainted air.

"Are you all right, Miss?" Lucy took her hands from over her eyes to see a uniformed policeman looking at her with concern.

She nodded. "Can I go home, please?" she said. She noticed the whininess creeping into her voice.

"We'd like to ask you a few questions first. Would you come and sit in the car?"

She didn't see how she could refuse. She allowed herself to be led round to the front of the house. Blue lights flashed silently in the street as a stretcher was bundled into the back of the ambulance. She stared out of the police car window as it sped away.

"Can you tell me what happened, Miss?" The policeman asked. He was sitting in the front of the vehicle, his female companion beside her in the back.

"I told the ambulance man. I don't know. I wasn't there. A friend fetched me."

"Who was this friend?"

Lucy hesitated. She didn't owe Marvi anything yet she felt a bit responsible. She had dreamed it and it happened

– or something like it. "Marvi Richards," she said.

"Where does Marvi live?"

"The flats off the Redditch Road. I don't know the number. I never went there."

"Was she here with the lad when the accident happened?"

"I don't know." I don't know much, Lucy thought. I shouldn't have let Marvi get me involved. "Can I go home, now?"

"We'll take you home in a little while."

Lucy pushed the car door open. "No. I'll walk."

The policewoman laid a hand on her arm as if to restrain her. "Let go of me," Lucy said. She threw herself out of the police car and set off at a brisk walk. If they wanted a statement they'd have to do it properly. And she wouldn't say any more without a witness. Right now, they'd have to arrest her to make her stay. And there was no way that she'd arrive home in the back of a police car. Her mother would have a fit and all the neighbouring curtains would be twitching like leaves in a thunderstorm.

She was no more than a quarter of a mile from home when Nathan met her. "Marvi said there'd been some trouble," he said.

Lucy carried on walking. "Yes."

"What over?"

"Ask Marvi."

"Hey, Lou. There's no need to get mad at me."

"I'm not." Lucy stopped. The wave that had been chasing her down the street rolled over her. Tears flowed. Nathan put an arm round her shoulders and pulled a rather grubby handkerchief from his pocket.

"Tell me about it."

"I just don't like being cross-examined by the police."

"Did you tell them anything?"

"I said it was Marvi's fault." She sniffed and fumbled in her bag for a clean tissue. "Can dreaming something make it happen?"

"I told you before. Course it can't."

"Then why did I dream Darren was being mutilated. By me."

"Perhaps it's what you hoped."

Lucy shivered. "I'm not that nasty, am I?"

"Course not. Say, do you want to give the cinema a miss tonight? You can take me to the Mop Fair next Monday instead."

~~~

The Kings Norton Mop was always held on the first Monday in October, though the nature of it had changed. What had originally been a hiring fair was now an occasion for fun. Lucy hoped that she and Nathan could enjoy it by themselves.

Every nook and niche around The Green had been occupied by fairground stalls. Cables snaked across the ground to trip the unwary. Generators hummed and fairy lights brightened autumn-dark trees. An ox roast had been set up in the roadway outside the butcher's. Lucy paid for two huge baps stuffed with sliced of beef. Fat and meat juices oozed between her fingers as she bit into hers, the lashings of mustard stinging her mouth and lips with its fiery warmth.

She almost choked as a fist hit her shoulder.

"Fucking bitch," Marvi screamed. "What you set the pigs on me for?"

Lucy gasped, spitting out the fragment of meat that caught in her throat and wiped saliva from her chin. She twisted round and stared into the other girl's fury. "I wasn't about to be landed with your mess," she said.

Marvi pushed her again. The force of the blow made Lucy step backwards. Her heel caught a curb. She staggered, trying to keep her balance and losing her grip on the roll. A passer-by trod on it just as screams of hysterical enjoyment ripped the air from the direction of the whirligig in the pub car park.

Nathan stepped between them. "Cool it, Marvi," he said.

"It's not your business."

"It is when you threaten my girl."

"You wanted my help," Lucy reminded her.

"So's I didn't have to answer stupid questions."

Lucy sighed. "And I thought it was because you were scared." She glanced around suddenly feeling that the three of them were the centre of attention, but people walked past, seemingly ignoring them as if they were an insignificant island in the sea of pleasure seekers.

"Why don't you stop thinking about yourselves for a minute?" Vinder appeared out of the crowds and came quietly to stand beside Marvi. He put a hand on her shoulder. It had a calming effect on her. The anger eased from her face and she looked away.

Vinder said, "I don't suppose any of you thought to go and visit Darren?"

Lucy hadn't. That she hadn't suddenly made her feel anxious; the way she always used to at school when she hadn't done her maths homework. Other subjects didn't matter, just made her feel guilty.

"Since you're asking," Vinder continued, "he is comfortable."

"You two gonna be friends again?" Nathan asked the girls.

Marvi shrugged. "If you want."

Lucy had never really been Marvi's friend but didn't

feel she could cope with her enmity. She noticed Stephen standing behind Vinder and gave him a little smile. "Okay."

Nathan and Vinder kept between the two girls as they strolled through the fair, Stephen tagging along behind. Marvi bought herself a giant stick of candyfloss. In texture, Lucy thought, it resembled her hair – frizzy. Nathan just missed out on a prize on the rifle range and Lucy won a plastic goldfish. She took one look at the pathetic simulation of the real thing in its plastic bowl and gave it to Stephen.

A fortune teller had parked a caravan outside the photographers. The paintwork was ornamented by a gaudy display of occult symbols, and a canopy had been erected around the doorway to give the impression of a tent. A small scruffy notice on the tarmac announced *Palm Reading, Crystal Gazing and The Cards* and declared *Your Future Revealed by courtesy of Madame Tracy*.

"Let's go in," Marvi said.

"You don't believe in stuff like that, do you?" Vinder asked.

"Nah, not really. It'll be a giggle."

"Do you want to go in?" Nathan asked Lucy.

She shrugged. "It's a lot of nonsense." Privately she thought the idea of trying to peer into the future slightly perverted.

Marvi was already pushing open the door to the caravan. Momentum carried the others forward as they crowded in after her.

Madame Tracy was not quite what Lucy expected. She had short mousey-brown hair. Her earlobes were stretched by heavy silver earrings that terminated in skull and crossbones on one side and a mermaid on the other. She wore a black low-cut T-shirt which exposed cleavage, and a short denim skirt. A black crocheted shawl – the only concession to gypsy-style – was slung across her left shoulder.

"Come in, come in," she said, her lips parting in a red enamelled smile.

Though Madame Tracy aroused feelings of charlatanism in Lucy's mind the caravan was another matter. Exactly what caused her discomfort she couldn't say. Disquiet oozed from the tasselled cushions and brocade curtains. The fringe around the silk cloth on the small round table behind which Madame Tracy sat trembled in anticipation. Lucy gripped Nathan's hand. She really didn't want to know her future.

Marvi was already seating herself at the table.

"I'll do three of you for a fiver," the woman said.

Vinder paid.

"Palm, crystal or cards?" Madame Tracy asked.

Marvi glanced round at the others as if looking for support, then held out her left hand.

"The other one," she was told.

Marvi rubbed the stickiness of the candyfloss on her skirt before presenting her palm. Madame Tracy ran a red-painted nail along the creases. "You are entering a troubled time," she said. "There are many changes coming. Maybe some are already here. Take care of your health."

Lucy thought it sounded suitably vague.

"Will I get married?" Marvi asked. "How many children?"

"There will be a child. Beware of loving it too much."

"Who's going to go next?" Vinder asked.

"Me, now," Stephen said. He had moved close to Marvi so that no-one else would be able to take her place when she stood up.

"Palm, crystal or cards?"

Stephen pointed at the crystal ball which stood near one edge of the table. Madame Tracy moved it between them, carefully polishing the surface with a scrap of green silk. Stephen hunched down and pulled a face. Lucy saw it distorted in the reflecting surface. For a moment his image resembled that of a horned demon, then Madam Tracy's fingers broke up the image as she cupped the ball in her palms. "I would like quiet, please," she said.

Lucy found herself involuntarily closing her eyes when the woman did, and breathing slowly and deeply in what she was sure was the same rhythm as Madame Tracy. She could hear their simultaneous exhalations. A wave of panic clutched her and she forced her eyes open. If Nathan hadn't been holding her hand tightly she would have fled. Then Madame Tracy was staring into the crystal ball.

"It's time to stop hiding," the clairvoyant said. She frowned. "Someone close to you, who you depend on, needs your help. A brother perhaps. I see an accident. To him or you, I'm not sure."

"Good," Stephen said. He stood up abruptly.

"You now, Lucy," Nathan said.

"I don't want to. Really." She took a step back, bumping up against the door jamb.

"Come on," Marvi said. "It's just a bit of fun."

Lucy imagined she heard something hard and threatening in the other girl's voice. Perhaps Marvi wasn't such a pudding as she thought. She conjured a picture of spiders in her mind. Marvi could never harm her while she kept that thought between them.

Nathan was pushing her forward, Vinder guiding her from the other side. She couldn't get out of it without creating a scene. The caravan was too small for that. The walls were crowding in on her. Madame Tracy's smile drew her forward. She was trapped.

Lucy sat, her hands clenched in her lap as Madame Tracy went into her deep breathing routine. That's all it was, Lucy told herself. She was creating a space while she invented something to say. Lucy stared at the ball. The reflection of the white ceiling gave the impression of clouds within it. They moved. The caravan's generator, the passage of people outside, the fidgeting of her friends, set up vibrations in the shell. The crystal amplified them. The clouds swirled. And parted. Feral eyes stared into hers. A long pink tongue snicked out to lick thin lips which curled back to reveal the delicate pointed teeth of a carnivore. The mouth smiled. The eyes blinked and were gone.

Madame Tracy sighed. "I can see nothing here. Give me your hand."

Lucy clamped down the question about what she had seen. She must have imagined it or, if she turned round, she would see a picture of a cat hanging on the wall. Except that Nathan stood behind her, his hands resting on her shoulders and effectively pinning her to the chair.

Vinder picked her hand from her lap and extended it until Madame Tracy could reach it. Lucy's skin tingled as they touched. She tried to pull away but was held tight. The clairvoyant's nail on her palm left a trail of fire.

"I've never seen a palm like this," the fortune teller said. "It is so smooth. The lines are hardly visible, almost as if they were fading." She seemed to be muttering to herself. "The lifeline stops, then starts again, like there's a bit rubbed out. It shouldn't do that."

Lucy's fingers curled against the other woman's grip. "You're tickling," she said.

"Sorry."

"Well, what's her future?" Vinder asked.

"I don't know," Madame Tracy said. "Sometimes the signs are hidden from me. I could try a card reading if you like."

"No," Lucy said firmly. "It doesn't matter. I didn't want to know anyway."

She stood and pushed her way out into the night air. Noises of the fair burst around her. She hadn't realised how much the walls of the caravan had muffled the sound. She was relieved to be out of the hot claustrophobic atmosphere. She didn't wait to see if the others were following her but began to walk. Away from the fair, towards the nearby park where Tonia had been raped. Others would say she was foolish but she just wanted to keep moving and she knew she would be safe. She wouldn't even be noticed.

~~~

The room felt reluctantly empty, as if it knew someone was missing. Their mother had made Darren's bed though she expected them to do it themselves. She'd also done a bit of tidying. Happily, she'd left all Stephen's things alone. He reached for his bag of counters.

When he arrayed them on the carpet, he flicked the yellow and green ones with his orange moon. The green skittered off under Darren's bed where he couldn't see it. The yellow one overlapped the black.

Leaning over, Stephen pulled a shoebox from under the bed. He peered into it before extracting a bottle of pearl-pink nail varnish. He unscrewed the lid of the bottle and sniffed. Nail varnish had a lovely smell, though not as nice as that which clung to newly dry-cleaned clothes or the special fags Darren wouldn't let him try. He examined the brush, then stood the bottle carefully on one side. He got up and padded into his parents' bedroom, appropriating his mother's eyebrow tweezers. He proceeded to pluck the bristles from the brush, regardless to the way they stuck pinkly to the tweezers. Satisfied, he threw them under Darren's bed.

Stephen picked up the black counter and painted a stick man on one side of it with the nail polish. He stared at it for a little while then drew another next to it. He had to curl it up to make it fit. He looked at his handiwork a while longer then blotted out the first figure. He smiled. Now it was just right. He set it down carefully to dry and sniffed the bottle again before screwing the lid back on tightly.

~~~

It was well after midnight. Lucy stood at her bedroom window staring down into the pool of mottled light cast by the streetlamp through the half-bared branches of a lime tree. A fox strolled up the road, its elongated shadow changing as it moved from bin to bin, all set out for next morning's collection. As it passed below it stopped and looked up, the light turning its eyes into orbs of brilliant topaz.

She shivered. The lino, exposed at the edges of the worn carpet was cold to her bare feet. There was no heating in the room. It cooled quickly in the autumn nights. She had hardly seen Nathan since the Mop Fair and nothing of Marvi or Vinder. Their paths hadn't crossed. Stephen, she avoided. It wasn't that she particularly disliked him; she just found his presence disturbing. That was partly why she'd seen less of Nathan. He appeared to have assumed responsibility for Stephen while Darren couldn't.

Lucy turned away from the window and climbed back into bed, pulling the duvet up around her shoulders. She didn't want to lie down. She didn't want to sleep. She might dream again. She had thought the strange dreams were over but this last week they had returned, this time as a recurring incident. They always started with her walking the streets in her nightdress but she wasn't aware of being cold.

~~~

Lucy paused in front of the derelict house and looked up. It was impossible to see that there was a skylight in the roof. At times she thought she might be mistaken in thinking that there was one there at all. It certainly wasn't visible from the outside. The urge to go in and climb the stairs to the attic was strong.

She set her foot on the first step and realised that it was concrete rather than wood that was in contact with her bare soles. The banister was painted metal. She turned the corner into darkness, smelling the stale odours of cat urine and cooking that always lingered around blocks of flats. Her feet encountered carpet. Emerging onto a landing, she found herself facing a white-painted door. A small china plaque stuck to it said *Marvi's Room*.

Lucy turned the handle and pushed the door open. She had never been inside Marvi's bedroom but she knew where she was. It wasn't just because the figure asleep in the narrow bed had Marvi's frizzy black hair. There were other clues, like the posters of Stormzy and Ed Sheeran on the walls, the untidy heap of clothes that exuded the sour smell of sweat. Where Lucy's room was almost bare of possessions, Marvi's was cluttered. Cheap ornaments crowded the dressing table, fighting for space with combs, lipsticks and used tissues.

In her bed, Marvi rolled over onto her back and began to snore. Lucy reached out and yanked the bedclothes back. The outsize T-shirt the other girl used as a nightdress, was bunched up around her waist. Lucy remembered seeing her like this once before.

Cold air touched her limbs, starting Marvi awake. "What the...?" The question hung in the air between them as Marvi stared at Lucy. Marvi smiled and held out her arms. "I knew you would come back to me," she said.

Lucy stepped into the embrace and breathed the other girl's body odour, suffocating in the intensity of it. Yet it aroused her. It aroused the male in her.

"Oh, Darren, Darren." Marvi murmured under her caresses, opening her fat thighs to receive the creature that in her sleepy state she thought to be her boyfriend.

Lucy grinned as she rode Marvi. Brutality edged her actions and the girl squirmed with pleasure as she pinched her flesh.

"You're hurting me, Darren." Marvi's eyes opened wide with sudden pain.

The fierceness of Lucy's efforts increased. She felt she was banging and tearing at Marvi's insides until she began screaming. Lucy expelled Darren's carefully hoarded seed and withdrew. She stared down at the writhing figure on the blood-stained bed.

Lucy tried to shut out the vision of Marvi howling with pain, her hands pressed between her legs. She shuddered, suppressing the dream and the pleasure she'd felt in inflicting torture on the other girl. And the delight of being male.

Two weeks later, when Nathan told her that Marvi was pregnant, Lucy laughed.

~~~

Stephen stood in the centre of the pool of orange light from the streetlamp, head back, eyes closed. He could feel it on his skin – not warmth but tingly. His eyelids glowed translucent red from his side of them as if the rays pierced his flesh. Black spots swam across his vision.

"You'll go blind if you stare at lights." The voice came from his left. Stephen tilted his head and opened one eye. It was Vinder,

"Moths don't." He had intended to say something different but the real words didn't come out. It often happened. Once he wondered if that was why people didn't stay friends with him. Vinder and Nathan and Darren were different though. They understood. He wished Darren would get better soon. He didn't like sleeping on his own in their bedroom. A moth brushed his cheek as it spiralled up towards the light, confused by the extra moon in its sky.

"No," Vinder said. "Moths burn their wings and die."

Stephen grinned. He was a moth. He came out at night but he wasn't going to be fooled by a silly streetlight.

"Were you going somewhere?" Vinder asked.

Stephen stopped grinning. Yes, he was going somewhere but he couldn't remember where. He looked around. The parade of shops started just ahead of him. One of them was owned by Vinder's father. Behind him was a roundabout, a pelican crossing and the pub he must have just walked past.

"Chips," Stephen said happily. He had only just had supper and he didn't really want any more food but it was the first thing that came into his mind. He knew that he shouldn't admit to not going anywhere in particular.

"I'll walk with you," Vinder said.

"Okay." Stephen was committed now. The chip shop was at the far end of the parade and set back a little alongside a tiny dressmaker's. He hoped there would be a long queue. Then he could say he had changed his mind. There was only one person waiting to be served. He ordered curry sauce and chips. When he dug into his pocket for change his fingers closed on a thin plastic disc.

He stared at Marvi's black tiddlywink and wondered how it had got there.

"What's that?" Vinder asked.

"Nothing." Stephen thrust it back into his pocket and counted out the money for the chips. He offered to share with Vinder, hoping the other boy would consume most of them for him, but he took only a couple and watched while Stephen forced himself to eat the rest. Afterwards, he felt a bit sick.

"You going to the park?" Vinder asked.

"Okay." It was dark. It was getting chilly, but Stephen always agreed with Vinder's suggestions. It was easier. Perhaps Nathan would be there. And Lucy. He didn't like Lucy, which was strange. Stephen usually liked everyone.

"Are you going to show me what you've got in your pocket?" Vinder asked as they ambled through the gates. The grass near the entrance glimmered in the streetlight where the dew had settled. Roses hung brown tinged heads where early frosts had nipped their petals.

"Nope." Stephen was prepared to share most things to others. It was easy to share. It helped people to like him and include him in their plans. He'd found that out a long time ago but no-one was going to see his counters. Not even Darren. Especially not Vinder – or Lucy.

"Go on. I'll show you what I've got in my pockets."

"Nope."

They were leaving the relatively well-lit formal area of the park. Here the shadows were longer and darker; the illumination was poor, relying on the distant houses that ringed the recreation ground, harder to keep to a path. Ahead and to the left the hillock that obscured the children's play area was a blot of black ink against the pearl rim of the amphitheatre of darkness. Stephen smiled to himself. He liked that image. He could picture the hedges as the seating around the stage filled with ghosts. Ghosts and goblins, all watching him. He often saw things like that in his head. The trouble was that if he ever tried to tell anyone else, the words would disappear. As if his mouth wasn't properly connected to his brain.

He was aware of Vinder walking next to him. There was no sign of anyone else. He took a step sideways onto the grass and stood still. Vinder carried on walking for a bit before stopping as well.

"Come on," Vinder said.

Stephen started to walk diagonally away from the path, towards the blot on the skyline. There was a maze on the other side made from logs hammered into the ground, and a wooden fort.

"Where are you going?" Vinder called after him.

"Play," Stephen shouted back. As Vinder began to follow him he started to run. He wanted to get there first, to hide in the maze.

Crouching down between the rows of knee-high wooden stakes, Stephen imagined himself as a cat. Vinder was looking for him but Stephen was also hunting. Body mingling with the black shadows, he lashed the tip of his tail to and fro. His eyes, large and yellow, reflected what light there was. If Vinder looked at him, all he would see would be his eyes. Then he would pounce. Vinder was the mouse. No. Stephen shook his head. Vinder wasn't small and furry. He was something else, something more. Stephen couldn't quite work it out. Dangerous was the nearest he came to it but he didn't understand why.

He could hear Vinder calling him as he searched. He didn't come anywhere near where Stephen lay, one flank against the rough wood, belly to the tarmac.

"You're being very silly, Stephen," Vinder said. "I'm going to leave you here."

A small growl formed in Stephen's throat. Vinder was playing games now. Sharpened ears would have heard him moving away. There was only stillness. And a slight scent of human nearby. Stephen could wait longer than anyone. He rested his chin on the ground between outstretched paws.

Eventually, Vinder gave up. Stephen heard the slight swish of his feet on the grass as he moved away. Stephen stretched and yawned. He resisted the temptation to lick at his fur – that would be taking the allusion too far. He set off across the park at an easy lope, taking the opposite direction to Vinder. The moon gave him all the light he needed until he hit the streets. There he trotted onwards, keeping out of the pools of mercurial light, blending with the shadows. He didn't feel at all tired or out of breath when he stopped outside the derelict house.

He had been there before, several times, but never on his own. Always Darren or Nathan or Vinder had been with him. Vaguely he knew that they weren't supposed to be there but it was fun having a hideaway, where no-one went except other members of your gang. Stephen thought he liked being part of a gang.

It was getting cold and he felt foolish being here. He dug his hands into his pockets for warmth and touched the black counter. It felt tacky as if the nail varnish he'd painted on it was still wet.

The boards creaked when Stephen pushed the door open. He breathed in the sweet muskiness of decay. Houses like this were not safe, yet they had met here without problems for months. When he reached the bottom of the stairs he remembered that he was supposed to be a cat – a black, sinuous panther. He dropped his front paws to the treads and lowered his head to sniff at a dark stain. It had a dull metallic taste like water that has stood too long in iron pipes. Perhaps he imagined it.

He padded upwards, pausing for a moment by the open door through which wafted odours of stale sweat. Two battered mattresses were visible and an old curtain that Stephen recognised as having once hung in his parent's bedroom. Downstairs, the air had been tainted with vinegar, melted wax and old beer. He didn't wonder that the smells still lingered from their first visit.

He was distracted by tiny sounds from above. Stephen continued up to the top landing. For a moment his senses wavered. Something felt wrong. His tail lashed in agitation. There was corruption here.

There were two doors to choose from – back and front of the house. Stephen stalked to the one at the rear. A muffled whimpering was coming from the other side of the wood. Then a scream. Stephen sprang. The door crashed back on its hinges.

Lucy, palely luminous in the moonglow from the skylight overhead, knelt facing him in the centre of the floor. She had her arm in what appeared to be a shapeless, overstuffed bag with a pair of legs sticking out of it. The bag moaned. Lucy smiled at Stephen. She pulled out her hand making the kind of squelching noise a Wellington does when withdrawn from mud. Red slime covered her hand and in her palm something pulsated. Ruby strands trailed from it.

"You are too late," Lucy said. She threw the object at him. It lay between his paws, a pink and white fish-like thing – bulging head, bud limbs and whippet curled tail.

Stephen stared at Lucy who calmly licked her blood-splattered fingers. He hunkered down ready to pounce. Her hands snaked out as he launched himself, her nails raking his face. Stephen fell back, whimpering.

His whimpering woke him. Stephen lay with his face

pressed against the cold tarmac, a taste of bile in his throat. His cheeks stung where the rough surface grazed him. Opening sticky eyes, a pink-red foetus resolved into frozen puke. Still feeling sick, Stephen used the logs of the maze to help him stand. Reeling from numbed feet, Stephen headed for home.

~~~

Lucy was beginning to think that her dreams were therapeutic. She felt calmer, more confident in the days that followed her nightmares. The problems of living in a small thin-walled flat with an anxious mother and an argumentative sister were more bearable. And the dreams seemed to come when she was most stressed, as if her sleeping mind was finding outlets for the build-up of tension. Last night she had gone to bed with a headache brought on partly by her mother and sister arguing about Donna's poor schoolwork. It culminated with Donna slamming out of the flat to meet her unsuitable (according to their mother) boyfriend. Even in the sanctum of her bedroom Lucy was bothered with extraneous noises.

Now, in the bright November sunshine she felt fresh, as though she had accomplished something. And last night's dream didn't worry her the way the others had. As Nathan said, they were all in the mind, they couldn't hurt anyone. She hummed to herself as she set out the baskets of cut flowers on the pavement in front of the shop.

"Lucy! Phone!" Ayline, the other assistant, called out to her.

Lucy hurried inside. Ayline held out the receiver. "Don't let Lorna catch you getting personal calls."

"Who is it?" Getting a call on the shop phone was weird. All of her friends knew to text her or leave a message on her mobile.

Ayline shrugged.

Lucy took the receiver. "Hello?"

"Help me, Lucy." The voice was faint and distorted.

"Who is this?"

"M— Marvi. Help me."

"I can't now. Get off the phone and text me if it's important."

"Please come."

"Not till after closing. I'm being paid to do a job, not to go running around after you."

"It hurts. I'm dying."

"Don't be—" Lucy bit off her immediate reaction. She could hear the hysteria in Marvi's voice. Why me, she thought. "Where are you?"

"At home. Please come."

"I don't know where that is."

Marvi told her.

"Look, Marvi. Put the phone down, then call 999 for an ambulance."

"Will you come?"

"If I can." Lucy dropped the receiver back into place then returned to her work. Her conscience was clear. She had told Marvi what to do though she was probably making a fuss about nothing. Probably trapped her fingers in a door or something. Or her father had found out she was pregnant and given her a good beating. She disliked the way Marvi kept trying to involve her in her problems. Take the business with Darren. Lucy hadn't really forgiven her for that. It was probably why she had dreamt about her the night before.

~~~

Lucy had stood naked in the room with the skylight. Moonlight streaming through the glass had bathed her body in cold fire. The frost of it felt delicious on her skin.

She held her arms out and turned slowly, letting it caress all of her body. She lowered her arms and looked at the figure at her feet. How Marvi had got there she didn't question. The other girl mewled in her sleep and Lucy knew that whatever she did, Marvi wouldn't wake. She couldn't.

Carefully, almost sensually, Lucy slid Marvi's nightshirt up her body exposing thighs and tangle of black pubic hair. Lucy ran her hands over the mound of Marvi's belly. As yet, anyone who didn't know wouldn't guess that she was pregnant.

Lucy pulled Marvi's legs apart and ran her hand between them, parting the labia until her fingertips found her vulva. Marvi moaned as Lucy probed her vagina. The sounds Marvi made were pleasurable. Lucy felt no emotion as she stretched the opening and thrust her fist inside. She opened her hand slowly, her fingers easing further into the passage. Flesh shrank away from her touch as her nails clawed their way in further. Marvi's moans changed to whimpers of pain. Instinct led Lucy to the cervix, that narrow opening to the womb. She worked her fingers into the gap, then punched her way through. Marvi screamed. Lucy's hand closed around a soft pulsating lump. She yanked. Marvi screamed again.

The door to the attic room crashed back on its hinges. Lucy looked up, smiling. A huge black cat crouched in the entrance watching her. She withdrew her arm from Marvi's insides and held out her hand to the animal.

"You are too late," she said, tossing the thing towards the beast as it pounced. It almost looked as if it were trying to catch it. Lucy licked her fingers, tasting the sweetness of fresh blood as the cat hunkered down, tail twitching, to spring at her. With lips drawn back from sharp teeth, it fixed her with its yellow stare. As it leapt towards her, she lashed out, her nails raking the side of its head.

Lucy had awoken before it could touch her, this time with satisfaction rather than terror from the dream.

Coupled with those memories, Lucy couldn't put Marvi's phone call out of her mind. At ten thirty, she grabbed her coat and ran for the bus. She sprinted from the stop to Marvi's door. Fighting for breath, she hammered on it.

"Whatja want?" the voice behind her made her jump.

The youth had the same round features as Marvi but looked several years younger. "Are you Marvi's brother, Micky?" she asked.

"Yeah. So what?"

"Marvi rang me at work. She sounded as if she'd hurt herself. She begged me to come."

"Oh, yeah?" The boy put his key in the latch and pushed the door. It didn't open at first so he heaved at it with his shoulder. Then it swung back easily.

"Shouldn't you be in school?" Lucy said.

He shrugged. She followed him in before he could slam the door in her face. Micky swaggered along the hall. He glanced in the sitting room as he passed and stopped.

"Shit," he said. "Shit, shit, shit."

Lucy looked in past him. "Call an ambulance, fast," she said, pushing him out of the way. She steeled herself to walk in to where Marvi sat slumped in the centre of the floor. She rocked to and fro, moaning and clutching her stomach. She was splattered with blood. More of it pooled between her open thighs.

~~~

"I don't seem to see much of you anymore." Lucy stirred her coke with its straw before bowing her head to draw a mouthful of the sweet liquid through it.

Nathan shrugged. "It's your choice."

They had taken the bus into the City Centre and had gone into McDonalds, more because it was raining than for any other reason. "Not completely," she said. "You don't often seem to be alone now."

"I do have other friends, too."

"Like Stephen."

Nathan shrugged again. "That's different. Someone has to keep an eye out for him while Darren can't."

"You're not his brother, or his social worker."

"No, but there's no reason to abandon him just because he's a bit simple. And Darren is a friend."

"Yours, not mine." Lucy could sense that Nathan was getting annoyed with her. Perhaps it was all to the good. Perhaps this was the time to break away from all of them.

"What have you got against Stephen?" Nathan said. "He's harmless."

"Is he?" She paused. "I don't like him. I don't like the way he looks at me."

"Do you expect him to go round with his eyes shut?"

"I don't expect to find him tagging along every time I see you."

"Like Marvi follows you around?"

"That's different."

"Is it?"

It was. Very different. Lucy's dislike for the other girl hadn't changed. She still thought Marvi to be an unimaginative fat lump and found her puppy-like gratitude rather pathetic, but the thought that someone needed her, however silly the idea was, was quite nice. The knowledge that she could hurt Marvi with just a few words gave her a feeling of power. Marvi had changed a lot in the last seven or eight months. She'd got fatter, too, so much so that when she'd slipped over in the park she'd hardly been able to get up. Lucy's feeble strength hadn't been much help.

"You encourage Stephen," Lucy said.

"You're turning into quite a nasty little bitch."

"And you can find someone else to pay for you in future." Lucy noisily drained the rest of her coke and walked out of the restaurant.

Initially, she was glad of the crowds of Saturday shoppers as she could use them to make sure Nathan didn't follow her. She felt a certain relief at having broken away from him. Her mood was as fresh and light as the rain falling on her face. After a while, as her hair became limp and straggly and water trickled beneath her collar, her spirits dampened. The freedom became emptiness and the purposeful pace became aimless wandering. With the exception of Marvi she didn't think she had any friends left.

It was about five-and-a-half miles from the City Centre to her home. Lucy drifted the distance; the tarmac, the cars, the houses all blurring as if seen from the inside of a bubble of water. As she passed the road that led to the derelict house she paused but didn't stop. She hadn't been there for a long time.

~~~

Stephen wasn't sure that he liked his brother anymore. Darren didn't seem to go out much now. He didn't hang around The Green and do clever things like soaking chips in gin and watching the pigeons getting falling-over drunk. In fact, since he'd come back from the hospital, all Darren seemed to do was sit in their bedroom drinking beer and playing loud music. He was uncommunicative – not that Stephen could ever think of anything sensible to say back – and frequently rude.

Stephen didn't dare leave his bag of counters in their

room in case Darren found them. He took them to the old house, the one where Darren had been hurt. He knew that because Vinder had told him. Sometimes he thought Vinder said things just to see if he could upset him. Stephen knew that if he stood there and smiled Vinder would soon give up.

Extra boards had been nailed across the ground floor windows and doors but Stephen had no difficulty prising them loose. He made himself a den on the top floor where the light sneaked in through the roof window.

He had his counters laid out in front of him. He liked the feel and texture of them and the warmth they retained after he held them in his hand for a while. The black one and the green one were at the opposite sides of the circle he had marked out in the dust. The yellow one was mid-way between, halfway around the edge at twelve o'clock from him. Red and blue were closest. He placed the purple one in the centre and the white one outside the circle directly in front of him. The orange Moon was his flicker. He wanted to see if he could get the white one to land on the purple but he didn't seem to be able to aim well enough. First it went to the green, then yellow. It landed on the black twice before skittering across the floor. He chased it and flicked it back, step by step towards the circle.

He missed again, the white counter landing on the far side. He tried once more. It slithered across the red one to rest next to the black one again. It was because Lucy and Marvi were friends, he supposed.

Suddenly, Stephen froze. He thought he heard a sound on the stairs. There wasn't supposed to be anyone else here. It might be rats, but he knew them. He had chased them and killed them, and it didn't sound like them. Quickly, Stephen gathered his counters and put them back in their hiding place – the bag fit snugly in the space behind the broken wall socket – and wedged the plastic back into place. He knew they would be safe there.

Stephen lay flat on the floor behind the closed door, his head tilted so that he could peer through the inch high gap under it. In the darkness of the landing there was little to see. He heard the huff of trainers on the steps below. The door opposite opened and he could see feet in a patch of diffuse street lighting. Stephen shivered. He hadn't been in that room. Not since he had dreamed of that creature in there. He knew that if he'd gone in it would have been there, waiting. He didn't want his insides ripped out. He scrambled to his feet, ready to rush out and warn whoever it was of the danger. There was a snarl and a scream.

Stephen scrambled to his feet and eased the door open. The house was silent except for the creaks it made as the temperature dropped after the warmth of the day. He pattered down the stairs and let himself out, carefully pushing the boards back over the window so no-one could see the way in. He could do things right sometimes. It was just that his body didn't always do what he wanted it to. Then he was clumsy and people laughed and said he was stupid.

He hoped Darren would be asleep by the time he got back. He probably wouldn't be.

~~~

Lucy was angry. She hadn't realised it at first but after she had dried off and settled down to an evening of her mother painting her toenails in front of the television, and her sister whingeing about being unable to go out even though it was a Saturday, the emotion began to seethe in her stomach. How dare Nathan equate Marvi with Stephen. Everyone knew that Stephen was brain damaged, Marvi was only thick. And the cheek of him to suggest that she had actually picked Marvi as a friend. Lucy didn't have friends; she had always hovered on the fringes of groups. When she was at school it had mattered, she had wanted to belong. She didn't care so much now.

Eventually, she could stand no more of the cramped atmosphere in the small sitting room and retired to her bedroom. She stood in a patch of diffuse light coming through the curtains from outside. She couldn't sleep. Behind her, the bed was rumpled and the sheets were sweat slicked. What she would really like to do was to scratch someone's eyes out. She imagined it.

She crouched and held her hands in front of her as claws. She drew her lips back from her teeth and ran the tip of her tongue along their edges, feeling the sharpness of incisors and canines. There was a sound outside. Like trainer-clad feet climbing bare-wood stairs.

Everything had fallen silent; the TV from down below, the cars in the street, the gurgle of water from next-door's toilet. The furniture was insubstantial, disguised by the shadows, existing only because she knew it was there. The floor felt rough beneath her bare feet.

The sound came again. The door opened. She couldn't see who was there as no light came in from the passage.

"I have come for you," he said.

Lucy felt a growl rising in her throat. She wasn't going with anyone. As he stepped into the room she sprang, snarling. Her nails raked his face and he staggered back, screaming. Lucy retreated to the centre of the room and the patch of light. She felt safe there – and glanced up at the skylight. The day's cloud was thinning and the occasional star gleamed.

She blinked. The ceiling light swung gently. She

looked at her hands. Two of the nails were broken, dirt caught under them and she shivered. It was a long time since she had been to that house, yet for a moment she had thought she was there. And she had been awake this time. Was it possible, she wondered, to be awake and dream at the same time?

~~~

Stephen was practicing stalking, following people without them noticing. He had seen it done on TV plenty of times and the shadow never got spotted. He wondered why people kept giving him funny looks as he tracked one person, then another, at random through the City Centre. Sometimes he was a detective on a case but it worked best when he was a cat. When he was good enough he would follow Lucy. Now she didn't hang out with Nathan anymore it was getting harder to watch her.

Something odd was happening to his counters as well. One of them had got scratches on it and he couldn't remember putting them there, and the Lucy white one was getting thinner. He could almost see through it.

~~~

Lucy hadn't seen Marvi for a couple of days. She hadn't really seen anyone recently. She seemed to be wandering through life in a haze of exhaustion. At work she did things automatically. Her nights were sleepless or broken by dreams. Not the invigorating kind but ones that left her more tired than when she went to bed. She almost walked past Marvi, who was seated on the bench on The Green where they were going to meet.

"Lucy." Marvi's squeaky voice penetrated the fog that filled her mind and she stopped.

The other girl looked dreadful. Her eyes were sunken into a puffy face that made them look smaller than ever. Food stained the clothing that hung sack-like over her misshapen body and her hands and ankles were swollen like an old woman's. A mess of congealing burger and chips lay on the seat beside her.

"You look awful," Lucy said.

"I feel awful," Marvi said miserably. "My belly hurts."

"I'm not surprised, the junk you eat," Lucy said, indicating the greasy food at her side.

"I didn't eat much. It made me feel sick."

"Why don't you just go home and go to bed?"

"I can't."

"Why not?"

"I can't get up," Marvi said miserably. "And I've wet myself."

Lucy suppressed a snort of laughter. "There's not much I can do here."

She carried on walking.

~~~

Stephen watched Lucy stop to talk to Marvi, then walk away. He was standing in the Newsagent's staring out of the big plate glass window. Vinder's father didn't seem to mind, even when Stephen took the girlie magazines from the top shelf and looked through them. He didn't really like the pictures but felt that he was expected to. He couldn't understand why his father had got so excited when his mother had found some under Darren's bed. Or why Darren had said they were Stephen's. She shouldn't have been looking under there anyway.

His fingers closed around the two counters he had in his pocket. He tended to carry the black and the white ones with him these days. He moved the white one to his other pocket as Lucy's figure receded.

Stephen had been watching Marvi. Part of him wanted to stay and see what she did but an equally strong compulsion urged him to follow Lucy. He closed his eyes and did an *eeny meeny miney mo* in his head. Lucy won. It was time to do what he had practised for real.

All she did was go home.

~~~

Lucy squatted on the edge of the bath and watched Marvi lying on the tiles and squirming. Her overlarge feet gripped the slippery surface and she felt perfectly stable balanced there with her body crouched so that her knees were level with her ears. All her limbs seemed longer than usual. Every so often she would reach out a thin, bony finger and prod Marvi with a sharpened nail.

The T-shirt Marvi wore as a nightdress was stretched around her obesity and soiled. As she writhed, Marvi spread the shit, blood and urine about the floor. Lucy was enjoying the other girl's pain. It didn't bother her when Marvi's groans became a continuous scream. No-one in house would wake, not as long as Lucy was there.

Lucy grinned as Marvi thrashed about. She could see the muscles of her belly rippling beneath the layers of fat as though something was trying to claw its way out of her abdomen. Marvi's knees were drawn up now. Her legs splayed, trying to ease the agony. A small deformed limb flopped from her vagina. Then another. Marvi's screams reached a crescendo as the thing emerged in a spurt of blood and mucus. Lucy leapt from her perch with a cry of triumph and snatched up the creature with its swollen head and stunted limbs. She bent her head to bite through the cord, and vanished.

~~~

Stephen saw the wraith ahead of him, pale against the darkness of hedge and wall. He, too, kept to the shadows, padding along on silent feet. His tail stretched straight behind him, his ears were pricked forward in concentration. He had followed it to Marvi's house and waited, crouched under the bushes under the front garden opposite. He'd tried to get closer but couldn't – his eyes closed and his head drooped with fatigue so he'd backed away and sat, cat-patient.

Now Lucy was on the move again. She was as insubstantial as the counter in his pocket.

It was the derelict house that she went to. And there, Stephen had a problem. As a cat he couldn't get in. He had no hands to ease away the boards. Reluctantly, he changed and shivered in the June-night air. As human, he was afraid to be seen. Quickly he climbed in and out of sight. Then he had to go through the whole process again – curling up small, then gradually stretching out one limb at a time, extending his spine into a sleek arch.

He soft-footed up the stairs.

The door to the attic was ajar. He sidled up to it and laid his length against it. A nudge of his shoulder would swing it open when he was ready. Then there were voices.

"Give it to me."

"No. I made it. I need it." That was Lucy.

"Give it up. Free yourself."

"Never."

Stephen crept closer, tail lashing. He pushed the door.

Only Lucy stood there, a nimbus of silver from the skylight surrounded her. Her neck was bowed over the baby in her arms. She raised her head as the door hinges creaked. Blood stained her mouth.

Stephen sprang. His weight bowled her over. Instinctively his mouth clamped on her throat. His jaws worked as his teeth crushed her windpipe. Heels and hands drummed on the floor. Stephen's hind legs gouged at her stomach, ripping the flesh. The cat in him desired to feed.

"Such a pity," a voice said from behind him.

Stephen looked around. It sounded like Vinder. "She clung to her own body too long," he said.

Stephen unwound from cat form. For once his thoughts came clear and lucid. "And you haven't?" he said.

The figure that stepped from the shadows wasn't Vinder, though it looked like him.

"No, I only borrowed this body," Vinder said. "I left my own behind a long time ago."

"I will find you out," Stephen said.

Vinder smiled. "I doubt it. You won't remember long enough."

~~~

Stephen wondered why he was lying in someone's front garden. There was a taste of blood in his mouth and his head ached. Perhaps he had drunk too much and fallen over.

The white counter in his pocket had disappeared.

~~~

They knocked down the derelict houses in October. The old man in the end house had finally been persuaded to move. Stephen watched as the workmen moved in, then was chivvied away as the police moved in. It seemed that they had found the skeleton of the girl who had disappeared more than a year ago.

From across the road, Vinder winked at him. Stephen wondered why.

Life Marks

I discovered science fiction while
Lurking in the A to Cs of the school library,
Devouring Asimov, Bradbury and Clarke instead
Of doing my French Homework.

Reflecting the church on the other side of the green,
The octagonal library housed spies, thrillers –
Deighton, Eliot, Fleming and Greene, the masters
Who travelled secretly on the bus with me to college.

But it started long before in a Victorian red-brick;
Dark wooden shelves lined with children's heroes
From Haggard, Ingelow, Johns, Kipling and Lewis
Joined me under the bedclothes with a torch.

And later, on tiny tables cramped between the tiers,
Heavy tomes divulged snippets of fact
On Metamorphosis, Niobium, Obsidian, Palaeontology
And Quartz in the depths of the university stacks.

Replaced by a book park of concrete, the elegant
Companion to Town Hall and Art Gallery
Blossomed with the civilisations of
Rome, Sumaria, the Tudors and Ur.

Snug in its Birmingham suburb,
The Poetry Place waits to speak the words of
Vaughn, Whitman, Yeats and Zephaniah.
Xs mark the libraries on the map of my life.

Dreaming Of Dragons

Eyes big as saucers light the lonely road.
The beast growls, straining,
As it hauls its bulk over the crest of the hill.
Long body, twisting and turning,
Following the contours of the descent,
The sound changing to a purr
As it coasts downwards.
Ahead, an unsuspecting village
Glitters like massed fireflies.
The leviathan roars through,
The fire in its belly swelling the night.
Lesser creatures scuttle from the path
Of the wingless behemoth.
It yearns skywards
Seeking the distant horizon
Longing for the freedom of flight.
Grounded, it challenges the stars
And thunders northwards into the dark.

The woman driving the juggernaut is
Dreaming of Dragons again.

Underrated

It seems unfair to have
The fewest number of pages,
Even in Chambers –
The work I have to do.

Without my help there would be
No unfrocked bishop, divorced spouse,
Dumped girlfriend or former boss.
Vermin and The Doctor would not be
Threatened with termination
By rat catcher or Dalek.
Courts would be devoid
Of the witness with knowledge
Of forensics or entomology.

Yet I need no help.
My rays penetrate your body,
Let the bone-setter do his job;
The entertainer with my factor
Rises to become a star.
And the Romans valued me –
Trusted me to mark decades.
A saltire, in Northern climes
I fly above civic buildings
Symbol of saint and loyalty and pride.

In older times the illiterate would
Mark me as substitute for a name,
Yet politicians crave, plead for you
To put me against theirs.
I strike through the unwanted,
Indicate the wrong, and show the spot
Where pirates hid their treasure.
I am the unknown.

So rate me, like the censors do,
To show that within lies material
To shock, corrupt, offend.
I am a warning but remember
You always seal that letter to
The one you love with xxxxs

Birmingham Mythic

Deep beneath the still dark water of
The Worcester Canal, what lurks?
Is it the rotting remnants of city living,
The dead bicycles and feral trolleys
Or does the water kelpie hide
Awaiting the unwary, lured south
With the Scottish engineers who
Created Birmingham's waterways?

Does the trickster who always pays his debts
Saunter through Handsworth Park,
A bounce in his step, a smile on his lips,
Eyes shadowed by yellow, red and green,
The colours of a continent, spun
With webs of playfulness? Has Anansi
Crossed oceans in the wake
Of those who sought a finer life.

On a hot day in Edgbaston when dust
Whipped up by the cooling breeze
Spins, does a dervish dance
At its centre, dreaming of
Saharan deserts from where
His people migrated in search
Of a greener land, where goats
No longer count as wealth?

Behind closed doors in, Ladywood,
Do Parvati, Shiva watch over the folks
That celebrate every year
With a carnival of lights?
And down Digbeth way, does
The leprechaun smile thinking
The gold shimmering off window glass
Is better than that left behind?

And in Deritend where once cavaliers
Fought Cromwell's men, do you hear,
On quiet nights, the tramp of feet
The musket fire, the ghastly scream?
And at Five Ways, where canal
And road and railway all converge,
Does the Spirit of Birmingham
Still await her tribute?

Lost

(i.m. Joel Lane)

I stand amidst the debris of your life;
You never threw anything away but let it
Accumulate around you, just as
Your mind never lost the snippets,
The ephemera that most forget.
You didn't know whether an object,
An idea would be just what was needed.

Beneath the layers, the detritus of fifty years
I find the hidden the nuggets, brought home
Lost amid time's accumulations, just as the gold
You would have shaped into poems, stories
But which now will never be unearthed,
Buried forever in darkness.

Around me, shelves are stacked with
Your passions. Amongst them the books,
The CDs, the DVDs you bought
That remained unwrapped, unused
Like the ideas still packaged, sealed within
Your mind, forever out of reach.

Devolution

One minute to midnight.
A walk along Broad Street
Spills light and sound, alcohol and crisps
Along the walk of stars.
In frost sharp air, the young sashay
In high heels, short skirts, backless tops
Revealing swathes of goose-bumped flesh.
Survival instincts forgotten.
From Five Ways to Paradise Circus
Past Revolution and the Sports Café
Language is the first to fade,
Philosophy, cultural conservation
Degenerates to grunts, gestures
Bodies shimmer as primal urges
Surface.
Walk into the Australian –
Emerge on all fours,
Bipedal motion unlearned
As the canal's primordial stink
Permeates hands and hair and clothes.
Saturates the soft tissues of the brain.
Crawl on from Hyatt Hotel
To Centenary Square,
Collapse beside the fountain,
Half within the water,
A gill-less fish returning to the sea.
Giggle helplessly, vomit,
Squirm amoeba-like in search
Of a taxi to next morning's hangover.

It is Saturday night on the Golden Mile
And Darwin is revolving in his grave.

Leaving

The telephone rings.
She does not answer.
I need to tell her to
Set out my blue suit for the journey,
And the black shoes.

It continues to ring
But is not picked up.
I want to tell my wife
About the flowers and that I love her.

The answerphone cuts in
And I remember,
No-one is at home for
They all left for my funeral
At twelve-thirty.

The machine beeps.
I leave no message.

AWAY WITH THE FAIRIES

"This is likely to be a difficult one," Greg said. The group were seated around a table in the back room of the local pub, the rain hammering down outside, raincoats on the backs of their chairs dripping onto the floor. Tess couldn't remember how many times Greg had started a planning meeting with those words. Often he was right. A fit fifty-year old, Greg was the leader of the local Hill Rescue team, and those present were those he had decided would be most useful for a particular rescue.

"What made them want to go caving in this weather?" Iain said.

"Wasn't raining this morning," Stuart said.

The door to the pub was yanked open and a wet figure stumbled in followed by a gust of rain-bearing wind. "Sorry," Aslan said, shucking off his yellow waterproofs. "The roads in the valley are beginning to flood."

"We've only just started planning," Greg said. He spread a laminated map of the area out on the table – it was easier than everyone trying to follow the maps on their phones. "I'm sure you are all aware of the rock slide a couple of weeks ago."

There were nods around the table. Tess said, "I heard it exposed a new entrance to the cave system."

"Let me guess," Aslan said. "Some idiots decided it was a good idea to explore."

"Nearly. It's a zoological team from Birmingham University who have been surveying the caves. They were already in the area when the slip occurred. The two who went in the cave are experienced cavers. There other two members of their team are camped in the valley."

"Something went wrong, though…"

"They weren't far from the entrance when one of them fell. We are dealing here with a suspected broken ankle. His companion was able to alert the ground crew, who called us. I was just showing the others the images of the site when you arrived, Aslan. I'm sending them to your phone now."

The pictures showed the limestone cliff face riddled with fissures and darker splotches that were cave entrances. The debris from the landslide littered the slope at the base, large boulders mingled with match-sticked trees. Along the ridge, wind deformed trees leaned at crazy angles as if preparing to fall.

"How did they get up there?" Aslan asked.

"Climbed. From the valley. The ropes are likely to still be in place but they won't be much use to us. They followed a narrow track up the valley in an ancient Land Rover Defender."

"Good kit," Tess said. "Those vehicles last for ever."

"But the rain will make that surface treacherous," Stuart said.

"Which is why we will have to go in from the top," Greg said. "The cliff face is likely to be unstable but we have to risk lowering the casualty down." They could all see that with the weather and the terrain this wasn't a situation where a helicopter could be used. Greg had contacted the ambulance service already. He would liaise with them.

"How're you planning to get there?" Iain asked. "The maps not showing much except footpaths along the top."

"The quadbikes should be able to cope with the terrain. Tess, Stuart, Aslan, you'll climb down. I'll stay up top with Iain. I've already sent Jared to meet their ground crew, reassure them. Any questions?" There were none.

Greg directed them to the pub's storeroom where their rescue equipment was kept. Since he was the owner of the pub, it made sense.

~~~

Greg signalled a halt some distance from the cliff edge. They were two-up on two of the quadbikes and their equipment was stashed in the back of the third. All of them were wearing thick orange waterproofs – it was still raining – the kind designed for ice climbing.

Stuart edged closer to the cliff and peered over. "Rope me," he said. "I can't see anything from here."

"Wait up," Greg said, "Jared is at the cliff base. He'll be able to pinpoint the cave entrance more easily."

Stuart stepped back. "The edge is cracking. Not sure we can abseil down without dislodging more." He had to shout over the noise of the weather. "It's creating an overhang."

Tess had walked along the summit to where a gully was starting to carve itself into the thin turf. She could see the orange speck below that was Jared. She waved. The figure waved back. She called to Greg. "Have you got Jared on the phone?"

"Yes."

"I think he can see me. Ask him where the entrance is from my position."

"He's sending an image."

The faint ping announced that the message had arrived. She expanded the image.

"Is that it?" Aslan asked coming to peer over her shoulder.

"Their ropes are still in position, so it's about ten metres down and thirty across. Dead under the overhang. Can you traverse from here?"

Aslan was the best climber of the party. "Shouldn't be a problem. There are plenty of cracks for handholds and to stick in the tricams."

"Okay. Let's tell Greg."

~~~

Once Aslan had made the traverse, securing the rope at intervals, Tess followed him. She turned on her helmet light as she ducked into cave entrance. It opened up inside giving enough headroom to stand upright. A gleam ahead showed her where Aslan had gone; a kink in the passage hid most of his light and the casualty. Mindful of the slippery surface, she placed her feet cautiously. As she rounded the bend she saw the casualty leaning against the passage wall. Aslan was crouched beside him examining the damaged ankle.

"Hi," she said. "I'm Tess."

The man winced, breath hissing between his clenched teeth. "Murray," he said after a moment. "And I feel very foolish."

"Accidents happen. We were told that there was someone with you."

"Steve." Murray frowned. "I didn't … he must've gone further in. He said he heard voices."

"Is there anyone else in here?"

Murray shook his head. "Echoes. Or bats or birds."

"He should've known better than to wander off." Aslan said. "We'll have to find him."

Tess nodded. "No-one goes in the cave on their own. I'll appraise Greg of the situation." She headed back to the entrance to call Greg – the surrounding rock interfered with the phone's signal.

Stuart joined Tess at the cave entrance. Dirt and small pebbles pattered past, dislodged as Greg and Iain hauled in the stretcher. Iain joined them. Tess said, "I hope it's safe enough to lower it down to Jared."

"It'll be risky but at least Murray will be secure so he's likely only to get some more bruises."

~~~

Loading Murray onto the stretcher was straight forward, a routine they had practised many times. Aslan and Iain left the other two to lower the casualty down to safety.

Aslan punched Iain playfully on the shoulder. "Let's go find our stray."

"He can't have gone far." Iain adjusted the light on his helmet and checked that the battery was secure on his belt. Although he was an expert climber, his preferred pastime was speleology. The chance to explore these caves would be irresistible. "I brought down extra batteries."

"Good thinking."

"We're not sure how long ago he went exploring," Aslan said. "He shouldn't have gone off on his own. He's supposed to be an experienced caver."

"Let's just be thankful it's a dry cave."

"If by dry you mean there isn't a river running through it, yeah." Aslan wiped his fingers down the wall. "This isn't dry."

Iain looked at him. "Your fingers are glowing."

"Phosphorescence. Do we call out?"

"Too many echoes. But we don't need to be quiet. I wouldn't want to startle Steve when we find him. Look for his footprints."

They walked on a way, ducking under rocks protruding from the roof, casting their lights on the walls, ceiling and floor.

"It whiffs a bit," Aslan said.

"Reckon there are creatures living here. Bats probably. All the caves here will be interlinked."

"Bats pong. Why do you think I prefer to leave the caves to those who like squeezing themselves into small holes?"

There was only one route to follow, no side passages. After a while Aslan said, "Hey, Iain. Is that a light up ahead?"

Iain stared. "Nah. The walls are glowing."

"Weird. Is it our torches?"

"Dunno. Turn them off. It could be Steve."

With their lights extinguished, the walls continued to glow. "It's some kind of phosphorescence," Aslan said. "Not quite enough to see clearly."

"Pity. It would be good to save battery power. We don't know how far we'll have to go."

Aslan said, "The glowing walls are beautiful. Hey, there's a huge centipede."

"Careful. It probably bites," Iain said. "You know, I've never seen caves like this before. Not in this country."

Aslan brushed his hand along the wall. "It feels like velvet."

"Hey. Do that again."

"Do what?"

"Stroke the wall."

"Sure." Aslan ran his hands along the surface. "It glows brighter where I touch it."

"It changes colour too." Iain caressed the opposite wall.

They went deeper in the passage, the phosphorescence rippling in their path, seemingly enchanted by that effect, forgetting why they were there.

"I can hear music," Iain said.

"Who could be singing down here?"

"Fairies."

Aslan giggled. "I've never seen a fairy.

"Some people think they don't exist."

"They've never been here. We'll be famous. The first people to hear fairies singing."

"Perhaps we'll see them too." Iain picked up the pace. Then he suddenly stopped. "What are we doing here?" he asked.

"Exploring." Aslan giggled again. "Hunting fairies. Perhaps we can catch one."

"Did you bring a net?"

"Nah. My helmet will do."

Iain frowned. "I think there's something else we're supposed to do."

"What?"

"Can't remember. Let's find the fairies first. I can hear lots of voices."

"Lots of fairies." Aslan ducked suddenly. "One just flew past met."

"Was it singing?"

"It squeaked."

Iain laughed.

The passage opened out into a wide dark cave. A shaft of light lanced down into the space. Beside it, a cascade of water tumbled from an opening. Spray broke at the base causing a myriad of tiny rainbows.

"Beautiful," Aslan said.

"Where have the fairies gone?" Iain asked.

Aslan pointed. "There. There. There—"

"Can we get closer?"

They began to move around the wall. The phosphorescence was less intense in the shaft of light from above but brighter in the darker alcoves. Voices chittered at them from the darkness. The ground was soft under their feet. Aslan closed his eyes and stretched out his arms. "I could stay here for ever. It's so beautiful even with my eyes closed." He breathed deeply, relaxing, everything else forgotten.

"Hey. There's someone over there." Iain's voice broke into his non-thoughts.

He opened his eyes. "Where? Are they our fairies?"

"Over there?"

Aslan could only see shadows. The floor of the cavern was split by a cleft into which the water tumbled.

"I'm going to get him," Iain said. "I'm not having anyone interfering with our fairies."

"How are you going to get there?" Aslan asked, his mind dimly registering the problem of crossing the chasm. The way the water tumbled into the gap was fascinating. The spray was like jewels and the faeries skimmed in and out of the curtain. He wondered how they didn't get their wings wet. What would it feel like to flit between droplets?

"I can jump," Iain said.

"Jump what?"

"Over to there. And I can soar like the fairies." Iain stood on the edge of the cleft, arms outstretched.

Aslan screwed up his eyes in concentration. There was something he had forgotten. "I don't think you should."

"Why not? I fly every day."

He didn't – Aslan remembered that Iain had been terrified to go hang gliding. He said, "Your wings aren't big enough."

"I'll run. Like a swan. Watch me." Iain walked back to the side of the cavern. He held his arms out and flapped them up and down. "Here I come." He began to run. At the edge of the chasm he pushed off, up and out, arms waving, legs pedalling. About halfway he began to lose height. Aslan cheered him on. For a moment it looked as if he might reach the other side, then he lifted his arms straight above his head, twisted in the air and plunged down into the falling water.

Aslan threw himself down onto the ground to cheer his friend as he tumbled out of sight.

~~~

Tess and Stuart lowered Murray safely to the ground. Jared and the two others waiting below would ensure the casualty was taken to the ambulance waiting further down in the valley.

Aslan and Iain hadn't returned from the depths of thee cave. Tess was trying to decide if she and Stuart should go after them or wait. She glanced at Stuart. "You've got some glowing stuff on your shoulder."

He wiped his hand over the cloth and looked at his fingers. "Where did it come from?"

"It was on the cave walls, near where Murray was lying."

"Oh, shit!"

Tess gave him a startled look. "What is it?"

"Trouble. Big trouble. I've heard of this stuff. It's some kind of a symbiosis between a fungus and a slime mould. It's found in places like Borneo."

"What's the problem with it?"

"The spores are hallucinogenic."

"You mean those guys could be tripping out in there."

"Yeah."

"Oh, in that case we have to go after them."

"And get pegged by hallucinations, too? We need breathing apparatus."

"But if we know about it, won't we be able to work through it?"

"When was the last time you tripped out, Tess? College?"

"Something like that…"

"LSD?"

"Pot. And some E."

"We'll need breathing apparatus. Trust me. Get on to Greg."

Greg agreed with Stuart's assessment. Stuart climbed back up to collect the apparatus needed for them, including the missing Steve. Back at the cave entrance, Tess and Stuart checked masks, batteries and lights. They used sign language to indicate they were ready and then headed in. As they penetrated deeper into the cave the glow from the phosphorescent slime mould became stronger. A bright line ran through it at a level where a man might trail his hand. Though it seemed obvious where they had gone, Tess also kept an eye out for tracks on the floor. Eventually the passage branched. In one direction the glow was more intense. Footmarks indicated someone had passed down that tunnel.

The masks made it difficult to communicate. Both Tess and Stuart had found that using sign language was an advantage and were proficient at it. As they navigated the passage, Tess signed, "I hear twittering."

"Bats? Too high pitched for me," Stuart signed back. "Voices?"

"Could be. Sirens?"

"Good imagination." Stuart stopped. They reached another junction. "Left. Right too narrow."

Tess saw a footprint in the squishy layer covering the floor. It looked like bat droppings and she knew that stank of ammonia, and she was very glad she was wearing a mask. They continued until they reached a section where the roof lowered and they had to duck under an overhang. Something darted past them. Tess assumed it was a bat.

As the ceiling became higher again, and the passage

widened, Tess signed, "I think I hear birds."

"And water," Stuart responded.

Tess wondered what kinds of birds would be found this far inside the cave system. She knew that in some countries there were such things as cave swifts, but she hadn't heard of anything similar in the UK, though it made sense that some birds would nest in caves.

Moments later they stepped into a large cavern with a waterfall at its centre. Stuart turned and sprayed a marker on the wall at the mouth of the entrance they had just come through. A precaution against getting lost.

Tess took in the surroundings. The floor was carpeted with a mixture of bat shit and bird guano. The waterfall was illuminated by a shaft of light coming from the hole in the roof through which the water also poured. The water cascaded straight down into a chasm that cut the cavern in two. She scanned the floor. Cockroaches, centipedes and other insects crawled over the mass of droppings. She saw tracks that were probably made by boots, but their traces were confused. Casting around, it looked to her as if someone had headed towards the lip of the chasm. There was a silhouette of someone on the far side, standing in a pool of light. She pointed him out. From the light becoming brighter, it appeared to have stopped raining and the sun was making an appearance.

"How? Too wide to jump," Stuart indicated.

"Waterfall." Even if there wasn't the clichéd ledge running behind the curtain of spray, there would be hand and footholds – slippery but likely navigable.

Stuart went first, ropes joining them, a safety line if he slipped. He made it to the other side and signalled her across. It was easier than she anticipated. The rock surface was rough beneath her fingers and, surprisingly, very little moss had accumulated. There were fissures in the limestone to grasp onto.

Birds swooped about, heedless of the water and the humans.

The figure they had seen earlier was still in the same position, arms outstretched, staring up into the paler areas between tree roots protruding through the cavern's ceiling. The light that fell on his face showed an expression of awe. Tess wondered what he thought he could see in his hallucinated daze. She cast about looking for any others, for their footprints. Her torch beam caught the reflective strip on the jacket of another figure sitting by the chasm, hunched over something.

Stuart lifted the mask from his face. "We should be far enough from the spores for the effect to be minimal. I hope. The birds don't seem to have a problem and we need to talk to them."

Tess nodded and removed hers, clipping it to her belt. "We'll need them to get back."

Stuart moved towards the standing figure, Tess to the crouching one, approaching cautiously. People in the grip of hallucinations were unpredictable and could do the unexpected. She dimmed her head torch so as not to dazzle him – there was ample light from the rift in the roof and the distant glow from the slime mould on the other side of the cavern.

She recognised Aslan. He was oblivious of her presence, even when she said, "Hi."

Tess moved closer and touched his shoulder. He flinched away, huddling closer to whatever he was hunched over. Aslan appeared to be hugging a skeleton. Tess thought it looked like a sheep's, one that had died a long time ago. That wasn't a surprise, animals could easily wander about in caves, unable to escape until they died of starvation.

She squatted down next to him. "Aslan, it's time to go home."

He turned his head slightly to look at her, confusion clouding his face. "I can't," he said.

"Why can't you come home?"

"He's dead." Aslan stroked the skull. A cockroach crawled out of the eye socket.

"Who's dead?" Tess wondered who he thought the skeleton was.

"Gus. Gus is dead." There was a hitch in his voice.

"This isn't Gus."

He shook his head. "I know my brother,"

She didn't know if Aslan recognised her or was just responding to a voice. Tess knew that Gus was in Sheffield. "This isn't him. When we get outside, you can call him."

"I'm not leaving him."

She supressed an inclination to argue. Somehow, she'd find a way of taking the skeleton with them when they leave the cave. Once the narcotic was out of his system Aslan would probably be embarrassed. "Where's Iain?" she asked.

"He flew away."

"Where did he fly to?"

"He went to play with the fairies."

Tess glanced over to where Stuart was silhouetted with the other figure. It wasn't Iain. He was shorter than Stuart. It must be Steve. Was it fairies he was staring at, flitting amongst the roots? She returned her focus to Aslan. Getting him and the skeleton back past the waterfall wasn't going to be easy. Stuart would have his own problems.

The backpack she was wearing, that contained the air cylinder, included a thermal blanket, folded into a tight pack. It opened out into a strong sheet. "Let's see if we can wrap this around him," she said,

"Why?"

"When we carry him out of here we need him to be safe."

"Oh, right."

"Can you help?" The problem with skeletons was that they had a tendency to fall apart, especially the older ones. This one looked as if it had been here a long time. In his current state, she worried how Aslan would react if a leg fell off. They wrapped the skeleton, tucking the blanket tightly around it, securing it with a length of rope.

She glanced over to Stuart, the instinct to keep at least a visual contact with her buddy was entrenched in her training. She was about to stand, to assist Aslan back across to the other side of the chasm, when the light flickered. She felt vibrations coming from around her.

Moments later, a roar emanated from one of the passages. A gust of wind and dust blasted across the cavern. Instinctively, she reached for her mask but she smelt the mustiness of fungus before she had clasped it in place. She'd inhaled some of the spores. Would she know if they would impair her judgement? A glance towards Stuart showed him lying on the floor, Steve standing over him.

She began to run.

~~~

Stuart had crossed the cavern to stand beside Steve; his mouth was hanging open, a trace of drool collecting on his lower lip. He was enraptured.

"Hi," Stuart said. "What are you watching?"

Steve looked round, startled, then crouched down, covering his ears with his hands. "Go away, monster."

"Nah," Stuart said. "Friendly kobold, me."

"They's nasty."

"You're thinking of orcs. Not an orc."

Steve swivelled round, still crouching. "What you want?"

"To take you to safety. So the orcs don't get you."

Steve stared around. "Are they here?"

"Not yet but they are in the tunnels. We must sneak away before they find us." Stuart was unsure what the hallucinogens had done to Steve's mind. He was trying to play along with the clues the man was giving out.

"What about the angels? I don't want the orcs to eat them."

"They won't."

"How do you know?" His face took on a dreamy expression and he looked upwards again. "They are beautiful, aren't they?"

"Angels can fly, orcs can't."

"Oh? Can you hear them singing?"

"Yes. Is it the angels?" Stuart knew it was the birds flitting in and out of the opening above them, but going along with Steve's delusions was the best way of persuading him to leave the cavern.

"Isn't it lovely?"

"You can hear them better by the waterfall." Once Stuart got him moving it should be easier to herd him towards the exit. He put a hand on Steve's shoulder to steer him in the right direction.

"The angels say I can fly with them."

"I don't think that would be a good idea. You don't have wings."

"I do." He held his arms out horizontally. "Watch me."

Stuart made a grab for him, visualising Steve vanishing down the chasm.

The light flickered and he felt the ground vibrate.

Moments later a roar erupted from a passage expelling a cloud of dust. He instinctively reached for his mask as he tasted mushroom on his tongue. It sounded as if the overhang above the cave entrance had given way.

Steve yelled, "Monster!"

Momentarily disorientated, Stuart didn't duck fast enough as Steve swung a hand at his head. The rock in it connected painfully. Unbalanced, his feet slipped on the sticky bat droppings under his feet.

He felt himself falling.

~~~

Tess stumbled across the uneven slippery surface. She was shouting but the muffling caused by her mask made her voice more of a growl. Steve hadn't given Stuart a chance to get back onto his feet. He was kicking the fallen man, yelling "Monster! Leave them alone" over and over. He was seeing something Tess couldn't.

Tess grabbed at Steve's arm to pull him away from Stuart, but he rounded on her and started pummelling, screaming that they were both monsters. She backed away, while trying to stop his thrashing arm, anything to prevent him attacking Stuart. Her mask became momentarily dislodged. Suddenly, Steve broke away from Tess and stumbled off. She dropped to her knees beside Stuart, not caring where Steve had gone.

She turned up the light on her head torch to see better. Stuart was bleeding heavily from a scalp wound. He was unconscious but fortunately still breathing. He needed help, urgently. She would come back for Aslan, and find Steve, later. And Iain, wherever he'd gone. As she tucked a thermal blanket around Stuart, sparkles of light landed on him. She did her best to brush them off, but there were many more floating in the air, in all shades and colours.

Tess scrambled back across the cleft, under the

waterfall. She didn't need Stuart's marker to know which exit she had to go down. The slime mould waved to her in rainbow colours. She was hardly aware of her fingers skimming the mould as she used the rock wall to guide her. But she came to a dead end. Boulders were blocking her route. Had she taken a wrong turn or was the rumble she heard earlier the roof collapsing?

It didn't matter. The air around her was more interesting. There were brightly coloured fish looping between the boulders. She plucked at the jellyfish that covered her face. She breathed in deeply. She sank to the ground, the better to watch the marvellous creatures that drifted around her.

Tess would sit there and enjoy the show. Nothing else mattered.

NIGHT HUNTER

That woman has no right to be in a place like this.

When she pushed open the door to the bar and stepped through, those were the thoughts that went through Hunter's mind. He sipped his drink – just orange juice at this time of night – and watched her over the rim. She was tall and assured. Her dark hair, curling about her shoulders, had a degree of muzziness that was almost deliberate. Her leathers, red flashed with black, emphasised her figure. It was the kind of figure Hunter liked but rarely had a chance to get hold of. She paused just inside the room and scanned the occupants – a ragtag collection of locals and late season visitors. This was a drinking hole, not the up-market kind of bar he'd expect her to be at home in.

Hunter was here because he had to wait somewhere until after nightfall, and astride a bike in a lay-by was not the most comfortable place. Besides, locals like this were good for picking up rumours. He watched the customers' reactions as well as the woman. Younger lads stared openly while their elders shrugged and turned away. Hunter glanced at his watch. It was almost time to go.

The woman exchanged words with the barman but instead of buying a drink she looked over in Hunter's direction. He averted his gaze. Attracting anyone's attention right now was not on his agenda. If he hadn't been working he might have enjoyed attempting to chat her up.

"You are Hunter." Not a question, an assured statement of fact. Her voice was melodious. It matched her appearance.

He looked up at her then, deliberately giving her a lecherous once-over, noting that her eyes were not as dark as he had expected. The milk-chocolate brown of them was flecked through with amber. He leaned back in his seat and raised his glass in her direction. "That is what folks call me. I don't think we've been introduced though."

She pulled out a stool and sat on it. "My name is Phoebe Makhani."

She didn't hold out her hand for him to shake as many women would have done when introducing themselves. Instead, she laid her palms loosely upon her thighs in a very relaxed attitude. Her nail varnish, he noticed, was perfect and black.

"And?" He didn't feel quite as casual as he pretended. Something about her was unsettling.

"I'm here to offer you a job."

Hunter smiled. "I'm not interested. I've already got a job."

"I know. You hunt wild animals."

He bowed his head in acknowledgement of her correct information. He hunted with nets, traps and a tranquiliser gun. He rarely killed his quarry and they ended up in zoos. What he hunted depended on who was paying him, and why. Phoebe Makhani looked like the kind of lady who thought having a cheetah on a leash looked cool. He had learnt not to be taken in by appearances.

"I want you to hunt for me," she said.

"I'm not available. I already have a contract."

"Contracts can be broken."

"Not by me. And before you tell me you will offer me more cash the answer is no. So don't waste your breath."

"Don't you want to know what I want you to hunt?"

"No. When I've fulfilled this contract, ask me again."

"You won't succeed."

"In what?"

"Your hunt."

"That remains to be seen."

Hunter placed his empty glass on the table and smiled. He stood up. "I don't fail very often, Ms Makhani. Have a good evening."

As he walked towards the door he had an urge to turn round to see if she was watching him. He resisted it. Outside, the drizzle from earlier had stopped and the cloud cover had broken. There was an occasional star visible but better still, the clouds towards the horizon were rimmed with silver where the gibbous moon was rising. That light would make his pursuit easier. He headed towards the car park to the rear of the pub where he had parked his bike – a stripped down Suzuki painted totally in matt black. Even the exhaust and mirror rims had been persuaded to take the colour.

The other bike caught his eye. The Harley was scarlet flashed with black lightning. He glanced speculatively back at the pub. The woman was wearing the same colours. The machine was built for speed and would need strength to control it. She hadn't looked as if she had the muscle but appearances could be deceptive. Either it was hers or she had hoped to make an impression on him and its rider was lurking somewhere. Hunter smiled. Yeah, she was impressive. So was the bike but he had a contract to fulfil.

~~~

It was just before midnight when Hunter met with his client. The Sussex farmer was parked in a lay-by usually used by anglers to reach the river from the Old Shoreham Road.

Ellis scowled. "Yer late."

"I've been checking a few things. The cat's got to lie up somewhere." Hunter gestured along the road. "Is the lime quarry completely abandoned?"

"Ay." Ellis was peering through binoculars, hardly paying attention to him. "There's where I bin seeing the critter."

Hunter doubted Ellis could see much, just dark outlines of hedges against the paler grey of the fields, and the silvery glint of the River Adur. Ellis would have been working as much by memory as anything. Hunter raised his own binoculars and switched them to night vision. They gathered all the available light and enhanced it. Everything was still shades of grey, but the sheep – the bait – were clear as they moved restlessly in the enclosure. If he listened carefully, he could hear the occasional bleat as they protested their confinement.

"When were the buildings last used?"

"A good few years."

"Any chance of a buyer?"

"Doubt it. Bain't worth the money."

Hunter kept his thoughts to himself. He'd been over the place earlier in the day. The mechanisms for crushing the chalk and feeding it to the kilns were well rusted and any glass in the buildings was long broken. He had seen traces of a car having been parked, and more than once. The tyre marks in the white mud were deep and overlaid each other. It could be a courting couple but the wheel imprints were wide, the tread new, but the kind fitted to large cars owned by the type of men who could afford hotel rooms for clandestine meetings. He'd looked for shoe prints but none were clear; just a few indentations his imagination could interpret as foot marks pointed towards the building. It was possible that the cat was being kept there and the visitor was feeding it – or had released it to find its own food. Hence the sightings and Ellis's score-marked sheep. Only one had actually died and it had been well picked over by scavengers before the farmer had found it. The evidence pointed to a big cat. There had long been a tradition of a Sussex lion and that is what Ellis had hired him to catch. Hunter would reserve judgment until he saw it, though. A feral dog could cause similar damage.

"What time did you see it?" he asked.

"T'were dusk. No mistake. Cat it were. Big as me sheep."

Could easily have been a sheep, Hunter thought. Dim light plays tricks with one's night vision. Shadows change shape.

"Bain't only one that's seen it," Ellis said.

Hunter had previously spoken to the woman who claimed to have seen the animal crossing the road in front of her car. She was a townie and couldn't be expected to distinguish between a muntjac and a wild boar, and the odds were she'd seen a fox and not recognised it in her headlights. They had been sighted in the area, but hearing rumours about a big cat tends to colour perception. Her sighting had been along this stretch of road.

There were big cats living wild in Britain; he'd hunted them before. Usually ones that had escaped for one reason or another and the owner wanted it recaptured quietly, without the press scaremongering. What gave *this* sighting credence were the pug marks. There were plenty of prints here, wader, dog, sheep, especially in places where the riverbank crumbled giving access to the water. The larger tracks could have been made by a big dog – he'd seen an Irish Wolfhound on the track earlier in the day – except that the ubiquitous claw marks were not visible. The banks of the Adur were a favourite walking place for dog owners and he noticed plenty of evidence of their presence; and what made them think that just because their dog was crapping on grass the law about taking it home ceased to apply.

"I already talked to Maisie Collins," Hunter said.

"Right. Leave yer to it then." Ellis headed back to his Land Rover leaving Hunter scanning the fields below.

Some people might have wondered how Hunter carried the equipment he needed on his bike; his backpack looked too small to carry everything they thought he ought to need. Hunter lifted the saddle and began to assemble his tranquiliser gun from the parts nestling in the cavity. He'd stopped carrying it openly in Europe after having had to explain its purpose and his legal right to carry it to police in countries where he didn't speak the language. It was easier to keep it out of sight until it was needed.

Hunter fitted the night goggles over his face and set off down the narrow path. He could feel the slipperiness of the mud beneath his feet. The treads on his boots were deep enough for him to be sure they would give him the purchase he needed. There was a small foot bridge at the bottom of the slope, there to give anglers access to the path on the opposite bank. He ignored it, heading left into the scrub. Earlier, he had constructed a crude hide opposite the wallow where the cat had come to drink. The hide was high enough up the slope so that he could see the penned sheep as well as the river, but not too far; his gun was powerful enough to hit the target, if he had wanted to. He settled in to wait. There was no guarantee that the animal would appear. If it was in the area, perhaps the penned sheep would interest it. Otherwise he could be here for many nights – it was part of the job.

Stillness and patience were the qualities he needed. He just hoped that if the animal caught his scent it would assume that it was lingering from daylight walkers.

Chill settled over the fields. Mist shimmied across the water's surface, clinging to the banks. If it got any thicker, Hunter would have to abandon his watch. He needed a good view of the wallow to get a firm shot – there would be only one chance. The tawny owl that had been calling from across the field fell silent. Insect noises had been sporadic and now ceased. The sheep were quiet. Above on the road a lone car sped past. He heard it braking as it approached the bend before its sound died, muffled by the hedgerows.

He tensed as an animal trotted along the footpath and paused by the wallow, and relaxed again as he recognised a fox. It leapt down to the water's edge to drink. Suddenly, it raised its head and stared back along the track. Then it was off, ears flattened, tail between its legs. Something had alarmed it.

Hunter, checked his gun by touch, not taking his eyes from the opposite bank. Would it go for the sheep first, or the water? He heard the sheep beginning to move restlessly, the breeze coming from them towards him. One bleated – tentative, but not yet alarmed.

Then it came. Even with the night goggles it was no more than a shadow on the path, a patch of darkness moving along it. Hunter bowed his head to sight along the barrel steadied on the branch of a tree. He took long shallow breaths as he waited, gauging its nearest approach. A sheep cried. The shadow stopped. Its head lifted as it turned, scenting prey. It gathered itself. Hunter held his breath and fired. At the same moment the creature leapt, vanishing into the darkness.

Unsure whether he had hit it, Hunter lowered the gun,

leaning it against the tree. He unclipped the detector from his belt and switched it on, scanning the darkness ahead of him. The dial lit up with the trace of the tracker embedded in the dart. He allowed himself a small smile: the trace was moving. As long as it had struck hard enough all he had to do was follow. Eventually, the tranquiliser would do its work and the animal would drop. At first the creature appeared to be heading towards a wide pipe that crossed the river, affording an easy place to get from one side to the other that wouldn't smell strongly of human or dog.

Hunter scrambled along the muddy path, reloading just in case, but he set the weapon on safety before setting off at a lope although there was no hurry. The detector indicated that the animal was headed into the quarry and seemed to be somewhere amongst the spoil heaps of uncrushed chalk. It stopped moving. Either it was holed up or it had dropped. Hunter moved cautiously.

He saw the dart lying on the ground as he threaded around one of the piles. He slipped off the gun's safety and crouched, making himself smaller. Darts did fall out but usually sooner than this. He scanned the tops of the heaps first – a dark shape should stand out against the chalk – before beginning a sweep at ground level.

A whisper of tumbling scree gave him a fraction's warning. As he turned a patch of darkness detached itself from the shadows and flowed towards him. He had time to raise the gun to his hip before firing. The weight of the animal hit him. He felt the prick of claws pierce his leathers. Its momentum propelled him backwards, his feet going out from under him, slipping on the chalk mud. A hard landing punched the air from his lungs. The goggles showed him fangs inches from his face.

A snarling streak hit the beast in the ribs. It twisted

sideways, striking out at its assailant. For a moment the air was filled with hissing and spitting ferocity, then one of the creatures leapt for the top of a spoil heap. The other followed it and both animals disappeared over the top. Hunter picked himself up and winced. The claws had dug deep and his butt was bruised. The creature was real and big – panther sized, he reckoned. His pursuit though was over for the night.

Reaching his bike, he stowed the gun and prepared to return home. He'd come out to inspect the area again in the morning. Unless there was torrential rain he ought to be able to pick up prints and try to make sense of what had just happened. As he settled his helmet in place another bike roared to a stop across his path. The big black and red Harley.

Phoebe Makhani raised visor. "I said you would fail," she said.

"There's always tomorrow," he said. He switched on the ignition. "You gonna get out of my way?"

"Since you've nothing to do for the rest of the night, perhaps we could talk."

"I was planning on using it to sleep. Besides, I've still got a job."

"That's what we need to talk about. And you really do need to dress those scratches."

"You offering?"

"No."

"Didn't think so." He backed up his bike and then swung it in a tight arc before climbing on and heading back towards Shoreham.

In his wing mirror he saw her following him. He didn't try to shake her. She had found him in the pub; she probably knew where he lived. Besides, she intrigued him. There were not many women who were prepared to ride a such a large bike. He was tempted to put her through her paces. He pushed his own machine along stretches that he knew were unmonitored by the police and swung around the A27 interchange. At this hour traffic was almost non-existent. At the Beach end of Norfolk Bridge he slowed and bumped up across the pavement and onto the footpath that followed the river bank. The boats moored here were permanent fixtures, with connected water and electricity, and post codes. The owners paid council tax and got the same services as land-based homes. Hunter's was one of them.

He wasn't supposed to ride along the footpath but at night no-one bothered. He dismounted to push the bike across the gangplank and locked it in the metal shed that was bolted to the deck. His home had once been a longboat. It was Birmingham registered and he had no idea how the previous owner had got it here, but once in its permanent berth the man he'd bought it from had built an extra level onto the superstructure so that the foredeck was level with the path. Hunter bolted the gate and unlocked the hatch, stepping down into the neat room that was his lounge and extended most of the length of the boat. On the lower level was the galley, two bedrooms, a shower and the head, each separated from the other by a folding door. Where the engine had been was his workshop. The place was neat. It had to be.

Hunter changed quickly and fetched a beer from the little fridge. He wasn't intending to go anywhere else tonight.

His visitor turned up a few minutes later.

Phoebe scanned the long room, virtually no expression on her face.

"I hope you parked at the foot of the dyke," Hunter said.

She nodded. "It wasn't easy finding my way here in the dark."

"I don't remember inviting you, but now you're here, would you like a drink?"

"Do you have any honey?"

"Yeah."

"Then warm water with a spoonful of honey stirred in would be good."

It was an unusual request. Hunter disappeared down the companionway to the lower deck to prepare it.

"I hope that's the right temperature," he said on his return, handing her a mug.

She sipped. "Acacia honey?" she said.

He nodded. "I'm still not interested in a job."

"Will you listen to what I have to say before making a final decision?"

"No harm in that. Besides, throwing you out physically could be a bit tricky."

"My offer will not necessarily interfere with your present contract. It may well help you fulfil it."

"Go on."

"I'm looking for someone who can be my ears and eyes during daylight hours."

"Why?"

"I am not normally active while the sun is up. I am nocturnal."

Hunter grinned. "You some kind of vampire, then?"

"Don't be insulting. Vampires – at least the kind that appear in Stoker or the current romantic fiction – don't exist."

"So what are you?"

"Bengal tiger."

Hunter laughed.

Moments later he was staring into the amber eyes of a

big cat, its fangs inches from his face. He froze. "Fuck me," he eventually said. Then the beast was gone and Phoebe was sitting opposite him sipping her honey water.

Much as he tried not to show it, Hunter was shaken. His mouth was dry; his heart raced. He had to press his hand to his thigh to stop it trembling. He didn't dare pick up his bottle to take a drink. As calmly as he could he said, "I thought were-animals had to get naked to do that."

Phoebe smiled. "First, I am not a were-animal, I am a shifter. Second, clothes made from natural materials are absorbed. Remember that hair and nails are dead tissue. So is leather and silk."

"Zips are metal."

"So are the fillings in your teeth."

"I don't turn into a big cat when I get annoyed."

"Neither do I."

"What was that about?"

"A demonstration. It's what you're up against: hunting Michael Tan."

Hunter shook his head. "My contract is for the Sussex panther."

"Did you hit it with your tranquiliser?"

He frowned. Since he had found the dart by the quarry; it had to have been carried there in the flank of the animal. "Yes."

"Then why wasn't it out cold? How come it could still ambush you?"

"Perhaps there are several of them. There were at least two cats in that quarry."

"We are immune to that particular tranquiliser."

"So what would I have to use? Silver bullets?"

She smiled. Not much, just a hint at the corners of her mouth. "Silver nitrate solution would certainly make me feel sleepy. Lead would be a better bet."

For a moment he decided to play along. "Who's Michael Tan?"

"To the population of Brighton, he is a successful solicitor dealing mostly with business law. In reality he is an Amur Tiger."

"And I am expected to believe that?"

Phoebe shrugged. "What you believe is not important. What you need to know is that he imports narcotics. I need someone who can track him during daylight hours."

"What I don't get," Hunter said, "is that if both you and he are tigers, why he doesn't sleep during the daytime like you."

"I refuse to feed the tiger. I am a vegetarian by choice. Some of us can get by dining on rare steak. A few like Michael Tan develop a taste for killing. While he hunted rats and rabbits no-one noticed. Now he has turned his attention to sheep. There is a possibility that won't satisfy his appetite for long."

"He'll graduate to horses and cows?"

"They won't provide much sport."

Hunter considered her for a moment, then said, "If what you say is true, putting aside this tiger thing, he would need to import the drugs somehow."

"Yes."

"How?"

"By boat."

"I didn't think cats liked water."

"Tigers are very good swimmers, as are leopards and jaguars. But that is irrelevant."

"Where's his boat?"

"If you go up on deck you will be able to see it."

Hunter nodded. It made sense. There were a number of boats of all sizes moored in the Adur estuary, from small lobster boats to the more luxurious yachts that overwintered at the boatyard on the opposite bank.

"You're not suggesting I follow it, are you?"

"No. My sources suggest he will be going out over the weekend to pick up a shipment. I want to know when he gets back."

"What then?"

"That depends. I won't ask you to do anything illegal."

"But you want me to act as a spy. Because I just happen to be moored in a good position?"

"That helps."

"What's in it for me?"

"Do you prefer cash or a transfer to an account of your choice?"

"Whatever, but cash is always useful."

Phoebe stood up. She took an envelope from an inner pocket of her jacket and laid it on the table.

"We haven't discussed price," Hunter said.

"I think you will find that generous." She took two steps towards the companionway up onto the deck before turning back. "You interest me, Hunter. I will be seeing you again."

He finished his beer before touching the envelope. He counted the notes inside. There was twice as much there as Ellis was paying him to hunt the sheep-molesting cat. He had to admit that Phoebe fascinated him. It wasn't just that she was a good-looking woman or that she could turn into a tiger. It was more her certainty that he would do as she asked. He only had her word about the activities of this Michael Tan. He took the money down below and tucked it into a safe in the floor of his workshop. He wanted to learn more before he was prepared to spend any of it – just in case she was setting him up.

~~~

Next morning, at the edge of dawn, Hunter was back in the quarry. He recognised his own prints in the mud and followed them. The surroundings were deceptively different in daylight – the slopes softer, less angular now the shadows were gone. He found the place where he had been ambushed, and his dart on the ground. There was no sign that he had hit anything. Significant were the paw prints: two sets, one slightly larger than the other.

He scrambled up over the chalk mound in the direction the cats had taken. He lost them at the road. There was no indication where they had crossed over or doubled back, though if there had been muddy prints on the tarmac, passing vehicles using the road would have eroded them. As part of the fast route between Worthing and Brighton, even he had to watch his step as he crossed over. Cars tended to speed along this stretch at all times of the day.

He shrugged and walked to the abandoned building, looking for a way in that he might have missed when he had first checked it out. Though the windows were broken, they were small with shards of glass still lodged in the frames. The door was still rusted solid. He prowled around, paying attention to where he had seen the tyre marks. The tracks were still there. He thought they might be deeper and wished he had photographed the set he'd found earlier. This time he did. There might be wheel marks in the park at the foot of the dyke that he could compare them to. What was new were the motorbike tracks suggesting Phoebe had parked here, perhaps watching him. He photographed those, too. As he stood looking at the tracks he recalled hearing the car passing along the road the previous evening. The engine had changed as it had slowed for the bend. He returned to the road and looked along it in both directions. The bend was still quite a way ahead. It could've turned in here. If what Phoebe had said, it was a possibility.

Nothing was conclusive. The only thing he could report to Ellis was that there was a big cat in the area and that he had had no luck in catching it. Hunter would only accept payment if he had captured the beast – it was a matter of honour.

He headed back to Shoreham. The pace slowed as traffic snarled along the main street. The town wasn't built for so much traffic; a bus and a delivery van could cause chaos on the main street, and the back roads were even narrower. Hunter made better progress than most, riding his bike, slipping past stationary vehicles when the opportunity arose until he could turn into the sanctuary of the boatyard. Hunter pulled into the small car park and propped the bike next to a neat Smart Roadster. He admired the glossy black finish and its yellow striping over the wheel arches.

The boatyard was one Hunter had used frequently over the past few years. Owning a boat, even a stationary one, meant keeping on top of the maintenance. He didn't wish to find himself sinking on a high tide, and he preferred to get his repair items from the chandlery than the B&Q just a little further down the road. Doug Winterton, the chandlery's manager, was always ready to discuss problems and what might solve them. Doug wasn't in the shop – that was being overseen by Betts, the daughter of one of his neighbours.

"He's down on the slipway checking the winches, Mr Hunter," Betts said when he asked. "Got a careening coming in on the high tide."

"Thanks." Hunter made his way down to the quayside between the yachts propped up on their fixed keels. Some of them hadn't seen water for several years but as long as the owners paid their mooring fees, Doug wasn't worried.

Doug waved to Hunter as he approached. He wiped the oil from the winch mechanism off his hands on a rag as he came to join Hunter on the hard. "What can I do for you?" he asked.

"I noticed that some of the paint is beginning to flake from my boat's superstructure and wondered what the best was to redo it?"

"Seaward or Landward side?"

"Seaward."

"It gets the sun and the salt spray. Come up to the shop and I'll show you the options."

"Sure. Is that your car parked up at the entrance?"

"The Smart? Nope. Belongs to Michael Tan. He parks it here when he takes his boat over to the continent."

"Which is his?"

"The blue and white one. The *Dynasty*." Doug waved and the figure on the deck waved back.

Hunter was gradually learning more about boats. The *Dynasty* certainly looked as if it was capable of a Channel crossing. Probably slept four at the most and, like many of the yachts in the harbour, had both an engine and a mast, now with its sails furled. It was moored in the deep channel so could leave at any time though there was currently a bank of sticky mud between it and the shore. "Does he sail it on his own?" he asked.

"Not always. I think he's alone this time. Went out in the dinghy as the tide dropped. Do you know him?"

"No. Just curious about the boats I can see from my deck." He changed track. "What range of paint colours do you stock?"

Distracted, Doug was happy to sell Hunter the supplies he needed – a two litre can of paint with another of the same batch put aside in case he needed it. After strapping it to the back of the motorbike Hunter took the opportunity to examine the tyres of the Smart. Small pieces of chalk were lodged in the tread of one. There were plenty of ways that could've got there. Hunter photographed them anyway.

Back on his boat, Hunter spent time sanding down the area he intended to paint. The activity gave him a clear view of the river and the traffic on it. He was able to watch Michael Tan's *Dynasty* slip her moorings. Then he called Ellis. He confirmed to the farmer that he had seen something and found cat-like prints in the quarry but had had no luck in capturing it. He assured Ellis that he would be out again that night, though if Phoebe was to be believed there would be no sign of it. That still had to be put to the test. He didn't want to rely only on what he had been told. He did some online research and found lots of rumours and dead ends as well as a few verifiable facts.

~~~

"You do realise you are wasting your time?" He hadn't heard or seen Phoebe until she spoke beside him in his stakeout a little past midnight.

"I have a job to do," he said. "I can't take everything I'm told on trust."

"That is commendable." She didn't sound as if she was being sarcastic. "Was Michael Tan everything I said he was?"

"I can't verify the bit about him being a tiger, or that he's a drug smuggler."

"There's nothing about that on the internet."

"And you don't exist," he told her.

"You are just looking in the wrong place. Tell me when he returns."

"Even if it is daylight?"

"I will see the message when I wake."

"What if you were killed in your tiger form, would you change back to human?"

"No. We keep the forms we have when we die."

He was about to ask something else but she had gone. The crickets became louder and he gave up at moonset. He swung past the quarry buildings on the way home. His torch didn't show up any activity more recent than the night before.

~~~

On Sunday afternoon Hunter had finished applying the undercoat to the superstructure of his home and was preparing to start on the first of two topcoats that Doug Winterton had recommended when the *Dynasty* rode back up the channel. The blue and white yacht came in on the tide. The only person he could see on deck was the man steering. Although tempted to use his binoculars, Hunter restrained himself. He waited until the yachtsman was lowering his dingy. Then, he locked the brushes and paint away in the bike shed and rode round to the boatyard.

"Do you still have that paint Doug put aside for me?" Hunter asked Betts as he entered the chandlery.

"Yep, Mr Hunter. Do you want to take it now?"

"Please. The paint isn't going as far as I hoped."

"I'll just get it."

The girl's disappearance into the back room gave Hunter a chance to look over the man Doug was talking to. He was a slightly built man who looked as if he had Malaysian ancestry. It fitted with the name. Doug beckoned him over. "Hunter, this is Michael Tan. Mike, Hunter was admiring your car the other day."

Hunter grinned. "I don't think I've seen one of the Smart sports before. Heard of them, though."

"It's a stylish answer to driving in city traffic," Tan

said. He had no trace of an accent. "Will the yard be open tonight, or should I tie up at the hotel wharf?"

"I'll give you the code," Doug said. "Just make sure you close the gates behind you, and remember to show riding lights on the dinghy when you cross the river after dark."

"Thank you. Good day to you, Mr Hunter." Tan walked out as Betts brought over the tin of paint.

"Do many people have the gate code?" Hunter asked.

"Only those who'll be going to and from their boats at night," Doug said, "And I change it every month."

"Good idea. How much do I owe you for the paint?" It was never a good idea to appear too curious. He wondered if he was beginning to believe Phoebe's story.

Once he got back to his boat he retrieved the envelope Phoebe had given him and called the number written on it. Then he returned to his painting, while keeping one eye on the *Dynasty*.

~~~

The evening was pleasant. Hunter sat on his boat's deck sipping a concoction of lime juice, elderflower cordial and tonic water. There hadn't been much activity on the *Dynasty*. Tan had gone back on board and disappeared below soon after Hunter had returned to his own boat. Tan hadn't been up on deck since.

As the tide receded Hunter noticed the channel cut in the mud leading from the boatyard to deeper water. He hadn't seen it before but then he wasn't usually watching the far shore. It enabled dinghies to reach land whatever the height of the water. There was another alongside the back yard of the pub on the corner by Norfolk Bridge.

The sun was slowly setting and once it was properly dark, he would have to go back to his stake-out.

"What is the situation?"

Hunter didn't change position even though he hadn't heard Phoebe approach from behind him. He didn't want to give her the impression that he could be startled easily. "Michael Tan has been below decks since four. Would you like something to drink?" He held out his glass in her direction. She leaned forward to sniff the contents.

"Could you stir some sugar into it?"

"Of course. Take a seat while I get it."

On the way back from the galley, Hunter took the opportunity to appraise Phoebe properly. In profile she had strong features. Maybe her nose was a little too prominent and her chin too square for classic beauty. She still wore leathers, the only clothes he had seen her in. At the sound of the cabin door shutting she turned toward him and smiled. There was beauty in it.

"I hope that's the right amount," he said handing her the tall glass. "I've brought the bag if you want to add more."

She sipped. "This is good. Thank you."

"What happens now?" he asked.

"I watch and wait."

Upriver, over Norfolk Bridge and the hills of the South Downs, the sky was turning red, sending shafts of light that reflected orange pink off mud and water. A kayaker was silhouetted against the glow as he paddled down river. He passed behind the *Dynasty*. A light came on aboard the yacht.

"I thought you didn't wake up until sunset," he said.

"The sun needs to be low in the sky, not below the horizon. It is dependent on the amount of UV getting through the atmosphere. I am quite comfortable and awake at this time of day."

"I'd have expected that canoeist to have got past by now," Hunter said.

At his words Phoebe stood up and worked her way along the narrow ledge of the superstructure. She crouched on the stern staring at the yacht. Hunter just made out a figure coming onto the deck, a shadow in the gloom. He suspected Phoebe's eyesight was better than his in low light.

"Have you got a dinghy?" Phoebe whispered, her voice barely carrying the few feet between them.

"No."

"Damn. I hate getting muddy. Watch where the kayaker goes." She morphed faster than his brain could register. The tiger leapt from the stern, a shape skimming the mud. A roosting duck took off quacking in protest.

Hunter raced to the bow to where he had left his night goggles, ready to leave for the night-time stakeout. He scrambled back onto the roof, awkwardly holding the goggles in front of his face. He could see ripples in the water and Phoebe's human form hauling herself up the anchor chain. There was too much on the deck of the yacht for him to see clearly. The *Dynasty* rocked. An unhuman-like cry echoed across the water. Hunter thought he saw the shadows on deck merge. Something went over the side.

Hunter had his night-vision goggles correctly fitted on his head by now and even with them it was hard to make out what was going on. There seemed to be two figures in the water. They parted and came together. They could be fighting or trying to save each other. The current was carrying them towards the harbour. He didn't doubt that one of them was Phoebe.

Someone, something, hauled itself out of the water. Another tiger emerged onto the mud behind it and leapt, raking claws along its flanks. The first one twisted round, lashing out, trying to sink its teeth into the neck of the other. Both slipped and skidded on the slick surface, releasing their grips on each other. Hunter thought he could hear growling. The first, slightly larger tiger pounced as the second reared up. They clashed, rolled together, slid, still thrashing, back in to the river.

Hunter jumped from the roof, grabbed up a boathook and ran. He knew where they would come ashore: the place where things that had been washed down the Adur.

The residential road disgorged into a muddy anglers' car park. A low chain-link fence was all that separated it from the shingle bank. Hunter scrambled over and slithered down, pebbles rolling beneath his boots. He scanned the ruffled surface, hoping their thrashing hadn't carried them out into midstream and the deep water where the undertow sucked the effluent out to sea.

Then he saw the cat, head held high, paddling for the spit of pebbles he stood on. Just one animal. He could not tell which. He picked up a broken boathook from the shoreline and stepped back, feet apart, and firmly gripped the hook near one end with his left hand. His right hand rested more lightly halfway along it. He waited as the tiger waded from the river. It looked at him and shook itself, spraying water. Hunter didn't move. He had to be sure. It took several steps.

As the tiger morphed into Phoebe, the water behind her exploded. A wet, spitting ball of fur and fangs launched itself shoreward.

"Down!" Hunter yelled.

Phoebe dropped. Hunter ran, his right hand sliding down the shaft to join his left hand and he raised it high and swung it.

The tiger landed, claws raking Phoebe's legs. The metal hook connected with its head. The tiger staggered. Hunter brought it round and down again, this time with less power. The creature caught it in his jaws, smashed at it with a massive paw. The wooden shaft splintered. Hunter rammed the broken end into the animal's throat. It pushed towards him, digging the stake in further. Its eyes went wide as it slowly subsided.

There was a hiatus as Hunter waited for it to move, to burst into action again. When nothing happened and the only sound was the harshness of his own breathing and the rush of water on pebbles, he hauled the carcass off Phoebe's body.

"Are you okay?" he asked.

She pushed herself up onto knees and arms. "Battered." She winced. "I'm not sure I can walk far."

"If you can get over the fence I'll carry you to my boat."

The glare she gave him was almost a snarl.

"It's either that or you crawl."

She held up a hand then for him to help her to her feet.

As soon as he had got Phoebe to his boat, he called the coastguard saying he thought he had seen a man go into the water from one of the moored boats. Then he had dressed the nasty gash the other tiger's claws had made down her calf. It could have been worse – her boot had partially protected her. He told her that she ought to go to hospital and have seen to properly. She'd shaken her head.

"It really needs stitching," he said.

"Can you do it?"

"Not well. It will hurt. It will scar."

"Do it," she said.

The maroon flare was launched and saw the coastguard's vessel quartering the river, heard it down in the harbour. He sat on the stern of his boat watching the activity. A member of the coastguard team came to ask what he'd actually seen.

~~~

It was mid-morning when the police came calling. Now there was a policeman sipping tea.

"You'll need to come over to the station to make a written statement," the officer said.

"Did you find him? The man who went overboard?"

"Not yet, but he may have swum ashore further along. We did find one strange thing."

"Oh?" Hunter tried to sound suitably curious.

"There was a dead tiger on the shore below the car park."

"Ah. I wondered what had happened to it. Are you sure it was a tiger?"

"Not a doubt. Do you know something about it?"

"Thomas Ellis, who farms up towards Steyning hired me to catch the big cat he thought was mauling his sheep."

"The Sussex panther? That rumour's been around for years."

"I shot at something with a tranquiliser a couple of nights back. It didn't go down straight away and I lost track of it. I assumed I'd missed. Maybe it went in the river and got swept down."

"So you think this might be your big cat?"

"It's possible. If no-one else claims it, I'll tell Ellis the cat won't be bothering his sheep anymore."

"You do that." The officer stood up to leave. "Thanks for the tea."

"You're welcome." As Hunter escorted him off the boat he wondered what the officer would think if he knew there was a Bengal tiger bunked in his guest cabin.

PLANT HUNTER

It is the sound you notice first as you step out of the car. Inside, you are insulated but open the door and your ears are immediately bombarded with the mewling screams of gulls wheeling across the rooftops. They begin to settle, squabbling over the best spots. In a momentary lull the shrill twitter of starlings fills the silence until the gulls erupt again into raucous laughter. You pause. An empty crisp packet skitters over the tarmac. It is May but your car is alone in the car park. Visitors prefer the congestion of Brighton to this more easterly stretch of coast by Shoreham Harbour.

As you sling the camera bag over your shoulder and lock the car door you become aware of another sound. A muttering from the direction of the sea. You walk into the breeze following the shushing of pebble upon pebble. Beneath your feet the stones are hard. They roll under the soles of your trainers, crunching.

Lying low to the ground and hunkering behind a slight ridge, sea kale and mallow seek protection from the prevailing wind. Tough salt-resistant leaves provide shelter for the small birds, the little brown jobs that flee, scurrying from the sound of your steps.

A little further on, the beach falls away. The tide is out exposing patches of sand at the lower reaches. You trudge down, the stones shifting in small cascades beneath your feet, threatening to unbalance you. Sea rushes up to greet your toes and retreats leaving a lather of surf.

You watch for a while wondering if the combination of foam and pebbles will make a good enough picture. You decide not and amble along the margins towards the Worthing end. As you go you watch the tide line, looking for that piece of flotsam that will make the perfect photograph. It is all too mundane: dried seaweed, fragments of plastic, broken shells. You are looking for that special image. You still need a last picture for your exhibition in the Croyden Art Gallery at the end of the month.

The sun is lowering towards the band of cloud that smudges the horizon. There might be a chance of a sunset shot, especially from the foot bridge over the Adur, looking up-river towards the Downs. For now, though, the sun casts long shadows. You eye the sand pebbles, seeing the way the retreating sea has created patterns, miniature landscapes. You consider the effect of light and shade, the shapes of object and umbra, and take a few pictures. You might get one good enough to enlarge for the exhibition.

This is a deserted stretch, there are few footprints to disturb the pristine markings that wavelets leave behind. A man walks his dog along the shingle breakwater. In the distance, in Worthing Bay, the wings of kite-surfers spiral for height. Largely, there is only you, the beach, the sea, and the distant smudge of a tanker heading out into the Channel. And the gulls.

It would be good to get an in-flight shot of birds lifting over the waves but they keep their distance from you, rising when they are just within range and settling back further along. The feathers of the juveniles make them almost invisible against the mottling of the shingle.

At the far end of the beach, huge boulders of Norway basalt form substantial groynes. They are there to keep the stones from migrating. You suspect that in a contest the sea would win but they will do for now, preventing the erosion from washing the foundations from beneath the houses built on the shifting shingle. You examine the crystals within the boulders and decide they need a higher sun to show the glints to best effect.

The shingle is steep here. You scramble along, pebbles shifting underfoot, and you are breathless from what seemed to be an easy climb up the slope. The ground is firmer at the top, compacted by the machines that have placed the boulders. You can look down into artificial coves. You notice the sign prohibiting fires right next to a patch blackened by last November's bonfire.

You glance at the sky. The sun has reached the stage of a huge red ball rapidly descending towards the skyline. You think it is time to strike inland, to get shots of it sinking over Norfolk Bridge. Perhaps, like the last time you were here, it will turn the river pink and the silhouettes of the fishing boats will stand out as a contrast to the shine of wet exposed mud.

You begin to walk a little faster. Ahead, a column of thick smoke rises from one of the man-made bays. As you reach a point where you can look down into it you see a gang of about five youths – boys and girls. The murmur of their voices wafts towards you, scarcely louder than the breaking surf. They have started a blaze, probably from bits of driftwood gathered along the foreshore. The plume, as it rises from the centre of their circle forms a smear of black across the flaming disc of the sun. If you listen hard you can imagine the crackle of flames and smell the acridity of fumes. The salt in their fuel gives the fire a brighter tinge. It is orange enough to match that of the sky.

"Oi!"

The human voice startles. For a moment you think it is directed at you. The man stands teetering on the lip of the shingle bank, gesticulating. He brandishes a rake. He plunges down towards the youths who step away from their blaze.

"Can't you bloody read," the man shouts. "No fires on the beach."

"Go fuck yourself, granddad," one of the girls calls back, her voice carrying thinly on the breeze.

They see the rake he is waving at them and take off, seawards, splashing round the rocks into the tide which is now on the turn.

The man begins to pull the flaming pile apart with the rake and to stamp the life out of the embers. You slither down to help. It's not just driftwood they were burning. There is the remains of a cloth bag among the cinders. It could have been a rucksack. There is charred paper and a variety of debris. As you join in, treading out the fire, you notice a notebook. You grab it just before the pages incandesce, brushing ash from the scorched edges. It is probably of no worth. You slip it into your pocket on impulse. It seems to be the right thing to do.

"Are they local kids?" you ask as the man leans on his rake, his task complete.

"Nah. Holiday makers. Bored outa their skins. There's nowt for the likes of their age around here. Worthing's almost as bad. Their parents shoulda booked a place near Brighton."

He turns away to scramble back up the slope. You look at the spread of incinerated rubbish and decide it is not worth wasting film on. A glance at the sky shows that you have missed the sunset. You follow the man up the slope and head back to the car.

~~~

In the room of the Stenning Hotel, you examine your prize. The notebook is small, and despite the damage most of the pages are readable, though crumbling at the margins. The writing is small and neat, occasionally illustrated with ink sketches. It appears to be a naturalist's observations. The name inside the front cover sounds familiar. You begin to read, turning the leaves carefully with the blade of a penknife.

At ten o'clock you lay it aside. The BBC News is a ritual you seldom miss. You are momentarily surprised by the local news. *South Today* is the station in this part of the south-east. You are used to receiving *London*. The geography is unfamiliar and you pay less than full attention until a name catches your ear. The naturalist whose notebook lies on your bedside cabinet has been missing for a week now. He was last known to be heading for the South Downs in search of rare plants.

You think you should hand the notebook to the police explaining where and how it was found. The local with the rake is sure to identify you as the stranger with the cameras, if any suspicion of wrongdoing should fall on you. But you will examine the rest of the book first. The constabulary can wait until morning.

Often there are bits missing from the beginning and end of lines. The writing scarcely conceals a growing excitement. The naturalist believes he has discovered the site of the Mare's Tail Orchid. If he is right, this will be only the third recorded flowering in Britain for a hundred and fifty years. There is a sketch, or more rightly, two-thirds of one. It is enough.

You lay the Ordnance Survey map of the area on the floor to trace the route the naturalist describes. This could be the picture you have been looking for. That special image to take centre stage in the exhibition. A photograph of a flower that has never before been captured on film. If you can confirm the spot.

It does not occur to you to wonder how the notebook got to the beach.

~~~

The field seems no different from the others in the area. It is a sloping Downland meadow. You hope you have deciphered the notes accurately. If so, the plant should be growing just below the brow of the hill. The grass comes up to mid-calf and is dotted with spectacular wildflowers: the brilliant yellow of rock roses, the white stars of the ox-eye daisy, its central eye mirroring the sun. Tinier vetches swagger between grass blades, showing hints of purple. You watch out for the spotted *orchis* leaves as you climb the slope. Butterflies, blue and brown, flit ahead, startled by the passage of strange feet. Hoppers leap unexpectedly from underfoot, chirruping a warning to their fellows once the danger has passed.

The field rises. So do your hopes, your excitement. Just below the summit you see it. The stem carries the flower-head proud of the surrounding grasses. The stamens and anthers, fine and thread-like, stream from the centre of the chestnut red petals. As the breeze catches it, the filaments seem to flow outwards. It is well named. You get your camera out of its bag, carefully selecting lenses and filters. This will be perfect, just what you hoped for.

You become aware that you are not alone. Five pairs of eyes are watching. The horses form a line on the horizon. You hear mundane sounds – the buzzing of bees in the flowers, the distant slur of traffic on a road below. Suddenly, as if the pitch has changed, they no longer seem so comfortable. The heat of the day presses down despite the breeze that ruffles the horses' manes.

Another horse joins its fellows. Lips draw back from yellowed teeth. They make no sound. For a while they stand and stare, assessing you. Then, as if a signal has been given, they begin to walk forward. An arc of horse flesh steps towards you, menacing in the synchronicity of its paces.

From your position kneeling in the grass, you see their eyes. White shows around the dark irises. Saliva drips from the mouth of the lead stallion.

You glance behind, thinking you can retreat down the hill. Several other animals are beginning to climb towards you. Perhaps they are just inquisitive. You look back at the stallion. He is closer now. The set of his shoulders, the look in his eyes, do not convey curiosity. You see menace there.

You edge away at a slant, across the slope. You had not realised how uneven the ground was, pock-marked with rabbit burrows. Your foot slips. Your ankle twists beneath you and you give a cry at the sudden pain. A velvet nose nudges your back. You feel a quick nip where neck meets shoulder. A hand clasped to the spot comes away sticky.

As the stallion rears above you, you realise what happened to the naturalist.

You scream.

ANGELO'S BAR

Alexis felt out of place. The sky was grey, the water the colour of pewter, the buildings dowdy, and her mood gloomy. She should never have come. It was Suzanne who had persuaded her, against her better judgement. There were too many memories in Venice.

"Surely you have happy memories," Suzanne said. "It's where you came with Daddy on your honeymoon."

And where he died, Alexis thought.

"I might never have another chance."

"You have the rest of your life," Alexis said. "I'm sure Danny will take you some day."

Suzanne pulled a face. "If you can't scuba dive it's not interesting," she said. "Besides, it will be the last chance we have to go away together before I get married. And," she added slyly, "I really would like to see some of the places you went to with Daddy."

Alexis gave in. They had been here less than twenty-four hours and she was already regretting it. It had started to rain as they had left the airport and had done so intermittently ever since. At least it suppressed some of the odours from the canals. She was sure she had seen a rat bumping along the wall of the buildings on the other side. A little way to her left, a number of gondolas were moored to posts emerging from the water like dead fingers. Alexis shook herself mentally. She had to stop feeling morbid or she would spoil the holiday for Suzanne. She turned as her daughter came towards her along the quay from where she had been talking to one of the gondoliers.

"Best time to take a gondola is early morning," Suzanne said. "Before the traffic gets too heavy."

And before the water gets a chance to heat up and smell unbearably, Alexis thought. "Do we have to book?" she asked.

"Not at that time of day. You never told me Venice was wet." Suzanne turned up the collar of her jacket. "We should have brought umbrellas."

Alexis surprised herself and laughed. "What do you call that?" she said indicating the canal.

Suzanne hunched further into her jacket. "That doesn't count," she said. "Let's go somewhere dry."

"We could go back to the hotel."

"Why? I want to see the sights now that we're here."

"Because your father and I spent the first two days in our room," Alexis said wickedly, "and I thought you wanted to do the things we did on our honeymoon."

"Mum!"

"Okay. Since we're here, we might as well take a look inside St Mark's Basilica."

~~~

Nicolo throttled down the engine expertly, slewing the motor launch alongside the jetty in the smooth movement of someone who was well practised, or showing off. As Alan Giles had only met the man at the airport four hours earlier, he wasn't sure which. The third passenger, Giuseppe, looped the bow rope around the water-gnawed upright and hauled the boat in the last few centimetres so that it touched along its length and he could easily step ashore. As Giuseppe tied the stern off, Nicolo gestured to Alan to disembark. The boat felt as though it was rocking precariously as he stood, dipping alarmingly to one side as he clambered up onto the boards of the jetty. These were water-stained and slippery, and looked rotten in places.

Alan glanced first over the water. The island was in the lagoon between Venice and the sea. The main cluster of islands that made up the city seemed far away even though it had only taken fifteen minutes to reach here. This island was covered with a tangle of vegetation poised above a skirt of mud. A vaguely unpleasant odour rose from it where the waves lapped at land that didn't seem very permanent.

Two other boats were tied up the other side of the jetty to where Giuseppe had moored the motor launch. One, open and weather-beaten, looked slow and had seating for more than a dozen. The other, resembled a larger version of the boat that he had just arrived in. The archaeological team was already at work.

A narrow path was cut through the plant growth and Alan thought he could see vague outlines of old buildings within it.

"Come this way," Nicolo said. He spoke precise English. Alan's Italian was adequate for the translation of written texts – with a good dictionary at hand – but not for everyday conversations. Giuseppe spoke with a heavy accent that Alan sometimes had problems understanding.

Nicolo led the way along the path. It rose slightly over what Alan suspected would be a buried wall, before dipping again. About a hundred metres in, it opened into a clearing. Dying vegetation had been heaped up on either side to expose a structure some three metres high.

"This is all that remains of the west chancel wall," Nicolo explained. "The entrance to the vaults is in this direction." He indicted to the left.

Alan stopped to run his hands down the old stonework. So far it tallied with what he had been given to expect. "How much have you excavated?" he asked.

"Come with me and I will show you." Nicolo led Alan along the edge of the wall which ended with a tree. It had grown so close to the wall it was now welded to the stonework. A carved stone column was embedded in the trunk. The pattern was similar to that common in fifteenth century churches and would have formed part of an ornate entrance arch, though, from the thickness, probably not the main one. Beyond the wall the area opened up. The ground sloped away to a surface half a metre below the top of the soil level. Half-a-dozen men were kneeling within the large trench, carefully scraping away at the exposed floor surface. Two others consulted in hushed tones, almost as if the Gothic church still soared above them.

"I hadn't expected it to be quite so large," Alan said.

"The Italians of Venice built with style," Nicolo said. "The island was much bigger when it was originally built, and other buildings also once occupied the site."

"Have you traces of them?"

"Alas, the waters have claimed them."

"What have you found?"

"Several sections of floor tiles are intact; fragments of masonry give us sufficient evidence to begin to reconstruct an image of the church."

"You are using computer graphics?"

"Of course. That is Giuseppe's function. The vaults are over here."

They doubled back towards the position of the north transept and where Alan estimated the altar would have stood. He wondered if any trace of it had been found, or whether it had been plundered. To the left of its position a huge hole gaped. Brick and stone rubble formed a huge pile glued together with drying mud.

"Part of the roof to the vaults collapsed into them,"

Nicolo explained. "Water has seeped into the foundations, and the inundations of the past few years have filled the cavity with lagoon mud. As you can clearly see, we have already commenced the removal of the accumulated debris."

"What have you found?" Alan peered into the darkness. The cavity ran back under the body of the church. He couldn't see how far the excavations had extended, but shadows of roof supports were visible in the gloom.

"The tomb of the Mazarini."

Nicolo was obviously proud of the fact. Alan tried to recall the contents of the notes the Italian archaeologist had sent him. The Mazarini were the family that had endowed and built the church in the fifteenth century. The last of the family to live in Venice had not had a particularly savoury reputation, but it wasn't clear whether the church was pulled down because of this, or whether it fell into disuse because the sea was reclaiming the island. Perhaps a bit of both, though that was one of the questions that Nicolo hoped to find answers to.

"Can we go down?" Alan asked.

Nicolo called to one of the diggers, simultaneously tapping the top of his head. The man hurried across carrying two bright yellow building-site helmets on which lights could be attached. "We must wear these for our safety," Nicolo explained. "The batteries are to be strapped around your waist, like so." He demonstrated. "The light attaches here."

Nicolo helped Alan adjust the helmet and switch on the light. It felt a little precarious, perched on his head, and wobbled a bit despite the strap firmly fastened beneath his chin. At least it kept his hands free. He followed Nicolo down the aluminium ladder while the digger held it firmly at the top. Nicolo didn't give him much of a chance to look around but took him straight to the end of the tunnel. Most of the vault was still blocked with a mixture of rubble and mud. Water oozed from this making a slurry at his feet. Alan could feel it squelching under his shoes and wished he had been warned to change into wellingtons. A tarpaulin covered the lower section. Nicolo lifted the edge to one side. Alan reached up to adjust the light onto the exposed surface. A beam of wood protruded about half a metre from the mud.

"A roof beam?" Alan asked.

"It is what we supposed at first, although it would seem strange to find any in this position in the vaults."

Nicolo produced a trowel and carefully cleaned back some of the mud on the top surface. He exposed what appeared to be broken fingers carved in relief from the wood.

"The crucifix?" Alan asked quietly.

"We think it may be. That is why we have asked you to advise us. If we are fortunate, it may have been preserved in the mud for three hundred years."

Alan nodded, his light bobbing over the surface. Alan's expertise was the preservation of objects like this, his reputation earned by working on artefacts discovered in the Cambridgeshire fens.

~~~

The hotel had changed. Or maybe Alexis's memory of it had. Once the building had been one of Venice's many palaces. A grand staircase swept up from what was now the reception lobby. It seemed smaller. The carpet, deadening the sound of footfalls on wood as they ascended, seemed more worn. It had been then, but the colours were faded and it seemed grubby. Suzanne doubted it was the same one, or even the same pattern.

Twenty-six years was more than one carpet could survive, considering the number of feet that must have trodden on it. Alexis was sure, though, that the rooms had never been redecorated.

"How can you tell?" Suzanne asked, exasperation colouring her voice.

Alexis smiled sadly. "That is supposed to be part of the charm of these hotels," she said. "The decayed grandeur."

"It's an excuse," Suzanne said. "It's just gone to seed and they want to make money out of gullible tourists like us."

"We could have stayed somewhere else."

"I thought you wanted to relive your honeymoon." Suzanne crossed to the window and forced the reluctant pane open, then closed it again quickly. "That canal stinks."

"You wanted to go all the places I went with your father," Alexis reminded her. "We stayed here, in a canal-side room."

"I didn't expect you to take me this literally. How did you stand being cooped up in a room like this for two days?"

"Ask me that again after your honeymoon," Alexis said.

Suzanne snorted. "Danny is more likely to spend the first two days totally submerged in warm Caribbean waters."

"He'll have to come up for air."

"Only to change tanks. Which bed do you want?" Suzanne indicated the twin beds that occupied most of the room.

"I thought we might push them together to get the full flavour of that time," Alexis said.

"Mum!"

Alexis held her hands up in surrender. "Okay. Make a list of all the places you want to see. It's your holiday more than mine."

"What about restaurants?"

"Anywhere not too expensive." Alexis glanced towards the window where splashes indicated that it was still raining. "One place I would like to go back to, Angelo's Bar. We ate there on our last night in Venice. I think you would like it – it's a converted church on one of the outer islands."

"I'd like to visit this," Suzanne held up one of the brochures she had piled on one of the beds. "The glass factory."

"I remember that – there's a little museum attached to it. Your father visited it a number of times. He said it was a good reference base for the stuff he was buying."

"Let's reserve that for Sunday, then. Many of the shops may be closed, and the churches will all have services going on."

"Don't you want to go to mass?"

Suzanne pulled a face. "You can't see the architecture properly when the priests are fogging the air with all that incense."

"What about tonight?"

"Can we eat close by? It's too wet to walk far."

~~~

It was two days before they were ready to dig out the crucifix. Alan had been surprised at how quickly Nicolo had assembled the equipment they would need, and to locate a tank big enough to hold the artefact. Alan had used the dimensions of the exposed fragment to estimate the size of it; he had to assume that it was intact, although it was quite possible that it had been at least partly damaged. Nicolo said that they had found what they believed to be the remnants of the altar stone. The marble slab had been smashed into at least five pieces – not an easy job as it had been a good three inches thick.

Once they were ready they had to work fast. It was wet sticky work in cramped conditions. The wood had to be continually sprayed to prevent it drying out in the warm atmosphere. The rains of the last day-and-a-half had given way to hot sunshine, baking the mud and raising a stink from the canals.

"This is good," Nicolo said when Alan commented on it. "The rain has added sweetness to the water. The rain on the hills of Italia will wash down and take away the smell the visitors leave."

"It raises, too, the water level," Giuseppe said. "This is no good."

Nicolo and Alan were both pleasantly surprised how complete the crucifix was. The carving of the Christ figure was slightly knocked, most of the extremities having been lost. The wood was spongy on the surface but seemed to have a good solid core. Alan thought he could detect some remnant paint forced into deep crevices.

They lifted it first on to a solid cradle, but the tricky part was getting it out of the vault, though Alan was more alarmed at the way the launch swayed as the diggers transferred it from land to boat. There were one or two more anxious moments lowering it into the tank provided. Once submerged again, Alan could relax. There was still work to do but the worst was over.

"I'd like it dendro-dated before we do too much more work on it," Alan said.

Nicolo agreed. "I should be pleased to know if it is original with the church, or if the Mazarini purchased it at a later date."

"And if those are flecks of paint a spectrograph might

tell us composition and even indicate colour."

"I can have the samples flown to the laboratory in Roma," Nicolo said. "It is possible that we might get them onto the late flight."

"When will we get the results back?" Alan asked.

"I will phone. I will say that you do not have a long time with us. Perhaps we can hasten then to three or four days."

Alan nodded. He knew that some British labs would work faster, but only under extreme pressure. As everywhere, most tests joined the end of a queue. He had waited three months for one set of results, and only got them because he had made several phone calls. He wasn't too concerned about the time lapse. He wanted an excuse to explore Venice, and to see what else the excavation unearthed.

~~~

Giuseppe had been at the site some time before Alan and Nicolo arrived the next morning. He had set up a computer in a hut outside the church boundary and brought in commercial batteries to power it. He had already fed in the geophysics results from the day before into the unit and was clearly excited. Alan waited patiently for him to finish explaining to Nicolo in Italian before asking him to clarify what he thought he could see on the screen.

"There is a chamber beneath the vault," Nicolo said. "Giuseppe hopes it is the Mazarini crypt. We would expect there should be one as they endowed the church. This is the first positive indication that there is one present." He broke off to speak to Giuseppe again. "There are already two diggers at work in the place from where the crucifix was removed."

They had cleared much of the muck left behind from

the day before. The slabbed floor was in reasonably good condition. It was pitted and worn in places – normal wear for a surface in use for a couple of centuries then covered with an acidic mud that might eat into the stone. If the flags had ever been decorated there was no trace.

One of the diggers looked up as Nicolo and Alan joined them, his head light swinging eerily around the damp walls of the crypt. He spoke to Nicolo who translated. "There seems to be an area here where the flagstones are not present," he said. "There may be a cavity beneath."

Alan looked around. "Is it possible to set up some lights down here. Maybe run them off Giuseppe's generator."

"It might be possible," Nicolo said. "We need to be able to see what hazards there are here."

"It is interesting," Alan said, "but the centre of the cross appears to have been placed exactly over the space."

Nicolo shrugged. "This might be a coincidence. or it might be that the altar piece was placed there for a reason. In days past, the people of Venice could be very superstitious."

"And?"

"If the Mazarini crypt is here they may have considered it necessary to detain their spirits below."

Alan didn't scoff. He knew that the English had similar feelings at the time this church had fallen into disuse. Instead he asked, "What had the Mazarini done to merit this?"

"Not all of them. The last of the family, Angelo Mazarin, was having the reputation of being a sorcerer. They were perhaps afraid that his spirit would continue to walk and feed on the souls of the living. At one time, such things were greatly feared in Italia."

"In some places in England, too," Alan said.

"Then you will understand that some of the less educated still have these fears, though you and I know it is nonsense."

By mid-morning a small generator had been acquired – Giuseppe was reluctant to give up any of his power – and the vault blazed with harsh light. The once soft shadows had retreated to the walls and crouched just beyond the ring of light. A relay of diggers started clearing the debris packed into the space below. Nicolo was eager to clear it as quickly as possible but sensible to the archaeological treasures the mud might hold. Everything that was excavated was carted into daylight, washed, sieved, and anything of remote interest collected and labelled. A lot of the work would be done long after Alan had gone home – it was laborious and time-consuming. Most of the debris would be similar to what had already been identified: building materials, fragments of window glass, pieces of broken tile, all adding to the picture, none of it complete.

By late afternoon the cavity was quite large. A metal rod thrust through the debris showed that the floor was about two metres below the ceiling. The remains of steps had been uncovered, though they were curiously smashed. Nicolo suspected that the solid object near one wall was a sarcophagus.

"We will stop now," Nicolo said as Alan began to scrape dirt from the corner of the stone block.

"It's just getting interesting," Alan said.

"It is time to tidy away for the evening," Nicolo said. "No-one will work here after nightfall."

"It will be no darker down here at night than it is now."

"Some of the diggers are superstitious. If we were to stay they would refuse to work for us." Nicolo shrugged.

"That is the way it is. Also, tomorrow is Sunday. They will not work here on the Lord's Day."

"Okay." Alan straightened up. If he was honest, he was glad of the chance to stop and unkink muscles cramped by working in the awkward space. His eyes were sore from the contrast of harsh spotlight and half-shadow. As he stood, a glint in the mud caught his attention. Rather than leave it, he grabbed the object. Normally he was scrupulous about uncovering and logging finds but this time something made him thrust the muddy item into his pocket as he turned to follow Nicolo from the crypt.

~~~

The tour around the glassworks on the island of Murano, was relatively brief. Alexis was more interested in the objects themselves than the process of making them. The displays traced the history of the industry through a wide range of artefacts.

"These are beautiful." Suzanne stopped before a case showing elaborate jewellery set with the swirling colours of the glass. "Don't you have a necklace like this one."

"Mine is only a replica. You can buy them in the shop here."

"Why did Daddy find this collection so useful?" Suzanne asked.

"He came to Venice because so many of the old nobility were having to sell up as circumstances changed. They often wanted to sell in the overseas market where they thought there was more money. The problem with glassware is checking its provenance. Your father often used this collection, and the pattern books in the library here, to help him authenticate what he was offered. Mostly he got it right."

"Why didn't you come with him that last time?"

"Because your aunt Briony was about to have a baby, and I thought you were a bit young to leave on your own – and it was school time, remember."

"I was thirteen."

"Twelve – just."

They moved slowly on. Suddenly Alexis realised that Suzanne wasn't with her anymore. She spotted her on the other side of the gallery talking to a man with fair curly hair. Suzanne was gesturing in her direction then walked back to join her, the man following. Alexis blinked. For a moment he seemed to have a shadow following him. A trick of the light, she decided.

"Mum, this is Dr Giles. From Cambridge. He was my tutor in Church Architecture."

Dr Giles held out his hand. "It's Alan Giles, Mrs Wakefield."

"Alexis."

"Dr Giles is part of the excavation of one of the old churches here," Suzanne said.

"And since the diggers don't work on Sundays I was taking the opportunity to explore some of Venice. Can I treat you both to a cappuccino?"

"Thank you," Alexis said. "That would be nice."

Alexis liked this man; he was very easy to talk to. She vaguely remembered Suzanne talking about him. She had certainly enthused about that section of her course. Alexis estimated that Alan was about her own age.

"Do you know Venice?" Suzanne asked him when they were settled in a street cafe.

"It's my first visit," Alan explained, "but the archaeologist I'm working with has suggested several places I should go."

"Including churches?" Suzanne asked.

Alan laughed. A pleasant sound. "Especially churches.

But is there anywhere you can recommend?"

Between them, Alexis and Suzanne told him of a few of the places they had managed to see. "There is one place, though, that we haven't been able to find," Alexis said. "The first time I came here we went to a restaurant called Angelo's Bar. It was on one of the outer islands but we haven't been able to find out which."

"If you want, I'll ask Nicolo if he knows where it is."

"Please."

Alexis gave Alan the name of the hotel they were staying at and surprised herself by agreeing to meet him the following evening for a meal.

"He's nice, isn't he, Mum?" Suzanne said as they walked back to the hotel from where the water-taxi had left them. It was raining again, and from the sky it looked as if the fine drizzle was set to continue for the rest of the day.

~~~

"I think that there is a possibility of serious problems," Nicolo said.

Alan looked up from the area he was cleaning the mud from. The stone sarcophagus was intricately carved, and in the spotlights it looked as if the relief might once have either been painted or gilded. "With the excavation?" he asked. "I thought it was going to schedule."

"No. There is no problem there. It is the weather."

"The rain will help if we have a wooden coffin to lift," Alan said.

"There may be a little too much water. There will be an extra high tide tomorrow night due to the new moon. The forecast is for a strong wind off the sea. Also, the rain inland is causing the rivers to flood. If the surge arrives on the high tide the whole island might be flooded."

Alan nodded. The vaults would fill again with water

and silt, undoing the past week's work. "Then we must be ready to open the sarcophagus tomorrow."

Nicolo glanced at his watch. "At dusk the diggers go home."

Alan sat back on his heels. "I am not superstitious. If I have to, I'll stay."

"I will not permit you to remain here throughout the night. It is too dangerous."

"Nicolo, do you really believe in ghosts?"

The Italian shrugged. "The waters may rise early. In the dark you may fall."

"Either leave me a boat, or I can use my mobile to call for a water-taxi when I'm ready."

"They will not come here," Nicolo said. "They are afraid. They do not even like us working here in the daytime."

"Then we had better get this job done as soon as possible." Alan returned to the task. As soon as the mud had been cleaned from the stonework they could photograph the entire surface. Perhaps it would be easier to ignore it and go straight for the contents. Archaeologists in other times and other countries would have done just that. Alan had been trained to be meticulous. Skimped jobs missed or destroyed vital clues. Nicolo was of the same mind.

They worked on in silence, Nicolo cleaning the top surface.

"We have it!" Nicolo broke the silence. Alan stood up and leant over the sarcophagus to see what Nicolo had found. In the torchlight the plate glinted yellow. He could make out a mud-filled inscription.

"Can you read it?" he asked.

Nicolo moved the torch to better illuminate the markings. "It is Angelo Mazarin. Strange."

"What is it?"

"Someone has added something in another script. I think it says, *May your soul let us rest in peace*."

Alan shrugged aside the incongruity of it. "Any chance of a look inside to see what problems we will have tomorrow?"

Nicolo glanced at his watch. "We have already stayed too long," he said. "It will have to wait until tomorrow."

Above ground, the sky was already darkening. Alan turned up his collar against the drizzle which seemed to be a persistent feature of his visit. He thrust his hands into his pockets while he waited for Nicolo to extinguish the lights. His fingers encountered the pieces of glass he had dropped in his pocket. The sharp edge stung his thumb. He pulled his thumb out quickly and stuck it in his mouth. He tasted a mixture of mud and blood.

The spotlights went out leaving the entrance of the vaults as an unnaturally dark hole. "Come on." Nicolo was already partway up the nave and waved his torch beam in Alan's direction.

As the launch pulled away from the jetty Alan looked back. The bushes and trees were just dark lumps against the grey of the sky. For a moment Alan thought he saw them move. An onshore breeze clawed at his hair and he attributed the movement to the wind.

~~~

"How did you and Daddy find Angelo's Bar … before?" Suzanne asked.

"I think he asked someone at reception." Alexis frowned. "We hadn't booked anywhere but we got dressed up anyway. The receptionist wasn't much help. Suggested we went down to St Mark's and asked the boatmen for suggestions."

"And?"

"One of them took us there."

"Then that's what we'll do," Suzanne said. "We'll go down there tonight and ask all the boatmen if they know where the place is. Can you remember anything about the driver?"

"I was looking at your father."

"Okay. Don't forget to wear your necklace."

The rain had stopped by the time they reached the square but the water was rising. The river emptying into the lagoon had flushed a week's rainfall into the canals. Two inches of it covered the flags. A network of planks and orange boxes criss-crossed the area allowing pedestrians to keep their feet dry.

Alexis hung back, letting Suzanne to do the talking. She watched her daughter move from one to the other, gesticulating and using the little Italian she had. The first five or so shook their heads or shrugged. Suzanne approached the boat towards the end of the line. It looked older, in poorer condition than most of them. The owner glanced over towards Alexis. She shivered and raised one hand to touch her necklace. The glass beads were warm to the touch, warmer than her skin temperature.

Suzanne waved to her. "He'll take us there," she said excitedly. "He knows where it is."

Alexis looked at the boat dubiously. He wouldn't be allowed to ply his trade if it was unsafe, she decided. The taximan held the launch steady against the jetty while they clambered aboard inelegantly in their heeled shoes and long skirts.

As the launch headed out into the lagoon Alexis could feel the unevenness of the water's surface, roughed up by the increasing wind strength. Behind them the lights of the main islands dwindled to bright pinpricks.

"Look," Suzanne said, drawing Alexis' attention to the

island ahead of them.

The central building was lit by the soft orange of sodium lamps making the stone glow. Even after nearly twenty-six years Alexis felt the excitement of finding something that was exactly as she remembered it. As they walked up the steps and through the huge wooden doors that stood open to receive them, she had to glance at Suzanne to remind herself that she hadn't been transported back into the past. If she had found Paul walking beside her she wouldn't have been surprised.

"It is wonderful," Suzanne said. The interior of the fifteenth century church was brilliantly lit by electric chandeliers. The outside spots had been positioned so that the light shone through the stained-glass windows casting bright patterns over the diners below. Where pews would have been, now there were tables set with snowy cloths, polished cutlery and crystal glasses.

Although they hadn't booked, they were quickly and deferentially shown to a vacant table. Alexis gazed around, letting her eyes linger on the other diners and the staff who moved efficiently between the tables. They had sat on the other side, last time, between two of the pillars. A young couple had that table this time. He was dark and good-looking, like her Paul, while she had brown hair, worn long and straight, the way she used to. They gazed at each other, scarcely aware of their surroundings – just like she and Paul had all those years ago. Now, all Alexis wanted to do was soak up the atmosphere. She scanned the menu, trying to remember if there was anything on it she recognised.

"Mum?"

Alexis looked up. "What is it?"

Suzanne smiled. "Nothing. I thought I saw Dr Giles walk through. I must have been mistaken; they'd never let anyone in wearing dirty overalls."

"True," Alexis said. "Have you decided what you want to eat?"

"It all looks very expensive."

"Ignore the prices."

"Okay. What did you have last time?"

"I was trying to remember. I have no idea."

Even this meal seemed to pass in a haze. Alexis wasn't sure whether it was the wine, the atmosphere, the idea that they were going home the next day, or the memories that hovered at the edge of her mind. Eventually she found the need to visit the ladies. A passing waiter directed her to the end of the church, where the altar would have been. She vaguely remembered a crucifix having stood there last time, but shrugged and made her way down two flights of stone stairs. It was less well-lit than she had expected though the bottom step was pooled in brightness.

She turned a corner and stopped. A man in dirty overalls was leaning over a big stone box. He turned at the sound of her footsteps.

"Alan?"

~~~

It took six of them to lift the lid from the sarcophagus. Alan and Nicolo stood impatiently to one side waiting to see what was within. Eventually it was safe to peep over the top. The lid had been a tight fit and, although water had obviously got in, there was very little silt. The wood of the coffin looked fragile but through it they could see lead, whitened by reaction with the brackish water of the lagoon.

"Can it be lifted in one piece?" Nicolo asked.

Alan reached over and touched the wood with his penknife. It was very spongy and oozed liquid. "I doubt it," he said. "But…"

He tried to explain what he had in mind. A thin flexible metal edge – like a spatula – with a plastic sheet attached to it. They might be able to slip it under and lift the whole thing.

Nicolo looked sceptical. "The coffin will be too heavy. It would be better to remove the wooden lid, then take out the lead lining."

Alan acceded. It was Nicolo's site. Both agreed they would have to move fast. Giuseppe reported that the water levels were already rising along the canals and some of the lower lying plazas were already flooding.

The team worked together smoothly and by early afternoon both the wooden lid and the lead one were on their way to the mainland for preservation. Lying on planks set across the stone rim, Alan and Nicolo gingerly began cleaning the debris inside. Both were now wearing full coveralls and masks to protect the skeleton from their breath. There was nothing left except a badly corroded skeleton and pieces of metal and glass.

"It is strange," Nicolo said when they took a break, "that he was buried with no head."

"But not unknown."

"True. They do this, too, in England?"

"They did, if they thought the person was a witch, or would rise from the dead."

"I think there are many things similar in both our histories. Where would you English bury such a skull?"

"Face down at a crossroads, under a rowan tree."

"There are few such places in Venice."

"But a crucifix was placed over the entrance to the crypt."

Nicolo shrugged. "There have ever been persons of a superstitious nature."

Alan had never considered himself one of these, yet now he felt uncomfortable with the sarcophagus in the shadows behind him. He also had an urge to take his torch and search in the corners.

That evening, as he was packing, ready for the next day's flight home, he pulled the glass piece out of his pocket. It was set in a gold mounting that had broken. It was that which had cut his finger the day before. He thought it might be part of a pectoral. As he looked at it he felt an urge to return it. He knew he should not have taken it from the island, and wondered if he could post it to Nicolo from England, with an apology.

He put it on the table beside his bed and glanced at his watch. It wasn't on his wrist. His first instinct was to look in the bathroom but he didn't remember taking it off when he had showered. He did a quick search of the room, then a much more thorough one. No trace. The only other thing he could think of was that he had dropped it in the crypt. He didn't want to leave it behind, even though he was sure Nicolo would post it on, as it had been a twenty-first birthday gift from his father. The only thing was to borrow a launch and go there himself. He could return the glass relic at the same time.

Nicolo was reluctant. "How will you find the island in the dark?"

"I have to try. If the excavation gets flooded, I might never find my watch again."

The argued a while. Finally Nicolo agreed to take him, but Nicolo would wait in the launch while Alan looked for the watch.

The trees on the island were thrashing around in the increasing wind. The tide was higher and Alan had to step down slightly onto the jetty.

"Do not take long," Nicolo said. "I will give you

twenty minutes."

Alan hurried, the light of his torch feeble against the shadows that seemed to reach out and grab at him. As he reached the ladder down to the crypt he remembered the generator. It only took a moment to switch it on. He turned off the torch and descended into the light.

He crossed swiftly to the sarcophagus and thumbed the torch to look inside. Something glinted there. He leant over to retrieve the watch. He turned suddenly, startled by the sound of high heels on the flags, banging his elbow hard on the stone. Alexis Wakefield stood within the circle of light.

"Alan?"

"What are you doing here?" he said.

"Eating," she said.

He didn't know what to reply. He felt totally confused.

She took a step towards him. "In the restaurant upstairs."

He wondered if she was an apparition. His eyes were drawn to the necklace she wore. Although the glass and gold suited her well, it seemed to have something missing. He put his hand in his pocket and drew out his fragment. It would fit perfectly in the centre.

"We found the restaurant," Alexis was saying, "Angelo's Bar. Remember we were looking for it. A taximan brought us straight here." She paused. "How did you get here?"

Alan realised he had his mouth open. He closed it and swallowed. "There is no bar here," he said. "Just a ruined church."

She laughed. "Don't be silly. I've just finished a delightful plate of linguini."

Alan's mouth felt very dry. "Is Suzanne with you?"

"Of course she is."

"Will you fetch her? Now."

"Why?"

"Please. I'll explain when you bring her." She must think he was mad. Perhaps he was. Perhaps he had found the wrong island and he was deluding himself that this was the crypt. Perhaps he was dreaming. Alexis disappeared up the steps. Alan blinked. There weren't any steps. It was his imagination playing tricks in the dark.

He should bury the relic and go. He looked around. If he dropped it in the sarcophagus, Nicolo would wonder why they hadn't spotted it before. He moved out of the circle of light and stood under the position the altar had had in the church above. Shining the torch around, he noticed that some of the flags were broken. If he could get it underneath.

One of the diggers' trowels had been abandoned in the shadows. He levered up the stone and began to scoop out a shallow hole. The trowel went down suddenly into a cavity. He heard a sound above him, almost like a distant scream. He ignored it and scrapped away at the dirt.

"What's going on?" Alexis demanded.

Alan hadn't expected her to come back. He had decided she was an illusion. He turned. She looked worried. "The lights all went out as we came down."

"There's water coming through the ceiling," Suzanne said. "I'm getting wet."

Alan turned back to his hole. He could just drop the relic in and get out. The trowel was stuck. He tugged. The cavity fell in. He reached in. His fingers touched the rounded shape of a skull. The Mazarin's skull.

"Let's get out of here," Suzanne said.

"Alan, why did you want us to come down here," Alexis asked.

He shook his head confused. "I don't know," he said.

He lifted the skull from the cavity and took two steps towards Alexis. He snatched at her necklace. The clasp broke. It splashed at her feet. She gave him a look of pure hatred and stooped to retrieve it. They were standing in two inches of water.

~~~

The passage changed. One moment, she was in the brightly lit sub-basement of Angelo's Bar, the next some dingy hole in the ground.

Suzanne screamed. "The steps have disappeared."

Alan grabbed Alexis' hand. "There's a ladder." He pushed her towards it. She looked at him as if he were daft. "And take your shoes off."

Alexis felt a rising panic. She didn't like ladders. This one vanished into gloom. Suzanne was standing at the bottom of it. Water was cascading down past it.

"Climb." Alan's voice urged her from behind. She felt his hand on her back. She felt cold water tugging at her feet.

"Go up, Suzanne," she said, her voice sounding calmer than she felt.

They scrambled up. "Left," Alan shouted after her.

There was another ladder.

There should have been a restaurant at the top. There was nothing. Only wind and darkness. And water. Someone gripped her hand; Alan pulled her along. She clasped Suzanne's wrist, dragging her with them. They ran in silence, stumbling over roots, dragged at by vegetation. Suzanne slipped on the jetty, almost pulling Alexis into the water. Alan bundled them aboard the launch. The man at the wheel gunned the engine and headed out into the lagoon. Alexis glanced behind. There was flash as the electric generator fused. It lit up the island

– and the huge figure that appeared to be reaching out after them.

The wind seemed to push at the launch, trying to tip it. The boat turned into it.

"Nicolo!" Alan shouted.

Alexis looked ahead. The shape of a gondola was approaching rapidly. They hit it amid ships. Their launch shuddered. Alexis looked over the side as they swept past.

In the water, the shape of the passenger's face gaped up at her in surprise. She shivered. It looked exactly like Paul.

~~~

The airport the next morning was buzzing with news. Alexis tried to ignore it, still shaken by the night's events. Suzanne insisted on finding out as much as possible. Many areas of Venice had had to be evacuated overnight as the flood waters had risen. A number of people, including tourists, were missing; presumably they were in boats when the rising tide, whipped higher by the storm, had hit the wall of flood water emptying into the lagoon. Alexis regretted the loss of her necklace.

In another part of the airport Alan Giles kept his holdall carefully at his feet. When he got home he was going to find a deserted crossroads, and plant a rowan tree there, along with the Mazarin's skull.

CLOSED BORDERS

To Jules Cullen, the juxtaposition of the words *closed* and *border* were a challenge rather than a deterrent. Getting into Armenia wasn't the problem. Some of the borders, especially those with Turkey, had been closed since before the country had been a part of the Soviet Bloc. There were official ways in, such as risking life and limb on an Aeroflot airbus by way of Moscow, though he had to admit that air safety had improved considerably over the last decade. The train from Georgia was a little more tricky.

No, Jules was quite happy to roam the small independent country, though usually news stories were a trifle dull.

Jules had made his reputation as a freelance journalist. He liked writing travel pieces, especially when he got his expenses paid to stay in high-class resorts. Back-packing excursions and adventure holidays he tended to leave to the younger generation these days. He'd got used to a comfortable bed at the end of the day. He was, like all in his profession, always hopeful of the big scoop, being in the right place at the right time when the dam broke. Some colleagues said you made your own luck, which is why he was stepping into Yeravan's summer heat.

It wasn't long before Arkady drew up in his battered 4x4. Jules threw his bag in the back and slammed the door shut. It didn't catch.

"Harder," Arkady said.

It was automatic for Jules to reach for a seatbelt that wasn't there. There might be rules about wearing them but no-one bothered, especially if they were heading away from the city. He tried to settle back and relax. He'd met Arkady some years back when he was covering the aftermath of an earthquake, and they'd kept in touch. Although he spoke Russian, as almost everyone in the country did, having an Armenian speaking guide was good insurance.

"Where is your story?" Arkady asked as they got on the road heading south towards Yeghegnadzor.

"Khosrov Forest Reserve," Jules said.

"What's there? It's just a huge area of mostly semi-desert scrub with a few wooded valleys surrounding the streams."

"Then why close it? One of my friends, a wildlife photographer, had all his routes planned and a written permission to visit the reserve. Day before, they rescinded it, no explanation given. Everyone very tight-lipped when he asked questions."

"Maybe simple. Rare nesting raptors, perhaps."

"They don't even close whole reserves for that in the UK and the British are very paranoid about conservation issues."

"We have paranoia about foreigners asking questions," Arkady told him.

"The Russian legacy?"

"Maybe, but there must be another reason for you to come all this way."

"I'm curious."

"You are a journalist. Give."

Jules stared out of the window, watching the distant mountains to the east of the road. In the rear-view mirror, snow-capped Mount Ararat, twenty-five miles into Turkey, appeared to hover, mist hiding its lower flanks. He considered how much he should tell his friend. He needed his help but didn't want him to get into trouble with the authorities. At length, he said, "You remember the asteroid?"

"Some of us do. It was not as spectacular as the Russian one and no-one streamed it on your internet as it came down."

"Only because it was remote and those who saw it had no smart phones."

"But it exploded over the Khosrov Forest Reserve."

"I am sure it made a big crater, my friend. Maybe the Reserve is closed for the safety of visitors. We would not wish them to fall into it."

"Then why not close it immediately. John Winterton got his permit weeks after the event."

Arkady shrugged. "Departments in government do not always talk to each other. One decides tells others much later. Just delayed information. Maybe the Reserve was always closed."

"I don't believe that. There must be another reason."

"What kind?"

"That's what I aim to find out. It might not have been an asteroid. It could have been a Korean missile, or a Chinese satellite or a Russian military test that went wrong."

"The Russians would not dare."

"There's a story in this, somewhere. I know it."

"And you are asking what of me?"

"Just to take me to the perimeter. I'll go in on my own. If I upset people, it's my problem. I don't want to get you into trouble."

"I am a journalist, too. I just do not think there is anything to find."

"We can discuss it later. Right now I'd like a shower and a good night's sleep."

"We shall be in Yeghegnadzor in another hour," Arkady said.

~~~

The hotel, relatively new and set just beside the road running through the centre of the town, had the facilities Jules had hoped for, especially the free WiFi connection. The only thing lacking was a restaurant but Arkady quickly found a place nearby. Afterwards they settled in Jules room with bottles of coke stashed in the fridge. Both men opened up their laptops on the low table in the seating area.

Arkady searched recent local reports for anything relating to the reserve while Jules zoomed in to the Google Earth maps of the area. The Armenian looked over at the aerial view of the reserve. "No sign of anything there," he said.

"It's an old image from before the meteorite came down. I wouldn't expect to see anything. Is that the main track in?" Jules pointed to a line through the scrub going away from the main road. There was a cluster of buildings but any perimeter fence wasn't showing up.

"Yeah. The chief ranger lives there and the Land Rovers park up there."

"The rangers don't take them home with them?"

Arkady laughed. "These are rough-road vehicles for rough roads. The doors are tied on with string and they're powered by a propane gas cylinder wedged under the back seat. They break all reasonable safety laws."

"There are gas powered buses in Yerevan."

"Those are road worthy. These Jeeps aren't. Take a look at this." Arkady's screen showed an aerial image of what could be a crater. It was a bit fuzzy.

"Is that inside Khosrov?"

"The caption says so."

"What kind of terrain is that?"

"Semi-desert. At this time of year it is hot and waterless." Arkady leaned over and pointed. "About there on your map."

"Well away from the entrance. Are there any other ways in?"

"Always. Local people graze their animals there. There may not be road as such but there will be tracks."

Jules felt a frisson of excitement. "Which is the nearest to the crater? Can your 4x4 cope with the terrain?"

"I have not said I will come with you."

Jules grinned. "Just show me the track, then I will steal your car."

"And how will I get back?"

"I am sure you can phone for a taxi."

"Englishman, you are crazy."

"Just take me to an entry point," Jules said.

~~~

Next morning, Jules went down to breakfast with a list of things he thought he might need for the expedition. Top of the list was water. At the bottom he'd put tent, then crossed it out again. The temperature didn't drop much during darkness and very little rain had been forecast for the area over the next week. A night or so under the stars wasn't going to matter. His only worry was carrying everything if he had to proceed on foot. He needn't have worried; when he showed Arkady the list all the Armenian said was, "You need to add extra batteries. Recharging will be a problem in the wilderness. The rest is already in the car for us."

"Have you decided to come?"

Arkady shrugged. "You will need someone to explain that you are English and the heat has mixed up your brains."

Jules tried to follow their route on his map but so few roads were marked, and he had problems deciding what was road and what were wheel-ruts into a field. When Arkady turned off onto a tarmac strip laced with potholes, he asked. "Is this the road into the Reserve?"

Arkady laughed. "This is the main road to the Georgian border."

Fields of vines ran along the right-hand verge while the other was a steep slope of beige coloured rock. A spiny-tailed lizard leapt from the ground where it had been basking to flatten itself onto the vertical surface. It merged almost totally. If he hadn't seen it move Jules would have missed it. Reptiles, he had been told, were common in Armenia. Other than wall-lizards, he didn't think he'd seen any others.

The contrast of the two sides of the road was more marked the further they went. When he commented on it Arkady said it was different rock types. The road they were following ran along the route of a fault line, thrusting harder rocks to the surface on the left. It reminded Jules that Armenia was a country that at times had been devastated by earthquakes. He hoped this fault line didn't shift while they were on it.

Two kilometres along the road, Arkady paused by one of the roadside stalls. He returned with a bag of cherries. He offered some to Jules before taking a handful, spitting the stones out of the window.

"Woman wanted to know where we were going," Arkady said. "Told her you were a birdwatcher looking for Syrian woodpeckers."

"Good thing I brought my binoculars then," Jules said wryly.

"She said to stay on the south side of the road. They've put up a shiny new fence all around the reserve."

"Who have?"

"Sounded like militia but then our rangers go armed."

"Didn't think you had anything dangerous around here."

"Illegal logging goes on in the forests." Arkady said, as if that explained everything. "Strange thing she did say was her man lost two goats last time he grazed them on the Reserve."

"Lost? How?"

"Dead. He found fur and blood and not much else."

"Sounds like your rangers are helping themselves to a little extra meat."

"Maybe." Arkady put the vehicle into gear. "Let's go find out."

A further kilometre along the road, Arkady turned onto a track that was merely two deep ruts in the ground. Jules wouldn't have been surprised to be told that it turned in to a river during storms as it ran between steep banks and followed a winding, upward path. Rounding one of the turns they were confronted by a bright new chain-link fence.

"We have two choices," Arkady said. "Turn round or go through."

"Or I can climb over and leave you here."

"Englishman, you are dead crazy. You cannot carry all the water you will need to walk to where the crater is meant to be."

"There are streams."

"Not for a long way yet. There are bolt cutters in the back. If asked I can say I found it that way."

"Right, so crazy Englishman gets all the blame."

"It is you who are chasing the story."

It didn't take Jules long to cut a section out of the fence and bend it back enough to allow the 4x4 through.

The track became increasingly rough. No life was evident except the scrubby plants. As Arkady slewed around one bend Jules thought he saw a hump on the top of the bank, shaped like a lizard's head. Another glance at it showed just a heap of stones.

Arkady didn't stop until he turned into the shade of a clump of stunted trees alongside a dry stream. The mass of rounded stones at the bottom indicated the difference between it and the track they were following. Jules decided that he wouldn't like to be caught in it during a thunderstorm if flash floods could move boulders that size.

While Arkady ferreted out the food he'd brought for lunch, Jules walked a little way up looking for a suitable tree to piss against. On the way back he noticed a gathering of flies and a smell he hadn't been aware of before. He spotted the turd on a rock. Goat, he decided. It was large enough for that, not that he was familiar with the shapes of them. He might recognise a cow pat but other animals' faeces were a mystery.

"How much further?" Jules asked as Arkady disposed of the remnants of their meal under a stone.

"An hour or so."

~~~

The crater when they reached it was a disappointment. Jules had been hoping either for a bowl-shaped depression like the one in Arizona – though perhaps not as large – or a wide area of flattened vegetation like the Siberian meteorite that had detonated over a pine forest. Here there were a line of three shallow pits and a big gouge out of the hillside,

"Are you sure this is the place?" Jules asked.

"As near as I can work out. Not very impressive is it."

"I'll take photos anyway. One of my contacts might be

able to work out things like trajectory from the indents. I can't see why this would cause them close the reserve."

"I said there would be other reasons," Arkady said. "Do you still think you can make a story out of this?"

Jules grinned. "I can make a story out of anything. I can add in the missing goats for colour."

He hadn't heard the approach of any vehicle but Jules certainly heard the sharp click of a bolt sliding home on a rifle. He raised his eyes in the direction it came from. A man at the top of the slope in heavy body armour was levelling an automatic at him, one that looked as if it could take out a tank. He took an involuntary step back. "Arkady?"

"I see them. Leave the talking to me."

With a skitter of stones, Jules saw two more armed men sliding down the slope towards them. The leading one shouted something.

"Put your hands behind your head," Arkady said, "Slowly and carefully."

The man reached Jules and poked the gun in his chest, shouting in his face. These weren't rangers. He felt the first hint of fear, his mouth going dry. "What's he saying?" His voice came out as a croak.

"We have to go with them."

"Tell him okay. I don't argue with guns."

They were made to climb the slope the soldiers had come down. It was steep and Jules had to finish the last bit on all fours. He wasn't as fit as he liked to pretend. Over the ridge two armoured Jeeps were parked, soldiers standing by each of them. This suddenly felt like a serious miscalculation.

Jules and Arkady were bundled into the foremost vehicle, and as soon as the soldiers had embarked it began to speed off down slope. It canted at an extreme angle as it negotiated a gully. Jules hung tightly onto a stanchion, fearing the vehicle would tip over. Its windows were small and he could see little through them except the rocks and bushes whipping past. As the ground levelled out the other vehicle came alongside so they were running parallel.

"What the fuck's going on, Arkady?" he said once he managed to get his breath back.

"No idea."

Suddenly, the vehicle veered off at right angles, the sharp turn kicking up dust. Something slammed into the side causing it to rock. Jules' hold was shaken loose and he pitched into Arkady's lap. He slid to the floor and stayed there. Over the sound of the engine he heard gunfire. Then the vehicle slewed to a halt. Moments later the rear doors opened and two soldiers from the second Jeep piled in. In the moment it was open he glimpsed the other vehicle its side, smoking. A shape resembling a giant lizard lay close by. Jules blinked. The doors were slammed shut as the vehicle took off again. The rational part of his brain told him that he'd been mistaken.

Squashed in the back with four armed men and his friend, Jules was flung around as the Jeep hit bumps and swerved around unseen obstacles. When it finally jerked to a halt the doors were pushed open. Jules, infected with a sense of urgency tumbled out. He was hauled to his feet and rushed across open space and through a steel door. He had time to notice that the roof of the building was adorned with an image of a giant skink. He was hustled down a set of stairs into an underground bunker.

A man in military uniform stood up as they entered. Jules' arm was released and the soldiers stepped back and to attention. The officer began barking questions at Arkady. Although he seemed to be speaking Russian

Jules could only catch one word in three. When he gave a sigh of exasperation, Jules asked, "What is he talking about?"

"I don't think I should translate, but basically he is calling into question the reproductive habits of journalists and their parents."

The officer calmed down enough to say in slow clear Russian, "Mr Cullen, fences are always erected for a purpose. Your actions have put the lives of my men in jeopardy."

"I don't understand why."

At that moment, another man dressed in civilian clothes came through an inner door. "You might as well explain," he said. "There may not be a resolution to the situation, in which case we may need a good contact with the greater world."

"What situation?" Jules asked.

The officer said, "It won't matter. They will not be able to leave."

Before Jules could protest the civilian said, "I am Sergei Petrov. Please come through."

He led the way into a corridor and into a room to the left. There were scientific instruments in it that Jules didn't recognise, along with some that he did, including microscopes and incubators. Petrov indicated two stools. "Please." Once they were seated, he said, "You are aware of the meteorite strike?"

Jules nodded. "That was why I came here."

"It has long been suspected that some of these meteorites carry bacteria from other worlds. You may know of the controversy over traces found on pieces found in the Antarctic ice."

"Don't they think they come from Mars?"

"That is one theory. Most will be destroyed in the

atmosphere and are harmless scientific curiosities. This time a virus made it through. Its effect is to cause rapid growth in reptiles."

Arkady frowned. "Was that what attacked us? A giant reptile?"

"Wouldn't their bodies collapse under the weight?" Jules asked.

"Fossil records show that there were very large reptiles on this planet once. It may be that after their spurt of growth they will die like plants do if sprayed with weedkiller."

"And if they don't?"

"Then the age of the dinosaurs is back. We cannot contain them here for ever. They are hungry and there are billions of nice snacks out there beyond the reserve."

DEMON HUNTER

Durga rested one hand on the head of the lion as she watched the spiral of dust dwindle across the scrub land. At its heart, leading a party of *rajput* warriors, was the demon Kesin. She had hunted him for two years and had at last found his hiding place. She had to flush him out before she could engage him in battle, or the forces they would unleash would devastate the town. Kesin might not worry about the lives cut short, but in her aspect of Parvati, she was creator. The mortals were in her care.

~~~

Kesin threw the reins of his gaudily clad steed to a hovering servant and strode up the steps to the palace entrance. He glared at the low-caste *bhangi* woman sweeping the treads, causing twists of dust to swirl unnaturally around her feet. She dropped her gaze and stilled her movements until he was past, but he sensed eyes watching him. He had been watched ever since he had killed the traitor Bikramsingh in the forest four days ago.

Once in the shadows at the top of the steps, Kesin looked back. The sweeper had her back to him and the *rajput* troops were already moving away towards the stables. None of the people in the square below appeared to linger, and a lone pigeon pecking at fallen rice grains flapped away as a potter staggered past laden with earthenware gourds.

The *rajput* warriors who flanked the entrance and stood at intervals along the corridors within the palace remained motionless as he passed from the heat-fierce sunlight to the chill of the marbled passages. The city on the plain was less comfortable than the forests he had lately left.

Word had gone before him. His party would have been seen long before they reached the city's walls. The *raja* rose from his cushioned throne as Kesin entered the long audience chamber and waved away the woman who knelt at his feet holding an ewer of water.

Kesin prostrated himself at the base of the dais but rose quickly at a word from the *raja*, who descended part way to meet him.

"Well?" the prince demanded.

"It is done." Kesin untied the bloody bundle that was slung at his waist. He laid it on the steps and unwound the cloth.

The *raja* bent to study the severed head that tumbled free; he smiled. "Are you sure it is he? This looks too old."

"From his own mouth."

"It is good. Have it impaled before the temple of Shiva and proclaim that the slayer of my father's wife is brought to justice." He lowered his voice a little. "Criminals need to know that even twenty years is not long enough to escape my hand, or thine. Burn it after five days."

Kesin grinned. "Yes, Lord."

The prince turned away, dismissing Kesin, who backed out of the hall. As the doors were closed, he tossed the head to the nearest guard.

"You heard the *raja*'s orders. See to it."

The man caught the grisly object awkwardly. Supposedly deaf and blind to all that went on in the *raja*'s presence, Kesin knew that the news would be round the barracks by nightfall. He had often stood the same duty when Bikramsingh led the old *raja*'s personal guard.

A dark-skinned beggar-woman was sitting cross-legged by his gate when he returned to his home. Her hair and torso were greyed with dust, her eyes downcast, and she held her alms bowl before her.

"Get rid of her," he said to the group of warriors who lounged in the forecourt. These were members of the *raja*'s elite whom he had assigned for his own protection. Rank had privileges, he thought smugly.

Three of the men leapt to their feet, drawing curved swords from their belts as they did so. Kesin watched from within as they shouted at the woman, prodding her with the tips of their blades, careful not to touch her in case she should contaminate them. Her bowl was kicked down the street, spilling the rice someone had placed in it. She climbed slowly to her feet, her hair falling lank and greasy over her face. They continued to shout and wave their swords at her as she stooped to pick up the bowl. She scooped the rice from the dust. One soldier struck her with the flat of his blade. She gazed at him through the strands of hair as if marking him. He took a step backwards, fearful.

The others tired of their sport as she retreated, hobbling down the street.

The entertainment over, Kesin passed through the cool entrance to his house and entered the inner courtyard. Only the most favoured were permitted houses with their own wells. His was small but shadowed by a neem tree, the leaves of which remained fresh in the heat as its roots tapped the source of the well's water.

A woman scurried across to draw water for him the moment he stepped into the courtyard while another brought him a leaf of honey-sweet cakes. The strings of beads that they wore over their naked torsos chimed musically with their movements. Kesin chose his servants for their grace.

He took the bucket as it appeared at the lip of the well and upended it over his head. Green slime cascaded down his hair and face. Kesin roared.

The woman dropped the bucket back into the well. The honey-cakes scattered in the dust. Both hauled it to the top again and peered inside. One dipped her hand in the water and raised it to her lips.

"This water is clean," she said timidly, obviously expecting to be blamed.

Kesin examined it for himself before using it to wash the muck from his body. Then he dropped his clothing in a filthy heap by the well and strode into the shade of his house.

~~~

Kesin stirred only slightly when the woman, Shabana, left his bed. It was almost light and she would be returning to the temple before the sun rose fully. Though any of his body servants would willingly have slept with him he preferred the courtesan, perhaps because he had to charm her and she was not available at his whim. Shabana had been given to the temple as a child and could command high prices to permit clients to worship through her. Normally they visited her. Because of his rank, she came to Kesin, but he had to make some effort to please her or she would tire of him before he was ready to discard her favours for another.

Outside the arched window a pair of doves cooed to each other, welcoming the dawn. Disturbed by their sounds, Kesin rolled over, his arm resting in the cooling depression Shabana had vacated. He opened his eyes to gauge the hour from the brightness of the chamber. His fingers touched an unfamiliar length of silk. A sash perhaps. The growing light revealed its scarlet colour. He didn't remember Shabana wearing it.

"It isn't mine," Shabana said when he tried to return it.

They stood in a courtyard of the temple where Shabana danced for the pleasure of the gods. The ornately carved building rose behind them with its arched entrances to the inner shrines.

"Then I will give it to you." Kesin had noticed how her fingers had lingered on the silk when he held it out.

Shabana shook her head. "Better to give it to the goddess," she said.

"Which one?" Kesin said smiling.

"Parvati, the mother, of course."

Kesin shivered as Shabana led him into the presence of the triple goddess. The stone images of her incarnations stood on three sides of the *stupa*. Kali the destroyer leered at him malignantly, her necklace of skulls rattling and grinning eyelessly at him.

Durga, many-armed for war, looked coldly on him, though Shabana had said that she ought to be his patroness. But gentle Parvati smiled benevolently as on an errant child.

Shabana took the sash to lay it over the wrist of the Parvati's outstretched arm. Kesin felt as if Kali's eyes were burning into his back. He snatched at the silk and crossed the shrine to stand before the demon-slayer.

"Red suits her better," Kesin said, tossing the cloth at the foot of the image. It drifted down to lie across the throat of the demon her raised foot rested on.

"What did you do that for?" Shabana followed him into the sunlight.

Kesin shrugged. He didn't really know himself. "It isn't wise to neglect the harsher aspects of the goddess," he said.

"What do you mean?"

He wasn't listening. He was staring at the bronze

statue that stood just inside the gateway leading to the street. He hadn't noticed it when he entered, as it stood within the shadow of the wall. He was sure he hadn't seen it in the temple grounds before but he hesitated to ask Shabana how long it had been there. Instead, he turned to her with a smile.

"I hope you will dance for me again," he said. "Soon."

As he left the courtyard he ran his hand down the head and across the back of the bronze lion. For a moment the cold metal seemed to change to soft, warm fur. His pace increased in his eagerness to mingle with the populace abroad on this thoroughfare. He glanced back, half-expecting to see the lion's gaze following him. He breathed easier when it wasn't, berating himself for allowing the atmosphere within the temple to affect his senses.

~~~

Kesin struggled for breath. Something soft and yielding dragged at his windpipe. Was moulded to it. He tried to prise it away but his nails failed to catch at the edges. He heard his own breath rasping. Mingled with another sound. A purring. Coming closer.

A pad, like that of a large animal, pressed on his chest. The tips of extended claws pricked his skin.

As he struggled, his hands brushed soft fur. He felt carrion-warm air caress his face.

Then red washed the darkness.

~~~

He was awoken by one of the servant girls bringing him a jug of *lasse,* prepared from soured milk mixed with cold well-water and flavoured with cinnamon and salt. His throat felt tender, as though he had spent a day shouting. He probed at the spot and encountered silk. The red silk sash was looped about his neck, its ends weighted.

"Guards!" he roared and went into a spasm of coughing. It exacerbated the rawness.

"Drink this, Master," the girl said, offering him the jug.

Kesin snatched it from her and gulped down the liquid, the creaminess easing his throat a little.

Two warriors charged into the room, their swords drawn.

"Someone has been here," Kesin croaked at them. "Find him."

"Yes, Lord." They disappeared again.

Kesin twisted the *rumal* in his hands. He doubted they'd find any sign. And he wondered what the purpose was. From the way the cloth had been wound about his neck, killing would have been easy. Frightening him would gain nothing – if it could be done.

"There were lion prints in the dust beneath your window," the warriors reported.

"Nothing else?"

"No, Lord."

"Where did it get in?" he asked.

"The tracks only appear there."

"I want the patrols doubled at night. Anyone found asleep goes back to the ranks."

"Yes, Lord."

~~~

"There was a bronze lion there two days ago," Kesin told Shabana. He'd had business in the temple precincts and had taken the opportunity to speak with the courtesan. At this time of day the complex was busy with petitioners bringing gifts of intercession to the deities or thanksgiving for favours considered granted. Women in particular sought Parvati's help.

A handful of guards patrolled though it was rare for them to have to act – most thieves respected the gods.

And murder was best done in dark alleys. The inevitable beggars sat on the steps of the main temple waiting patiently for alms – a handful of millet, a portion of boiled rice.

Shabana shook her head. "You are mistaken, Lord. The only lion is the one Durga rides. That is made of stone, like the rest of her image."

Disturbed, Kesin left the temple complex, choosing one of the other gates. Normally, as he walked through the streets, two *rajput* warriors trailed him, a ritual but largely unnecessary guard of honour. Now they seemed to have deserted him, perhaps fooled by his departure in an unexpected direction.

Kesin walked quickly. He was less familiar with this part of the city and he intended to circle round the temple and regain the thoroughfare that took him to his home. As he turned between the houses he lost the sound of the usual bustle. The gaps between buildings were narrower, and cooler in the shade they created.

An old man squatting on a step spat betel juice into the dust and disappeared into his house as Kesin approached. The strings of beads, hung in the doorway to discourage the ever-present flies, jingled softly as Kesin passed.

He turned into another street expecting to see it widen out ahead. Instead, it was just like the last. A dog urinated against a wall. The only sounds were Kesin's footsteps and the buzzing of insects as they homed in on the patch of wet earth.

At the next corner he paused to get his bearings. In the silence vacated by his feet he heard a distant pad, pad. It sounded too loud for a dog and not sharp enough to be a mule. A sacred cow wandering through this maze would be heralded by the chiming of its bell.

He began to walk faster, listening intently for the padding that seemed to shadow him. He turned into another street. It was little more than a narrow alley between the backs of houses where garbage was thrown. As his attention was behind him he didn't see her at first.

She walked towards him out of the shadows. Her long, black hair fell to her waist, the strands lifting slightly in a faint breeze. There was a dagger in the top of her red *ghagra,* which was tied tightly against her dark skin leaving her breasts bare. In her hands was a *rumal,* and at her heels, a lion.

"I remember you," she said.

Kesin had a momentary vision of this girl standing barefoot in the water beside Bikramsingh's headless body. She had uttered similar words before she had turned and run. This time it was Kesin who retreated. He backed away wondering how she could have arrived in the city so soon.

He backed to the end of the alley, yelled once and ran.

Round the next corner the maze disgorged him into the busy thoroughfare before the temple of the triple goddess. Here was noise, colour and bright, hot sunlight.

Kesin looked back. An old man spat betel juice into the dust.

~~~

Kesin found it difficult to settle. Twice he had checked that the guards were alert but he wasn't sure that that was enough. If the lion were mortal it would have been seen in the streets and hunted down. He did not believe it was. And the girl. He had seen her – he was certain now – sweeping the steps of the palace when he returned with Bikramsingh's head.

And begging outside his gate. But that was impossible. Unless she was not human. Kesin remembered the feel of the red scarf tightening about his throat when there was no-one to hold it. Except the hand of the goddess, the enemy of his kind. He didn't eat what his serving-women brought him but paced restlessly from room to room. He called for lamps to be lit in all of them.

The household quietened as all except Kesin slept. The flames guttered and died as the wicks smokily consumed the last drops of oil.

Dawn lightened the sky. Kesin entered his sleeping chamber. A lump was silhouetted against the window slit. He held the last lamp out towards it. It illuminated the head yellowly. The distorted, rotting features of Bikramsingh grinned at him.

"Tomorrow," it said and rolled from its perch on the narrow sill.

Kesin leapt for the slit, determined to catch whoever had spoken. The courtyard was deserted.

The empty eye-sockets seemed to follow him as he backed across the room. The demon slayer was here. She had shown she could touch him. Durga was playing with him. He needed space to fight her. To win, he needed to choose the place of the encounter.

~~~

The coming of dawn saw the demon climbing into the mountains. He followed the stream as it twisted up the wooded ravine. In his present form, Kesin was a handsome man, turbaned and dressed in richly embroidered clothes which were now dusty and travel-worn. He was armed with both a sword and a spear. He carried shield, breastplate and helmet in a bundle at his back. He sniffed the air. His enemy was out there and coming closer.

Kesin called up a storm, a hurricane that plucked trees from the ground and disturbed boulders. He hurled one in her direction. She turned it aside. She quenched, too, the fire that snaked through the forest at his bidding.

He was close to the safety of Patala but she was tenacious and he would retreat no further. He had no intention of allowing her entrance to the demons' underground realm so she could cause mayhem and bring her slaughtering kin. Before the next sunrise one of them would be lodged with Yama.

Kesin looked up at the mountainside. In places weather had shattered the vertical walls sending swathes of scree scything through the vegetation. Such a spur jutted out into the valley a short way ahead. There, he decided, he would set his ambush.

He picked his ground and waited.

~~~

Durga had long discarded the illusion of human form. Her black skin glistened as the humidity increased with the rising sun. Warily she threaded her way through the trees in the ravine. She knew she was close behind the demon. Kesin was cunning and powerful.

In two of her hands she held her sword and shield. The third grasped a bow, ready strung, while her free hand rested on the head of the huge lion she rode. Sunlight glinted on her bronze helm and was reflected from the white bone of the skulls that made up her necklace. They clinked with the rolling stride of the animal beneath her.

Durga was weary. The turning of the storm had drained a lot of the strength she had borrowed from Indra – but the making of it must have equally weakened Kesin.

She had entered the valley soon after the light had first touched the mountains and knew that somewhere within it her enemy waited. At some point Kesin would turn and fight. She sensed it would be soon. He would not want to lead her into his homeland though the demons, by their numbers, would quickly overpower her. But once she passed through the entrance it would not close and others, Indra perhaps, could follow. The carnage amongst the dwellers in Patala would be great. If the great god Varuna permitted it to go that far.

A stream threaded between boulders in the valley bottom. The great lion bowed its head to drink. Durga listened to the wood. Birds sang and in the distance a monkey howled; all seemed normal. Durga slid from the beast's back, certain that it would warn her of the approach of any danger, and scooped up a handful of icy water.

Over her curled fingers she saw a figure seated in the shadows of the trees on the opposite bank. Shy pigeons accepted grain from his outstretched hands. When Durga raised her head to see him more fully, he wasn't there, only a bird pecking at the ground. It rose in fright at her sudden movement.

A shiver of apprehension ran down her spine. Remounting, Durga continued on her way, conscious of the passing time. The sun had reached the zenith and was poised for its descent towards night.

The valley narrowed, the stream twisting between spurs thrust like tentative fingers from the mountains. Ahead, a rock fall had cut a swathe through the vegetation. Loose scree prevented anything rooting there.

Durga thought she glimpsed movement amongst the precariously balanced boulders. A light touch and a murmured word turned the lion from the path. He bounded upwards, his pads scarcely touching the stones, shifting without dislodging them. Not a pebble fell to alert Kesin of their coming, the lion's colour blending with the rock.

The goddess nocked an arrow to her bow. She saw

Kesin now. He was on a level with her, crouched with his shoulder against a boulder near the top of the slide. He glanced up as the arrow hissed towards him and moved slightly. It splintered harmlessly against the rock. The second and third, loosed in rapid succession, disintegrated into a shower of sparks.

Kesin hurled his spear at the lion before drawing his sword. The lion turned aside and Durga reached out. Her fingers touched the haft. The spear stopped in mid-flight, dropped to the ground and the snake it had become slithered away between the stones.

The demon roared as Durga threw herself from the lion's back, her shield raised to ward off his blows. He staggered back under the onslaught of her sword and dagger. The shale beneath his feet shifted. The boulder, already unstable, tottered beneath his weight and began to roll. The scree around it followed, gathering speed as it plunged down the slope. Unable to keep their balance, both combatants were swept along with the avalanche. She glimpsed the lion surfing the pebbles before the rush overwhelmed it, its bloodied body carried out of sight into the trees at the foot of the slope.

~~~

Durga brushed the stones from her limbs and rose to her feet, bruised but unharmed. Her shield, still strapped to her arm, had taken the brunt of the fall. It was battered but still serviceable. Her dagger was still gripped in another hand but her sword was a few paces away, wedged between the stones. As she reached for it Kesin's blade sliced through the air and her fingers. Cursing her stupidity she whirled, switching her dagger to the uninjured right hand as she did so.

The demon had resumed his natural form. His skin was bright red, his eyes, iris and sclera, an unnatural blue.

He grinned, fangs protruding from an overlarge mouth. Muttering under his breath he rushed at her, his squat body nimble on the bowed, muscular legs.

Her shield took his blows. Durga felt the shock vibrating to her shoulder. Behind her she heard the grating of stone on stone. As the sound rose to a scream she flung herself sideways. More of the hillside slipped downwards. A few rocks struck her leaving bloody trails but most flew past to splinter on Kesin's armour. She twisted, stabbing at his feet, slicing his calf before he leapt aside. She tore one of the skulls from her necklace. Crushing it between her fingers, Durga flung the pieces skyward. Dark clouds began to gather over the gorge, obscuring the sun and lit internally with sheets of blue fire.

Demon and deva circled each other warily, Kesin glancing uneasily at the sky whenever he dared. Suddenly Durga snatched off her helm and hurled it away. She raised an open palm heavenward, made a fist and jerked her arm downwards. The lightning followed, drawn to Kesin's bronze headpiece. For a moment he was enveloped in blue flame. He rushed Durga. She dodged. His sword struck her shield. It blazed, then shattered. Durga was thrown back as the fire died. Both stood still, stunned by the shock.

Durga recovered first. Throwing down the remains of her shield, she dived for her wedged sword and yanked. It jerked free in time to parry Kesin's next stroke.

They fought now in silence, exchanging blow for blow, Kesin's shield and greater weight balanced by Durga's extra hands and longer reach. She noticed he tended to favour the leg she had cut; she kept her injured hand tucked in her waistband. It hampered her movements slightly. She dared not slacken her concentration to throw up another illusion lest he slip under her guard. Yet Durga knew she had to trick her way past the darting blade before the sun set. Kesin's strength increased with the declining daylight, reaching a peak in the first four seconds of twilight. Her own strength was waning.

She edged backwards towards the trees, the demon following. Both were breathing heavily. Durga's legs and her sword arm ached, the stumps of her missing fingers itched. She dodged behind a slender trunk. Kesin hacked it down.

Sweat and blood from various scratches ran down their bodies.

Durga put another tree between them, and watched it fall. A little further and there would be shadows she could hide in. She fingered a skull in her necklace. She feinted, retreated. She waited until Kesin's blade bit into the trunk, then dropped the ornament. She faded into greyness. Kesin struck at the dark after-image. She attacked from the side, her dagger sliding up between his ribs before his shield smashed into her face. Dazed, she fell back, leaving the knife in his chest, limiting the blood flow. The copper in the metal began its slow spread of poison.

A grinning Kesin thrust at her body. She rolled and came to her feet, shaking the stars out of her head. She loosened the sash from about her waist. The ends were weighted and it hung easily across two of her palms. She parried with the sword, feeling her knees give slightly. He played furiously now, each stroke seemingly stronger, more sure than the last. She was again forced to retreat.

Backed against a fallen trunk, Durga's eyes narrowed. Her sword engaged his, hilt locked to hilt. The sash lashed out, the weighted end snaking around his neck. Kesin threw down the shield to wrench at the cloth that tightened about his throat. She could feel his strength waxing as the sun touched the distant horizon. There were only moments left. Jerking at the sash she launched herself at his throat. Her teeth sank into his neck, meeting.

He gripped her hair. The sword blades slid along each other. The weight on her arm lessened as they fell apart. She felt the pommel strike the base of her skull as she attempted to suck the life from him. He struck again. Distantly she heard an owl calling.

~~~

Yama, Lord of the Dead, watched the demon limp up the slope, the head tied by its hair to his belt banging against his thigh. He was followed by the two smaller demons that had sprung from his spilt blood. The remains of Durga's body lay twisted at Yama's feet. The lion padded out from between the trees. Its ears were torn and its coat matted with dried blood from a gash in one flank. Its feet left red pawmarks on the stones. It sniffed the body of its mistress, then looked at Yama before passing on up the hillside, following the demons' trail.

Yama cast his noose. The loop sank into the torso of the dead goddess. He tugged gently and Durga's soul-form rose from it, the rope loosely about her neck.

"I am honoured that you have come for me personally, Lord Yama," she said.

"I regret it was not the demon," Yama said. "They are much more fun."

"I share your disappointment."

Yama chuckled, a deep, sonorous sound. "Nevertheless, I welcome the company of an intelligent guest."

Yama held out his hand. Durga took it and followed him.

CHAN CHAN

Hunter skidded his bike to a halt where the tarmac disappeared under a layer of sand. "Tell me you're joking," he said.

In the headlights, the terrain undulated, quartz sparkling in the beam. Behind him, the fishing village of Santa Paulo slept. Not a single light showed in any of the houses. His travelling companion Phoebe Makhani moved her bike up beside his. "Is there a problem?" she asked.

He gestured into the darkness. "Do you know what that stuff will do to the engine?"

"You could stay here … or walk."

"Your tiger can go a lot faster than I can." He couldn't see her grin but he imagined it. Phoebe was a shapeshifter, her other form being a Bengal tiger. Hunter was her daytime eyes since she could only be human at night.

She relented a little. "I am told that the road surface is firm, but that is where we must go to meet Que."

Hunter sighed. "How far is it?"

"Not more than two kilometres. I will lead."

She usually did, Hunter thought. Professionally, he was someone who was called in to deal with wild animals that were causing a nuisance to the people they shared their habitat with. A lion that had discovered village cattle were easier prey than springbok would need to be removed, either to a remote area or an enclosed reserve. There, worst cases might become breeding stock for zoos. Hunter only killed if there was no alternative.

Occasionally, as in this case, he had no idea what he was hunting. Phoebe gave him information she thought he needed, which was not necessarily what he wanted.

This region of northern Peru was desert. The winds streaming off the Pacific held their water tight until the land began to rise into the western ranges of the Andes.

Phoebe's machine moved away from him in the darkness, the sound of it reminding him of the purr of a big cat. His own was throatier. He followed. Phoebe's wheels kicked up enough dust for him to hang back. Overtaking wasn't an option as he neither knew exactly where they were headed nor how deep the sand was by the side of the track. He had to rely on her knowledge and instincts. To the right he could make out the sound of waves at the foot of the cliff.

When he pulled up beside Phoebe's bike he noticed that she had left her lights on. That was for his benefit – she was capable of seeing in much lower light levels than he was. He stood his bike next to hers and removed his helmet. The crash of the sea was much louder now but the overwhelming sense was the ammoniacal stench of guano. He wondered what kind of creature Que was.

Phoebe was standing much closer to the edge, her figure illuminated by the bike's lights. Despite the heat that still lingered in the air she wore her form-hugging leathers: red with flashes of black down the seams. She might be a shifter but he'd never seen her naked. The first time they'd met she'd disdainfully dismissed the usual folklore regarding her kind. As long as her clothing was natural, it changed with her, the leather becoming the fur of her tiger. She was a tall woman, only three inches shorter than his six feet. Currently, the dark hair that normally curled about her shoulders was being blown back away from her face. She was waiting.

Hunter moved to stand behind and to one side of her. The sky was cloudless and a three-quarter moon gave the pale sand an eerie gleam. He could see shadows moving at the edge of the cliff. Large shadows.

Then, there was the soft susurration of wings and an even larger shadow rose in front of them. Two beats and it was hovering in the headlights. Hunter got the impression of red and green amongst the feathers that formed a showy crest, as well as on the long serpent-like tail. It was something he'd seen in black and white drawings from mythology books. The creature alighted on the cliff edge and transformed, first into a pelican then into a small weathered man in cotton trousers and shirt cut in the Peruvian style. He wore a red bandana around his neck; Hunter estimated his age anywhere between thirty and fifty. He mentally shrugged; the man was just as likely to be twenty or one hundred and twenty. The only real knowledge he had of Phoebe's kind was what she had deigned to tell him.

He spoke in a Spanish dialect that Hunter just about understood. "Welcome, Tiger. Is this your human?"

"It is, Que," she said. "He calls himself Hunter."

Que nodded. "Jaguar speaks highly of him. Does he know why you are here?"

"He has not been so told."

"Is he a sceptic?"

"I have not asked. It did not seem relevant."

"Yet he accepts our kind." Que looked directly at Hunter and asked, "Do you believe in the unnatural?"

Hunter supressed a laugh. To most people, seeing a woman turn into a tiger was unnatural. Instead he said, "In my job I have seen many strange things."

Phoebe said, "Que means things that cannot be explained." She spoke to him in English.

"Like ghosts or vampires?"

"I have told you vampires do not exist. Ghosts do."

"Okay… So, Que has a problem that he thinks we can solve. Hit me with it."

"No. There is a problem that he thinks you can solve."

Que squatted down – a position that Hunter's leg joints refused to entertain, but it seemed only polite that he sit on the sand facing the man to listen. Que said, "In three days the moon will be full. It will be a blood moon. On that night the Chimú king will walk. This must not be permitted."

"What will happen if he does?" Hunter asked.

"He will demand sacrifice. The day of the Chimú has passed, so has the time of human sacrifice. It must not return."

"What is it you are asking from me?"

"When the last king died, he was buried in the royal compound at Chan Chan. In the days of Chimú, he and his advisors were disinterred every year so visiting dignitaries could pay him homage. Tributes were food, llamas and youths who came as willing sacrifices. On the night of the blood moon he would walk amongst his subjects and choose which of the tributes he would accept. When the Inca finally vanquished the Chimú, the king remained buried."

"What has changed?"

"Archaeologists. They have uncovered the burial place of the king."

"And? You need to explain more than that."

Phoebe gave him a dark look, the kind that made him aware of his ignorance of her assumed knowledge. She said, "Tourists have a fascination for the macabre. The tomb is still in situ. It is covered with glass so all can see the aspect of the dead. When the light of the blood moon touches him, he will walk."

Hunter glanced up at the brilliance of the stars in the absence of street lighting. "No chance of cloud," he said.

"Not in these latitudes."

"I assume you have thought of a solution."

"Yes."

Hunter had a feeling he wasn't going to like the answer. "Do tranquilisers have any effect on the dead?"

"None at all," Phoebe said.

~~~

It was mid-afternoon when Hunter arrived at the Museum in Leymebamba. Distances looked much shorter on maps but the road had twisted and turned as it climbed up into the Andes before sliding down into the village of Cajamarca. The Museum was two kilometres up the next ridge. Because of its remoteness, accommodation for visitors was part of the purpose-built museum. The purpose was to house the Chimú mummies in a carefully controlled environment.

He parked and headed for the reception area of the museum where Juan was serving a couple of Spanish visitors with cold drinks.

"You are Señor Hunter," he said. "Is your companion with you?"

He shook his head, "She will be arriving later."

"That will be Señorina Makhani?"

"Yes. She made the booking."

"It is a twin room I have for you."

"That is acceptable." Hunter wasn't going to bother explaining that it would be unlikely that Phoebe would actually be sleeping here, even during the daytime. He could imagine the hysterics of the cleaner if she found a tiger napping on one of the beds.

Juan lifted the key from under his counter. "You will

need to sign the visiting book. Please ask the Señorina to do the same."

"Si. After you have shown me the room may I look around the museum?"

"Of course. I lock the doors at five."

"That should give me plenty of time for a first look."

"You have an interest in our history?"

"I am fascinated by mythology. Ms Makhani prefers birds. The pelicans on the coast have delayed her."

Hunter followed Juan along a stone flagged passage that opened up to a small courtyard planted with orchids and palms. The rooms led off a balcony that ran round three sides of the space. Everything was constructed from highly polished wood, and the accommodation was spacious, carpeted with rugs in bright colours woven from llama wool. Juan left him to settle in. It didn't take long. He was used to travelling light and not staying anywhere for long.

Inside the museum, wall boards told the history of the Chimú civilisation but Hunter was only interested in the mummies. The whole of one side of the museum was a thick glass window allowing visitors to view them. They had been gathered from all over Northern Peru and were stacked on shelves in a controlled environment. Just inside the sealed door Hunter could see the meter indicating temperature and humidity. For most of the mummies it was the cold dry air of the Andes that had created them. Hunter shivered despite the room he was standing in being a comfortable temperature – it was the macabre sight of so many centuries-dead people that was disturbing.

Each was a bundle of bones tied up soon after death. Knees drawn up to the chest, arms folded into their sides to take up the smallest space possible. They were wrapped in hessian sacks with a crude picture of a face painted on the outside. All looked as if they were screaming. It reminded him of the Munch painting. The mummy he'd seen that afternoon in Chan Chan was merely a curiosity compared with the mass of them here. He turned away to restore his equilibrium before turning back to examine what he was really here for – the security system.

Juan locked the museum as he left – a simple Yale key – and set the alarm on the touch pad. He said, "There is a *restaurante* in the town. The food there is good."

"Gracias. I will ask Ms Makhani what she wishes."

Hunter spent the remaining daylight dusting down his bike. He knew that he'd have to take it back into the desert but he needed it running smoothly, for his own satisfaction.

~~~

It was well after sunset when Hunter heard Phoebe's bike pull up outside. He didn't bother going down to meet her as she had a knack of finding him wherever he was. She walked into the room without knocking and threw her helmet onto the bed he wasn't stretched out on. "Well?" she said.

"I thought Quetzalcoatl was a Mayan god."

"Que follows the pelicans. They range all the way up the Western Pacific seaboard."

"Quetzals are Central American though."

"Forget them. Que's true form is the feathered serpent. The pelicans are camouflage. Are you getting all this stuff from Wikipedia?"

"Seems a good place to start. I like to know what you're getting me in to. Didn't know you could have more than the two aspects."

"There is a lot you don't know about our kind."

"I'm beginning to realise that."

"Are you going to divulge your findings? Or do I have to scare it out of you?"

Hunter grinned. He had become used to her rapid changes in form from woman to tiger, but that didn't make him less wary. A Bengal tiger was all teeth and claws and she wouldn't hesitate to use them. He'd prefer not to have his hide shredded.

"Okay. Chan Chan…"

~~~

They had stayed overnight in Trujillo, Phoebe vanishing before dawn to find a place to hole up for the day. Hunter had ridden west out of the city to where the desert started again. The road cut through a plain humped with the remains of an adobe city eroded by centuries of weather. If all these had been houses it would have been an impressive city. He followed the signpost to the site and parked in the lee of the visitor centre. It would give the bike some protection, but wind eddies around and he knew dust was getting into the mechanism. Once he got home, he'd have to strip everything to its basics.

The walls of the central complex had been restored and the towering twenty-foot structure was impressive. Hunter tagged onto a group being shown around by a guide who almost spoke English. Though not particularly interested in the history of the place, it was hard not to be impressed. The Moon Pool, when they reached it, was the size of a standard swimming pool, only square. Sloping ramps ran along the walls forming a path down to the water's edge. The guide was explaining that it filled with rainwater and it and other tanks like it had supplied the city with water.

One of the group, an American tourist, said, "I heard they used it for sacrifices."

"It is one theory that young men and women would sacrifice themselves by walking into the water when the moon was full. More likely it was a bathing ritual."

"Wouldn't want to drink from it if there were bodies in it," the American said.

"Too true," his wife said, nudging him in the ribs.

Hunter stared down into the water, wondering how deep it was. The ramps disappeared under the dark surface, about ten feet below where he was standing. He could imagine it gleaming in the moonlight. He suddenly noticed that the group had moved on and he hurried to catch up.

The central courtyard, they were told, was where the king received delegations from outlying provinces, and that when the king died it was his mummy that was paraded to the visitors.

"Do we get to see the mummy?" a Goth-dressed girl asked.

"We will see the tombs of his advisors. This way."

The graves had been cut into the underlying sandstone. Now protected by a corrugated iron roof they looked unimpressive, just empty square slots in the ground.

"Where are the bodies?" the Goth girl asked.

"They were taken to be preserved," the guide said.

Her companion, a skinny youth with several pieces of metalwork adorning his face, asked, "Was the king buried here?"

"He is this way."

They were led around the other side of a mound. Here was a deep pit covered with Perspex. The party stood around staring into the depths. A light had been fitted inside and shone down onto a cloth wrapped bundle. The American said, "Sure is tiny. I've seen more spectacular mummies in Cairo."

The guide said, "Here it is the sand that preserves the king, not the priests."

The party moved away. Hunter stayed. As Phoebe had told him, all they had to do was exchange this mummy for that of a peasant. All Hunter had to do was work out how to get access to something sealed under plastic.

On his way out he stopped in the souvenir shop to purchase a map of the site. He walked past the Goth girl and her companion in the small café area. They were with a couple of lads that had the appearance of surfers. He heard her say, "Wouldn't it be great to see the full moon in the Moon Pool."

One of the others said, "It's nearly full moon. We could come back at night."

Hunter said nothing, hoping it would be a wish that was quickly forgotten.

~~~

Hunter relayed that information to Phoebe.

"As long as the king is not at Chan Chan there should be no danger. Can you get into the tomb?"

"Anyone with a screwdriver could. I don't know what you need me for."

Phoebe smiled. "You have talents other than being both a good shot and tracker. Someone has to lock the king away safely."

He ran his fingers through his blond hair. "Is there no other way? Like covering the tomb with sand?"

"We went over this last night. And it has to be done now. Tomorrow the moon is full."

"Right." Before he had changed careers to track down rogue animals and transfer them to places of safety, Hunter had been a locksmith. He'd been steered in that direction by a youth worker who had recognised his talent for opening locked doors – and had wanted to keep an East End boy out of trouble. The satisfaction was knowing he could open a complicated mechanism, not what valuables might be on the other side. He wasn't completely comfortable with the idea of stealing a mummy. Or even exchanging one for another, but Phoebe's reasoning was persuasive. A risen king would take his tribute from somewhere, and the nearest place was the streets of Trujillo.

With a sigh, Hunter reached for his kit. Basically, it was his bike's toolkit with a few added extras, a legacy from the day his ignition key had broken and he'd needed to improvise. He followed Phoebe outside.

He was already studying the mechanism that would let them into the museum when the moonlight dimmed. He straightened, looking over his shoulder. The shadow across the moon's disc resolved into the shape of the feathered dragon. As Que landed he shifted first to his pelican form, then into the wrinkled native he'd met before. He spoke animatedly to Phoebe.

She turned to Hunter. "We have a problem. There was an accident at the pass this afternoon, and it is still blocked. They won't be reopening the road until morning."

"Not even the bikes can get through?"

"Only emergency vehicles are being allowed up."

Hunter considered the implications. The intention had been to exchange the king's mummy for one in storage tonight. Then there would be no danger of him walking. "How much time will we have tomorrow night."

"Blood Moon is at three am."

One of the things Hunter had done while waiting for Phoebe the previous night was to Google the phenomenon. It was a reference to the colour the moon's disc went during a lunar eclipse. He'd never seen one but knew that, like solar eclipses, superstitions were woven around them. This was the first time anyone had suggested some real basis in truth. Knowing Phoebe, he was prepared to believe that something untoward was likely to happen. He said, "That's cutting it a bit fine. I wouldn't even risk opening the vault until after dark. Neither am I going to liberate one of these mummies tonight and stash it somewhere. It's asking for trouble."

"How so?" Phoebe asked.

"An observant curator will spot one missing. It will be bad enough breeching the atmosphere controls but as the only people staying here we can't afford to be suspected of tampering." He looked at both of them. "I suppose it's out of the question for Que to fly the mummy to Chan Chan and do the exchange."

"Totally. Neither pelicans nor tigers can keep up the pace to get there and back in a night. That's what the bikes are for."

Hunter held up his hands. "Okay. We leave it until tomorrow and hope there is enough time."

~~~

The part that concerned Hunter most was upsetting the delicate balance in the sealed chamber. He knew the mechanism was supposed to be able to adjust for small changes. He was going to have to let in the outside atmosphere, along with its potential pollutants, twice. Until he opened the room to check, he had no idea whether there was an alarm that alerted the curators of a drastic change in the room's atmosphere.

He had no clue as to where the big cat had spent the daylight hours but Phoebe had returned to the Museum at sunset. Que arrived a few minutes later. "The road is clear," he'd announced.

Unlocking the outer door had taken a matter of moments. The inner one longer. That did have an alarm that would warn of a breaching to the chamber and he had to work round it. "Which one?" he asked as the seal cracked.

"Any, Que says."

"Right." Hunter reached for one on the lower shelf and found himself apologising to the long-dead Peruvian for disturbing its rest. He grimaced at the stupidity of it.

Phoebe carefully packed the mummy into a box while Hunter resealed the chamber. She would take it strapped onto the back of her bike. He glanced up at the moon, newly risen above the mountain ridges, a swollen silver disc at its closest approach to Earth for a decade. It would be a ride of several hours. As long as there were no mishaps they should be at Chan Chan well before the Earth's shadow began to encroach on the moon's face.

~~~

Hunter had taken the lead along the twisting mountain road, with Que riding pillion. Less tiring than flying, he had said. The archaeological site was unsecured, with only a simple barrier across the approach road. It would have been impossible to secure such a vast area and the bikes easily shimmied around the bar. They swooped into the parking area between the visitor centre and the adobe wall. Hunter slammed on his brakes and swore – and not just at his rear wheel skidding in the sand.

Nosing the wall was a small self-drive mini-bus, eight-seater at most. He remembered the Goth girl in the café and swore again. He propped the bike on its stand and pulled off his helmet. "We've got trouble," he said as Phoebe pulled up beside him. He gestured at the interlopers' vehicle. "Gaggle of tourists wanting to see the reflection in the Moon Pool."

He didn't understand her response but guessed it wasn't polite.

"They may not be an issue should they stay by the pool," Que said.

"We'd better get moving," Hunter said.

Phoebe unstrapped the box from her bike and passed it to Hunter. She morphed into tiger. He followed her in. The moon gave a reasonable light but her cat-eyes were better in the darkness. He wasn't sure about Que who retained his human form. Pelicans usually flew by day but he had no idea of the abilities of his dragon form. He wasn't going to ask.

The way Phoebe headed unerringly for the grave suggested that she had scouted the area at night. He knelt beside the depression and brushed sand from the Perspex surface.

"I'm going to need more light," he said. "I can't remove the covering blind." He looked at Phoebe, who sat on her haunches staring at him. He added, "The walls will shield the light somewhat, but I'd rather that little group of hippies didn't wander over to see what was going on. I'd appreciate it if one of you kept an eye on them."

The look the tiger gave him was one of disgust before she stalked off in the direction of the Moon Pool. If he listened very carefully he could just make out voices coming from that direction.

Hunter glanced up at the sky. The moon seemed bigger and closer, its light reflecting off the cover he had to remove. He set out his tools – torch, screwdriver, lubricant and a container for the removed fastenings. When he'd been here in daylight he hadn't noticed any wiring that could be attached to an alarm. That was a minor mercy – the Peruvians trusted that no-one would vandalise their heritage.

The job took longer than Hunter expected. The screws had been set into the framework at six-inch intervals and he had to remove every one. The battery-powered screwdriver helped but it still wasn't fast enough. He steeled himself not to keep glancing at the sky. Already the edge of the Earth's shadow was creeping across the moon's face. Partly, he hoped that Phoebe and Que were wrong about the effect totality would have. At the same time, he didn't want to run the risk. She had been right about so many things in the past.

Eventually, the last screw came free. He beckoned Que over to help him lift the cover clear before he reached in to snag the king's mummy from its resting place. Hauling it out by its sacking covering was undignified so he tried to lay it down more gently. He could feel the thin and fragile bones through the cloth. He arranged the substitute as best he could in the same configuration as the original and set about replacing all the screws.

Concentrating on his task, Hunter hadn't realised that Que had disappeared, or that the king's mummy hadn't been placed inside the box, protecting it from the moonlight. He glanced up as the quality of the luminescence changed. The last of the earth's shadow slid across the moon, dimming its glow and changing it from silver to a dark orange-red.

He caught a whisper of sound, like sand grains moving over each other. Turning his head he saw the bag twitching. "Shit."

Hunter dropped his tools and lunged for the box. Upending it, he threw it over the mummy. He heard the aged sack tear as the bones knitted and stretched. The king rose from the sand, throwing the box aside. The skeletal form turned towards him, reaching out clawed fingers. Hunter scrabbled backwards. A furred form leapt past him, bowling over the mummy. As the tiger sprang clear the mummy twisted around, grabbing for her.

Phoebe crouched, weighing up her opponent, only the tip of her tail twitching. The king stepped forward as she launched her attack, paws batting at his skull. Thin arms swept up, throwing her away from him. He was stronger than he looked. She rolled and came lightly to her feet. She prowled in a circle with him in the centre, the moon's red light lengthening his shadow, turning his mottled brown hide the colour of dried blood.

Hunter moved out of the way knowing any interference on his part would hinder the tiger. The only sounds were the low growl from Phoebe's throat – and a distant shout.

She lunged snapping at its legs, fastening teeth onto one shin. Bony toes of the other foot raked at her throat; hands buried its nails into the fur of her back. She snarled, releasing her grip on his leg as he lifted her from the ground, flinging her to one side. Breath whooshed from her lungs. She grunted and rolled to her feet. The mummy strode past her. One of the tiger's paws snaked out to try and trip him. He stepped over it.

Hunter knew where the king was heading: towards the Moon Pool and the unsuspecting tourists. He wished he had his rifle although it only fired tranq darts – but he hadn't expected to be facing a wild animal. Anyway, they would have no effect on the mummy but the rifle's stock would make a useful club. He sprinted towards the Moon Pool while the tiger continued to harry the king.

The still surface of the dark water mirrored the swollen globe of the red moon. The Goth girl stood on the far edge, her phone held at arms' length as she videoed the scene. Her three friends were partway down the ramps leading to the water. Hunter shouted. One of the boys laughed and waved.

A sound from behind him caused Hunter to leap sideways. He didn't care if it was the mummy or the tiger, he wasn't going to remain in their way. As he rolled he glanced over. The king stood, its skeletal feet hooked over edge of the pool's rim. If the mummy had eyes, the king would be staring at the youngsters. The three on the ramp became still for a moment before continuing down, taking slow steady steps, almost as if compelled. He remembered the guide's answer to a question, that some thought the pool was used for sacrifices, and Que's assertion that the king would demand at least one. Here were three willing victims.

The girl filming started whooping with pleasure, obviously thinking the skeleton was a show put on for their benefit – until the leading boy reached the water and carried on walking. Her shouts turned to cries of consternation, then alarm. Hunter wondered where Phoebe had got to.

The boy was up to his waist when Phoebe, in human form, appeared behind the king, carrying a bundle of cloth. She called, "Hunter!"

As the fabric unravelled from her arms Hunter raced to her side and grabbed one edge of the cloth. He could guess what she intended – to make a barrier between the king and the moon. But they wouldn't be tall enough.

Que appeared then, the pelican morphing into the feathered god as he rose from the pool. Talons outstretched, he swooped down, swerving in time to avoid the mummy's arms that reached for him. Que's claws caught a wrist. He twisted in mid-air and brought his beak down on the skull. As the king stumbled Hunter and Phoebe threw the cloth over him.

The sky began to lighten as the Earth's shadow began to slide away from the moon. It would be an hour or so before it cleared completely but this was enough to begin the colour change back from red to silver. Beneath the cloth the king struggled, the force of the struggles lessening as the moon changed. Que untangled himself from the cloth and bones to become human, helping to wrap the skeleton. Hunter could feel its movements diminishing further.

A scream. They were dangerously close to the edge of the pool. Hunter glanced over. Two of the walkers had stopped and were staring round in confusion. The third had continued down; he was neck deep in the pool and he wasn't stopping. Hunter left Que and Phoebe to deal with the king. He rolled over the rocky edge, diving into the water praying it wasn't too shallow at this point. Hands touched slimy mud before buoyancy pushed him upwards. He surfaced and trod water, looking for the youth. He'd gone.

Hunter duck dived.

Fingers touched the surface of the ramp and he kicked along it, almost colliding with the body. He hooked an arm around its waist and pushed off for the surface. Gasping for air, he dragged the boy's head out of the water. The weight of water in his boots threaten to pull him back under. Then there were hands lifting the burden from him. The Goth girl and the other boys hauled their friend up the slope onto the level surface. Exhausted, Hunter flopped onto the ramp. Leather wasn't the best fabric to go swimming in.

By the time he staggered to the top the boy he'd rescued was spluttering back to life.

"What the hell was that thing?" Goth girl said.

"Rehearsal for a pageant," Hunter said. The lie came

easily as he wondered where Phoebe and Que had gone.

"We were told we'd have the place to ourselves."

"We just wanted to see the place at night. We didn't mean any harm."

"Take your friend back to wherever you're staying and put it down to experience. He was lucky," said Hunter.

"Yeah." She didn't argue and Hunter watched as the four disappeared into the maze that led to the car park.

"I will watch that they leave," Phoebe said. "Que needs your help in dealing with the king." She had appeared silently at his side. He noticed that the left sleeve of her leathers was ripped. It was the equivalent of having some of the tiger's fur torn out. He hoped there was no deeper damage but said nothing.

Now that the eclipse was over, Que had unwrapped the mummy. Now it was no more than a collection of bones. It was a case of arranging them and binding them together with strips of ancient fabric. Hunter worked carefully under Que's supervision, half-expecting the fragile cloth to tear – the bag it had been in was ripped. While Hunter held it still Que stitched the bag closed. The repair wasn't elegant but once the mummy was on the shelf in the museum it could be a while before it was examined. Only then would the archaeologists have a conundrum to unravel.

Of more concern was the broken window in the Visitor Centre. Phoebe had smashed it to get the cloth they'd used to entangle the mummy. Hunter carefully folded the material and replaced it on the pile with others. He checked for CCTV. Thankfully, there was none in evidence, though if he had to he was sure he'd be able wipe the footage. No-one wants to see a tiger rampaging through their shop.

~~~

Job done, Hunter stood in the parking area outside the Leymebamba museum. The king's mummy was tucked in safe storage, brick and mortar protecting it from the light of any moon. Above him, dawn light caught Que, a confection of brilliant feathers. It was easy to imagine why the Maya had seen his kind as gods. Then there was just a pelican flapping its way towards the coast.

Back in his hotel, Hunter hung the *Do Not Disturb* notice on the room's door. It wasn't just that he was exhausted and needed a good long sleep – he didn't want room service to be freaked out by the sight of a Bengal tiger curled up on the other bed.

RED SLAVE

The two undergrads hauled the wooden box into Cameron Morton's workroom by its rope handles. Godfrey Theakstone from the Modern European History department followed them.

"Thought this was more in your line," he said.

"What is it?" Cameron asked, knowing that the contents had probably once been alive. His section, which had acquired the nickname the Department of Death, specialised in archaeological funerary practices. The fact that it was only Cameron and one student didn't deter his colleagues. He also suspected that they referred to him as Dr Death when he wasn't in earshot. He always insisted, though, that he would have nothing to do with Egyptology. That province belonged to the woman irreverently called Queen Tut by her students. He amended his question to, "Where did it come from?"

"An old boy in Wolverhampton," Theakstone said. "His grandchildren were clearing the house and donated everything."

"I'm assuming you've brought me copies of authentication."

Theakstone dropped a yellow-edged notebook on top of the artefacts cluttering the desk. "By all accounts he was methodical in his collecting. This details what he knew about Jack in the box. I'll email anything else that seems relevant. We're still sorting through the bequest. Come on, lads, we have work to do." He swept out of the room, in as much as a short, portly academic could sweep.

Cameron had schooled himself not to show over-eagerness, especially in front of colleagues and deliberately finished the paragraph he had been composing before saving his work and reaching for his camera. Everything he did was precise and well documented. It was the only way he had of maintaining the respect of his peers, being not only the youngest in the History Department, at thirty-six, but also of mixed heritage. His mother was Dutch and his paternal grandfather had been a black GI who'd stayed after the war with his Scottish bride.

Cameron prepared to photograph and measure everything, not knowing which clue might lead in the direction of truth, rather than guesswork. He had other talents in his repertoire that he never let on about, but he needed solid proof before he could reveal his findings. They might mostly be regarded as speculative – much of what he examined was unassociated with written records – but his peers liked logical reasoning. He also preferred to see and, sometimes, touch the object before examining its provenance.

The box itself was unremarkable – sturdy, probably oak, water stained and at least a hundred and fifty years old. There was a catch but no lock. Cameron knelt beside it and slowly lifted the lid.

The contents were wrapped in what looked like an elderly piece of sailcloth, greyed with use and age. Dust had settled in the folds indicating that Theakstone had lifted the covering before deciding that this was a curio more suited to the Death Department. As it had already been disturbed and wasn't a relic *in situ*, Cameron had no qualms about touching it. The tingle in his fingers wasn't just anticipation. Lifting the cloth away, Cameron exposed a corpse and realise why Theakstone was so eager to pass this on. Cameron would have to do all the paperwork relating to the accession of human remains.

The body was curled into a foetal position and just filled the box. The skin, dried to leather, showed all the contours of the bones. The mummy was intact. Cameron laid his hand on the skull, feeling the wispy strands of hair that still clung there. In his mind he heard a murmur that could have been words, though not in the language he normally spoke.

Mijn naam is Ezra.

A ping from his computer indicating incoming mail broke the contact. Cameron checked, it was the data from Theakstone; he sent back a "thanks" and returned to his new acquisition. There was a lot to be determined. Age for one thing. It wasn't unknown for eccentrics to collect Egyptian artefacts, including mummies, but this wasn't one – the death position was wrong – and many other cultures preserved the dead. He also wanted to know about the method of preservation – were the organs intact, were embalming minerals used or was it a natural process – and how the person had died.

He spent the rest of the day taking the minute samples that would be needed for testing and arranging for an X-ray, knowing he was likely to be at the back of a long queue for any forensic analysis.

~~~

Mijn naam is Ezra. Ik gebruikte om te leven in Rincon met mijn familie... But since Pa went blind working all day in the salt pans, the owner says as I am eldest I have to take his place.

"Stick with me," Zak says. "I'll see you all right."

Zak's son is my best friend. Since we could walk we've worked side by side in the stony fields with our mothers, cultivating maize and growing the few crops to feed our families. We've seen older boys, and some girls, drafted south to work the salt but we never expected it to happen to us. But not for many more years. We'd not accounted for Pa. That sort of thing is always for others.

When Pa comes home that last Sunday, the overseer visits. He says, either I go work in Pa's place or all the family gets sold next Auction Day. I couldn't see the family split up and no-one would buy a blind man. So I go.

It's a long walk from Rincon to Red Slave, about as far as you can go on the island, and the men do it, six hours each way, every Sunday. If they don't they get no food. I am loaded up with my share – six jars of maize, some beef, coffee and rum. Ma gives me a small sack of what she can spare. She hugs me and cries. "See you Sunday," she says. I turn away so she can't see my tears. I am scared. I've never been away from my family before.

~~~

Cameron rubbed the sleep from his eyes and hauled himself out of bed. He'd spent too long reading through the notes Theakstone had sent him. The mummy box and the rest of the contents of the house had belonged to an old Dutch family and most of the curiosities had been purchased in the ports from sailors and merchants by the donor's father. He'd brought the collection with him after the war when his family had settled in the Midlands. It would explain why Cameron had been dreaming in Dutch. He'd learnt it as a child but rarely spoke it unless he was visiting the Netherlands. The dream had also brought back memories of a childhood visit to the Caribbean island of Bonaire. It was part of the Dutch Antilles and he had felt good to be able to talk to the locals in their language, and with his dark skin he felt he could almost pass for one of them. Almost, because he didn't speak Papiamentu, the island's patois.

His father and sister Alyse were both keen divers. Cameron preferred history. At the age of twelve he was into castles and pirates. His mother hired a car so she and Cameron could explore an island once owned by her countrymen.

As they drove beyond the narrow streets of Kralandijk he noticed white mountains. "What are those?" he asked.

"Salt," his mother said. "See the pink water. Those are the salt pans. Sea water is let in and the sun evaporates the water leaving the salt behind."

In the distance he could see yellow machines scooping up the salt and dumping it in lorries. The white peaks made them look small, like toys, but as they got closer he could see they were huge. He was the toy to their enormity. He frowned. "What did they do before machines were invented?"

"Slaves did the work."

"From Africa? Like those in America?"

"Yes, *liefde*."

He had learnt about the slave trade in school, and the campaigns against it. He couldn't imagine what it would be like to be owned. "Was Grandad a slave?"

"No. Slavery was abolished long before your grandfather was born – but his grandfather might have been. I don't know."

Ahead of them, Cameron could see a group of orange-painted structures. He remembered passing some white ones a while back. His mother pulled over to the side of the road and they got out to look. Two tall thin pyramidal obelisks stood nearby. One was red, the other orange. Cameron raced over to the information board curious to know what they were. He read, then turned slowly.

"Mum, the slaves lived in these huts." He walked over to one of them. The side walls only came up to his waist before the roof sloped steeply to a point. He peered into the small entrance that opened on the seaward side. Even he could only get in by crawling. There was a tiny square opening at the back and he could feel the wind blowing through it. There wasn't any room to stand upright except in the very centre under the peak of the roof.

Cameron sat down and closed his eyes. The notice board said six men would sleep here. There didn't seem to be enough room for that. He tried to imagine what it would be like and shivered. The sea seemed to whisper to him, *Mijn naam is Ezra*.

~~~

It is dark when we finally arrive at Red Slave. We can see because the moon's light shines on the salt and it gleams. I can hear the waves. They sound very close. Zak steers me towards one of the painted stone huts.

"This is where we sleep, boy," he says.

"Just you an' me?"

"Six of us. It's crowded but we are out of the weather. We built shelters from driftwood before the government made these. Your Pa's blanket is at the back, so you go in first."

As I crawl in through the small entrance I notice the smell. Even with the wind blowing through it lingers. It isn't quite as bad as having a goat in the house like back in Rincon. Even though I am tired – I don't think I've ever walked so far before – I'm not allowed to sleep. Zak insists I eat first. We have to shift for ourselves, he says. The overseers don't feed us and the water comes from a big cistern which collects the rain.

Despite my tiredness, I don't sleep much that first night. It is too bewildering. I miss my mother and sisters. I even miss the goat. Around me, five men snore and my place by the small square opening at the back lets in the weather. Added to that is the sound of waves slamming against rocks.

Zak prods me out before the sun has fully risen. I learn the work fast and hate it. All day, except when a ship is moored, I wade ankle deep in brine, breaking the crust that forms over it, my skin wrinkling. Or I stand on the pan, scraping up the salt, shovelling it into wheelbarrows for others to move to the growing heaps that already stand twice my height. The three hours when the sun is highest is a time to eat or catch fish. What we are given weekly isn't enough. And I am always thirsty. At night some men tell tales of those who have escaped, gone over the water to South America. They are our myths.

~~~

Cameron was unable to get back to his examination of the mummy for two days. His tenure at the university meant that a certain proportion of his time had to be given over to lectures and tutorials; the mummification and worship of ancestors in Northern Peru was a distraction. As soon as he could, he set about reading the notebook Theakstone had left with the box. The pages were yellowed and the ink fading. It was also written in Dutch. Cameron translated it with a dictionary at hand. He'd quickly discovered that not all the spellings in it were conventional and where the ink was least distinct he had to guess the word written from context and what was left of the faint marks.

His concentration was such that the ping of incoming mail startled him. It was from the forensic department. The preservative for the mummy had been salt. Nothing else. There were still crystals of the substance in the folds of skin. The X-ray scan showed no particular cause of death. All organs were intact, though shrivelled by the drying process. It would take much longer for DNA results to indicate the part of the world he originated from.

Cameron had known of bodies pickled in brine, the most famous being Nelson after his death at Trafalgar. It was a practical way of stopping decomposition. Using salt itself was wasteful as it had always been a precious commodity. He wondered if the salt crystals could have formed by evaporation of a brine solution, though to mummify a body that way it would need to be opened up to allow the liquid contact with the interior of the body cavity. It wasn't done in this case. He emailed back a few questions then asked when his corpse could be returned.

He rubbed his eyes. Tomorrow, he would finish translating the notebook.

~~~

I try. I can't do this for much longer. The heat scores its way into the skin. It is always windy and blown salt cuts and stings. Even weaving hats from grass doesn't keep the sun from scorching us, drying all the sweat the moment it forms. We may have a three-hour break when the sun is highest but sitting in the shade of our huts doesn't slake our thirsts. The glare from the pans is painful to the eyes as we work. They are always dry and red. If the overseer doesn't think we are working hard enough he slashes at our legs with his starter. Salt in the cuts makes them weep, develop into sores.

From the start Zak guides me, working alongside, taking more than his share of the loads. Then he dies. Just drops dead in the heat. He isn't the first. The walk back to Rincon the following Sunday is unhappy. I have to tell my best friend his Pa is gone.

I am already struggling but so are the crops my mother tends. The weather is too dry and even the aloe suffers. Maize withers away to nothing. The goat stops giving milk. The home plot can't grow enough to feed Ma and the littler ones so there is no extra for me. Our owner decides to sell my sisters. I like to hope they are going as servants on Curacao or Aruba. I don't know. I hear the other wives saying Pa won't be here much longer, he is just another mouth. I don't know what they do with slaves that can't work. There are always rumours. All I know is that a month later when I arrive home he isn't there and Ma isn't saying anything.

In the camps at the salt pans I'm always hearing the tales of slaves who have escaped. How can they know when no-one comes back? The only way off is by boat and there is nothing at the pans to build one.

There are boats. They come ashore from the ships that moor outside the reefs. The painted obelisks by each group of huts tell them the way through the coral shelf, and the colour tells them the grade of salt they are collecting. Trestles with planks are laid from shore to boat and the women walk along them carrying the baskets on their heads, tipping them into the bottom until it is full. As I load baskets ready to be lifted onto their heads, I watch. Is it possible to go, ride the boat back to the ship and escape? It seems unlikely. The sailors have muskets and cutlasses and keep good watch.

~~~

Cameron frowned at the notes he had translated. Most of the contents of the notebook seemed to relate to items that either no longer existed or that Theakstone had kept. Not only was Cameron not going to ask the man about them but he felt disinclined to pass on the information he discovered. Theakstone had an attitude which suggested that all other history departments were inferior to his own – even the more popular ones like Egyptology. Populist, he called them. It didn't usually bother Cameron – he just didn't go out of his way to be helpful. Neither did anyone else. He read through the notes again, then smiled. There was more here than he had thought. The previous owner of the artefacts had, when he began his collecting, kept a diary of where and when he'd acquired his finds. It wasn't as random as he had first thought.

The unnamed collector specialised in items from the colonial past of the Netherlands even though he'd never left Europe. The contents of the box, which included the mummy, were from the Caribbean. That gave him a frisson of excitement. The Dutch Antilles had included Bonaire as a centre of the salt trade. Some of the things referred to in the notebook pre-dated the European arrival in the area but others related to the period prior to the abolition of slavery.

He read: ... *my source tells me that the poor child whose body lies in the box was a refugee from the ABC islands, probably the salt island. He presumes the boy died on the voyage and his body was preserved until landfall in Amsterdam. Why he was not given shriven burial at sea I do not know, as that was the usual practice. The scrimshaw in the lot I purchased with the box has a date of 1852 inscribed on it. This might not be relevant ...*

~~~

I do not know how to swim, yet that is the only way to get to a ship. Fish swim. We do not leave the island so why should we? But at the height of the sun many of us sit in the surf as the best way to cool our bodies. While the others are just sitting in the water I splash about, thinking I might learn enough to carry me to one of the ships when they anchor overnight. I tell myself that I will get to a ship or sink in the going. A watery death seems preferable to continued toil in the salt pans. What I will do if I reach a ship I do not know. I will take that as it comes.

By the time I am desperate enough to try I've worked it so my blanket is nearest the entrance to our hut. All the others are snoring their exhaustion when I slip out into the night. I am not strong – though the work weakens our limbs I am resolved.

The sky is clear and the half-moon gives me enough light to see the anchored schooner.

The first few yards over the reef are rough. I can't see the coral beneath me and it tears at me. Once in deeper water it is easier but I've not reckoned on the chill. I've taken a plank of wood with me. I push it ahead, kicking and splashing, hoping that any aboard will take me for a shark or dolphin. It is only when I am in the open water that I think that being eaten by a fish is a possibility.

The ship appeared so close from the shore but every wave seems to push it further away. At times I rest on my wood having swallowed mouthfuls of the sea. More than once I consider allowing the tide to take me back. I am so tired, sleeping forever in the waves seems like bliss. Then I think that if I can get to South America I can get enough to buy my mother her freedom. It spurs me.

I don't realise that I've reached the ship until I crash into it. Either I'd fallen asleep and kicked towards it without knowing, or the tide has swung it round. From here it is huge. The wooden hull curves above me. I have no idea how I will actually get aboard. I am out of energy and cold. No-one on deck will be able to see me in the dark but that is of no help. Come dawn, they'll see my body floating alongside and if there is life in it I'll be thrown back ashore and whipped for my daring. I haven't planned more than getting here.

I pull myself slowly along the hull, scraping my hands on the barnacles encrusting the plating, fearing it will push me under every time it rolls. By the time I reach the anchor chain I am near ready to give up and sink under the surface.

Each link is a huge, fat oval of iron twisting on itself. It is slimy with weed but is my only way aboard. The hole it disappears through looks small from where I am – I only hope I don t get stuck wriggling through, or find I can't get in that way. It does occur to me that they might start raising the anchor and crush me.

As I begin to climb my feet slip on the smooth metal that shifts in time with the rocking of the ship. My fear is that a sudden movement will trap a foot or hand in the links. Already tired I soon begin to feel the pain of stretching and hauling myself up, one link at a time. My muscles are afire, my shoulders feel as if they are being wrenched from their sockets. And it is further than I thought. Always there is the fear that someone would see me.

I reach one last time and encounter wood. Struggling through the tiny hatch I lie on the deck, cold and wet, hurting all over and scared of discovery. Exhaustion takes my senses away before I can summon the energy to find a hiding place.

~~~

Cameron made sure that he wouldn't be disturbed by going into his office on a Saturday morning when there were few staff around. Other faculty members knew he obtained good results from his studies – he never told them how.

He wore linen gloves as he tenderly took the mummy from the box and laid it on the silk sheet spread on the floor. He didn't know why he could do this, perhaps a combination of Scottish and African heritage, but dead things spoke to him, told him their story. Later, he would try to find the evidence to verify their tale.

Cameron peeled off the gloves and knelt beside the shrivelled corpse. He placed one hand on the skull, skin to skin, and closed his eyes. It was rarely words he heard but he did see images.

The place he was in was dark. It rocked like a ship anchored near to shore. He smelled dampness and brine.

~~~

They find me. Instead of throwing me overboard they laugh. I am tossed into the hold. The landing is soft but the crystals of salt cling to my skin. The hatch is slammed shut and I lie in the dark. I am tired, and hungry and thirsty. More than anything, I am thirsty. I can almost feel the salt sucking the water from my body.

I hadn't imagined that dying could be so painful.

~~~

Cameron heard the whispers as the salt shifted under his – Ezra's – body, moving away from the unexpected weight. Grains slid over him, wrapping him in a white blanket. Crystals moved into every orifice, seeking out, sucking out every drop of moisture.

The whispers in his mind said, *Mijn naam is Ezra. Het zout is killing me.*

BENEATH NAMIBIAN SANDS

Elaine Harrison stared down into the huge, conical depression in the sand. Back in Koichas, she had seen the images that the drone had taken two days before but the reality was so different. The pictures didn't evoke the feeling of awe that the actuality did.

She crouched at the lip and picked up a handful of dry sand, allowing it to trickle through her fingers. With no cohesion the individual grains caught the light as they tumbled down the slope. The depression, maybe thirty feet deep, had sides with a perfect slope that allowed the grains to flow unopposed to the bottom. Wind had rounded the lip but for some reason hadn't filled up the space. Except for the wreckage of the Land Rover on its side near the centre, wheels towards her, she could almost imagine a giant hand smoothing the sides daily.

"What could have made a depression like this?" she asked.

"Kettle holes." Bayron Ndume stood beside her, also looking down into the hollow. Despite his name, he was as English as she was, his grandfather having emigrated to Birmingham long ago.

"What are they?"

Bayron was a landscape geologist whereas she was only an administrator for a charity providing clean water for villages in the south of the country. She still wasn't sure why she had volunteered for this search party in the middle of the Namibian desert.

"You know how glaciers move?"

"Vaguely."

"Imagine a boulder caught in a depression in the rock. As the ice moves over it, instead of going with it, it is trapped and turns on the spot, digging its way deeper. It makes a hole."

"I'm guessing it's a bit more complicated than that, and this isn't ice."

"Think of a stick being spun round in the wind. It could dig out a hole like this."

"Could it really?"

Bayron shrugged. "I haven't thought of a better explanation yet."

"But that is Laury's Land Rover down there?" Laury Bishop was Elaine's boss. She didn't particularly like him but when he'd disappeared she felt obliged to volunteer, but not expecting to be allowed to go. Her experience of desert conditions was limited.

"It is very likely," Bayron said.

The vehicle had sand piled around it and, except for its inverted position, didn't look too damaged. It was the kind of accident that people walk away from.

"We need to go down and look," she said. There had been three in the Land Rover, Laury, the driver, and a local guide. Well, local in that he lived on the outskirts of the desert. Not much could survive in areas this arid.

She rose to her feet and made to step forward but Bayron put a hand on her shoulder. "Not without ropes," he said.

"Why? I could get down there easily."

"But not back up. Have you tried walking up the face of a sand dune?"

"No, but—"

"Trust me. It is very difficult. Naheela will want to radio back that we have located the Land Rover. Then we go look."

"Okay." She didn't like waiting. It was frustrating. Elaine wanted to get this over and head back to base as soon as possible. The endless sand dunes stretching in all directions were oppressive. And she hadn't appreciated the strength of the sun would be magnified by reflection from the loose sand.

She and Bayron walked back to the two vehicles and trailer that made up the search party. There were four others. Naheela, the other woman on the team, handed her a bottle of water. "Is it them?" she asked.

"Bayron thinks so. He says we should use ropes to go down to investigate."

"Right. I'll report in to Koichas." She waved to the three men who were standing nearby – two were armed rangers, the third doubling as cook and mechanic. "Jamie, Matias, harnesses and ropes for three, Isra line up the Jeep as an anchor."

Elaine felt useless as the rest of the team hurried to follow Naheela's instructions. She felt she had only been included in the party because Laury was her boss. "I'm going down," she announced.

Naheela merely nodded; no trying to persuade her not to. "Follow Bayron's instructions," she said.

Bayron checked her harness was secure before allowing Elaine over the lip into the depression. Isra had the engine of the Jeep idling and was watching them in the wing-mirrors while Naheela stood on the shady side, keeping well back. Matias tested the security of her rope. She had watched Jamie begin the descent. He had gone over the lip backwards, his rifle slung over his back, as if he were abseiling a rock face. Elaine had seen the way that the sand had shifted beneath his feet, the dry grains sliding over one another. There was no cohesion.

Elaine copied his movements. The moment her feet

touched the slope she felt the sand move. The least pressure of her boots set up mini-avalanches. Unstable, she fell to her knees. If the rope hadn't been there she would have tumbled, unable to stop herself. This descent wasn't going to be as easy as she had thought. Her hand touched the surface. It was already burning hot, and the day had barely started.

She concentrated on moving her feet slowly until she backed up against the fallen Land Rover. With relief she unclipped the rope but reached to hold onto the superstructure of the vehicle. She yelped, her skin blistering on the hot metal. Bayron, who arrived moments after her, passed her a pair of cotton gloves.

Jamie had already worked his way round to the other side where there was a little shade and was scooping sand away.

"There's no-one here," he said. "Either they were thrown clear or they climbed out."

Not any other alternative, Elaine thought. The Afrikaner did sometimes state the obvious. "Is it Laury's Land Rover?" she asked.

Jamie reached in and yanked a backpack from under one seat. He opened the zip-pocket at the front. "Yep," he said. "Laurence Bishop's passport."

She looked up the slope, which from this angle was daunting. She couldn't see their vehicles, and Matias, standing on the lip, appeared small and far away shimmering in the heat. The sky overhead was an untarnished silver-blue. The surrounding dunes were invisible.

"Could they have climbed out?" she asked.

"Try it," Bayron said.

She did. Every step she took was like climbing on ice. Her weight made the grains move frictionlessly over each other and she slipped back. There was nothing to hold on to, except the rope. If they had climbed out they would be wandering aimlessly in the desert with no shelter and little water. They'd be lucky to be found. She understood why the advice was to stay with the vehicle if you break down. It was a larger target to spot.

"Does the radio work?" she asked. She knew that Laury always carried a phone and that out here there would be no signal.

"No. It was smashed in the fall."

"Then, where are they?" Laury might not be desert savvy but he'd travelled with two men who were.

"Hey!" Jamie called. He'd found a slender pole from somewhere – the radio aerial she realised – and was stabbing it into the sand, presumably looking for bodies. He had moved downslope a little to where it levelled out. From the top of the crater, the Land Rover had obscured the shape of the ground at the centre of the depression. Here the sand formed a circular hump. Bayron's kettle stone, perhaps, or like the peak you get at the moment a raindrop hits water. A meteorite strike? Would that make this kind of pattern in sand? She'd've asked Bayron but he was standing next to Jamie, looking down. She trudged over to them, the soft surface dragging at her boots.

"There's a hollow under here," Jamie said, pushing the pole into the centre of the mound. He waggled it and the sand began to cave in, leaving a hole surrounded by a foot-high barrier of sand like a much larger version of the ants' nests she'd seen around the village.

"They could have taken shelter down there," Elaine said.

"If it's big enough," Bayron said.

Jamie poked around a bit more. "It goes deep."

It started slowly, but the rush of sand rapidly increased

to a torrent exposing a huge cavity beneath.

"We need to go and look," Elaine said.

"Not without torches. Stay here." Bayron trudged back round the other side of the Land Rover and clipped on one of the ropes. After a few hand signals. Elaine saw him being hauled up the slope. Presumably he'd tell Naheela what they'd found as well as gathering the equipment they'd need to explore below. Elaine sat in the meagre shade to wait. Jamie passed her a bottle of warm water. She hadn't thought to bring any with her. At least she had her hat, even though she thought it made her look ridiculous.

"Why are you here?" Jamie asked.

Before she could answer, he pointed at the ground. "Not in Namibia. Here. You could have stayed back in Koichas."

She sighed and took another sip of water. "I'd never have heard the last of it if I hadn't gone looking for him – personally."

"I thought he was your boss."

"He is. My best friend, his wife, persuaded him to give me the job."

"So you could keep an eye on him?"

"I guess. She's heard about charity workers getting involved with local women."

Jamie laughed. "And she thinks Laury Bishop would do that? The only woman he'd be interested in would be one bringing him an exotic insect."

"That's what I told her." Elaine shrugged. "She's a bit of a worrier."

A scuffle of sand heralded Bayron's return. He was carrying more ropes and a rucksack. He pulled out three torches. "Naheela's told Matias to set up a tent and sort lunch while we explore. We are to be back by noon, whatever. Then we'll try to pull the Land Rover out of the hole."

"Can't afford to leave good equipment lying around," Jamie muttered.

"No, we can't," Bayron said sharply, "But we can use it as an anchor for our ropes."

"Do we really need them?" Elaine asked.

She felt a little stupid when he said, "How will we get out again?"

She wasn't an explorer and her skills didn't extend to caving so she watched as the two men set up the rope, dangling the ends into the cavity and checking they were secure. She worried that their weight would cause the vehicle to roll or slide but said nothing. She'd made enough stupid comments as it was. When they were satisfied Jamie went in first. She knew he had reached the bottom when the rope went slack.

"What can you see?" Bayron asked.

"It's a cavity, about eight feet deep and six across. The walls are disintegrating. Piles of sand all over the place."

"No sign of Bishop's team?"

"Nothing obvious."

"I want to go in," Elaine said.

"There's not much room."

"Doesn't matter." She was already clipping the rope to the harness.

"I'll lower you," Bayron said.

Jamie was right. With the two of them in the space it was claustrophobic. It wasn't just the size of the cavern but the smell. She'd once been in a loft housing a colony of bats. It reminded her of that, only drier, like the space was filled with the essence of moth wings. It was choking, tickling at her throat. She put a hand over her mouth and nose to keep out the most of it. Jamie hadn't mentioned the bones. The floor was littered with them. Most were small and crunched underfoot. She picked up the tiny skull of something that might have belonged to a lizard. There were bigger ones, too. She spotted something that resembled the tooth of an elephant. She knew that some small herds survived on the fringes of the desert. One falling into the pit wouldn't have been able to climb out. Some of the bones had what appeared to be skin clinging to them.

Elaine noted the falls of sand that obscured a lot of the bones but in one place there was a lump that didn't fit. She hadn't seen it when she first entered as Jamie had been standing in front of it.

"What's this?" she said, touching it. She'd expected it to be hard, a boulder perhaps. She still had the kettle-hole image that Bayron had described for her. The surface gave. It was more like touching the skin of a balloon that was beginning to lose air. She rubbed her fingers together. It was slightly sticky, enough for sand grains to adhere to it. She tried pinching the surface between her fingers. It was resilient. She pulled and sticky strands came away. They had the texture of spider's web or a fungal mat.

Jamie, seeing what she was doing said, "Hey, I want to collect some of that."

"Why? It's gross."

"Aren't you curious about it?"

"Not really. I want to find out what happened to Laury."

"Well, he's not here."

Something glinted in the torch light. She pulled the object out from under a pile of sand. She held it up in triumph. "He was. He never goes anywhere without this."

Jamie glanced at the iPhone she was holding. His voice

had a tightness when he said, "You go up top and report that to Naheela. Bayron and I will search this pit more thoroughly."

She was about to protest when Bayron called down having obviously been listening to the conversation. "We've had more experience with this kind of thing."

"What kind of thing? You think he's dead, don't you?"

"That's not what I'm saying."

"You're thinking it, though."

"We know the desert, Elaine."

She laughed. "You don't. You spent most of your life in Birmingham."

"That's true but I have been working in Namibia for three years longer than you."

"And I'm just a useless passenger in this search!" She was angry but she also knew that he was right. Until yesterday she hadn't gone further than the outskirts of Koichas. She knew nothing about the desert or its dangers. "Pull me up then. I might be more help helping Matias cook."

By the time she got up to the level plateau, she was exhausted. Not just from the climb, which was assisted by Isra hauling on the rope, but from the heat and the frustration of feeling useless. He picked up his rifle when she was safely at the top. Naheela was in the Jeep acting as the anchor. She gestured for Elaine to join her in the cab. As she opened the door a blast of cool air greeted her. She hadn't realised that the vehicle had air conditioning.

Naheela handed her water and said, "I'm going to keep nagging you to drink more. You are not acclimatised to these conditions."

Elaine climbed in and accepted the water. Naheela was right but it niggled. It was another indication that she was the passenger and not a functional part of the team.

"Tell me what you found." Naheela said.

"Laury's iPhone. He was in that cavern."

"Describe everything."

Elaine wondered if she was being humoured or distracted but did the best she could. "Where could they have gone?" she asked.

"Jamie and Bayron will be checking to see if there are any tunnels leading off the cavity. Many desert animals burrow to keep out of the heat."

"Mighty big rabbit," Elaine muttered.

Naheela laughed. "Rivers run underground as well. I wasn't aware of any in this area but there is so much unexplored out here."

"Even with modern technology?"

"That only scratches the surface, literally. When the others come up I'll update Koichas and decide the next move. Okay?"

Elaine sighed. "All I really want to know is what happened to Laury."

"We all do. We can learn from mishaps. Then they might not happen to anyone else."

"You call the Land Rover falling into that pit, a mishap."

"Until we find out otherwise, that's what it will be classed as."

~~~

Over lunch it was decided that Bayron and Isra would attempt to drag Laury's Land Rover out of the pit while Jamie collected the bones from the cavity. They would give him an idea of what animals ventured this far out into the desert. Naheela planned to fly the drone over the area and see if there were any more similar pits. Knowing how they formed would be useful information.

"And what do I do?" Elaine asked, hoping Naheela

would let her help with the survey. Computers was something she could do.

"You can help me," Jamie said. "We won't be able to carry all the finds back so photographing the bones will be the best bet."

"All of them. They are horribly mixed up and we crushed a lot."

"Just the skulls. They'll give a good indication of species and give us a count."

She wasn't too happy going back underground with the pervasive musty smell but she was tired of feeling like a spare part. "Just show me how you want it done," she said.

Elaine found the situation frustrating. The space was really too small for Jamie to root around sifting the bones to find skulls and for her to set them out on the squared cloth he'd laid out on the floor. The fungus ball thing didn't help. It took up space and she was sure the funny smell was coming from it. She had to keep looking behind her at it. Her imagination told her it was flexing, almost as if it were breathing.

"We've got an ape skull here," Jamie said plonking the object in front of her. It made a change from all the tiny lizards. As she set it in position the jaw fell away. Elaine stared at it for a moment then said, "Er, Jamie. This is human."

"It can't be,"

"It's got fillings."

Jamie snatched up the skull, then whirled round.

"Where did you fund it?" Elaine asked.

"In the sand, beside the cocoon thing."

"Are there other bones?"

"It won't be Laury. It's too clean. A skull can't get this clean in a week."

"It's someone. He'll need a proper burial."

"This could have been here for years."

Elaine snatched the skull from his hands. "You look for more bones. I'll take this up to Naheela."

"Now look here…"

Elaine didn't listen. She clipped her harness onto the climbing rope and tugged twice, sharply, the signal to be hauled up.

Bayron helped her over the lip, "Given up already?" he asked.

"We've found something," she said, refusing to be baited. She crossed to where Naheela was sitting under the canvas shelter with her laptop open before her, and placed the skull beside her. "We found this."

Naheela glanced away from her screen for a moment. Then closed the lid. "This was in that cavity?"

"That's what I said."

Naheela looked up at Bayron. "Forget the Land Rover. Go and join Jamie. If there are human remains down there they must be collected."

~~~

By dusk there was an argument in the camp. Naheela made it clear that they were going to be spending a second night in the desert. It was too late to set out for Koichas and travelling in the dark was not a good idea. It made sense to camp where they were and reassess in the morning, especially as Naheela's drone had located another pit. It was old, half-filled with blown sand. Bayron was keen to examine this one more closely to work out how it had formed while Jamie wanted to examine the other one, hoping to find more animal bones. Elaine wanted to go back.

The excavations had revealed three human bodies in the cavern, all of them covered with a layer of desiccated skin. The other items found with them confirmed that it was Laury's party. Elaine felt it more important to take the bodies back for a decent burial and to inform families properly. At this moment she wasn't quite equating the skeletons with someone she'd known. That would come later. Currently, she felt the reason for them being out here was over. The others seemed to have lost the focus for their purpose. If they couldn't travel at night, her vote was to return at first light.

Naheela wanted an explanation. Yes, there had been an accident; yes, the men had probably sheltered in the cavern and without much in the way of food and water, they might have died – temperatures here dropped well below zero at night. That didn't explain the state of the bodies. Jamie said they had not been there long enough to be mummified and it was too cool underground for that. There were beetles who would clean bones that precisely and perhaps leave the skin but there wasn't any sign of them and it would take weeks to do.

"Why did Laury say he was coming out this way?" Naheela asked.

"He'd heard that big insects had been seen in this direction."

"Laury would go chasing any insect," Jamie muttered.

Elaine glared at him and continued, "He was worried that there might be a swarm of locusts forming. He'd want to stop them before they reached the crops. The growing season's been too short for several years."

"It's much too dry for devourers to emerge. There's been no rain here," Jamie said.

Elaine didn't know the exact life cycle of locusts but she could understand why Laury was concerned. "How do you know?" she said.

Naheela raised her hands. "Isra, you haven't said

anything. What is your advice?"

Unlike the rest of them, he was the only one who had actually lived all his life in Namibia. He largely kept his opinions to himself. Now he said, "We should leave. There are no small devourers, only big ones."

"What about you, Matias?" she asked.

The cook/mechanic shrugged. "I go where I am told."

"In that case," Naheela said, "I will decide in the morning. But I do want a watch kept. Jamie, sort that out."

~~~

The two women shared the tent while the men bedded down in the Jeeps. Elaine had been surprised by the thickness of the sleeping bags on the first night out but as the temperature plummeted after sunset she appreciated the warmth.

She lay awake listening to Naheela's gentle snore. In her mind she could see that leather-clad skull. She didn't consider herself particularly squeamish but the image of swarms of small, flesh devouring beetles was unsettling. In the end, pressure in her bladder forced her up. She remembered to put boots on before she left the tent – Jamie had pointed out scorpion tracks the previous night – grabbed a torch and stepped out into darkness. Above, the sky was a deep black punctuated by pinpricks of stars. The moon was nearing full, casting weak shadows across the sand.

She saw a gleam of torchlight beside the silhouette of one of the Jeeps. Ducking behind the other one she quickly relieved herself – the wet patch would quickly dry and she didn't want to venture any closer to the pit. She walked over to where she had seen the light, making sufficient noise to alert whoever was on watch. Matias was leaning against the hood of the Jeep. He looked around as she approached.

"Couldn't sleep," she said.

"And I would like to," he said.

"I don't see why there has to be a watch. There can't be anything dangerous bigger than a scorpion."

"There are Isra's big devourers."

She laughed. "Do you believe that?"

Matias shrugged. "Who knows what is out here? Do you hear that?"

"What?"

He held up a hand. "Listen."

She stood quietly. All she could hear was the shifting of sand grains and a popping sound as the metal in the vehicles cooled.

"Nothing."

"That is what is creepy."

Elaine shivered. Even if she couldn't sleep, it would be warmer in the tent. "Goodnight," she said.

As she bent down to unzip the tent flap Elaine though she heard a rustling. It reminded her of moth wings against a light, only more expansive, a host of moths. She could see nothing and assumed it must be one of the men moving around. Before she ducked inside, she glanced up at the moon. A shadow flitted across its surface. Her imagination, or one of those birds she'd heard about that made daily trips to the sea to soak their feathers before carrying the water back to their chicks hidden from predators in the desert. She tried not to picture flocks of insects pouring from the ground and she crawled back into her sleeping bag. Myriads of beetles was bad enough.

When she awoke at dawn Naheela was already about. As Elaine emerged she saw her in earnest conversation with Bayron and Isra.

"Did you see Jamie when you went out last night?" Naheela asked as she approached.

"No. Only Matias. Why?"

"He's disappeared."

"Where would he go?"

"Devoured," Isra said.

"Don't be ridiculous," Naheela told him. "And he's got too much desert craft to go wandering off."

"Maybe he fell in the pit," Elaine said.

Naheela scowled. "Get some breakfast from Matias. I'll do a drone sweep of the area. Bayron, Isra – see about getting that Land Rover up. I'm not wasting time waiting for him to show up."

"Bossy," Bayron mouthed as he moved away.

Matias had boiled water for tea and handed Elaine a mug and a meat-filled flatbread. She didn't ask what the meat was. Some things were better not to know.

"Has Jamie gone off scouting the other pit?" she asked.

Matias shrugged. "He relieved me after midnight. Not seen him since."

"Will this change our plans? Will we go straight back to Koichas?"

"Naheela won't want to abandon him out here."

"Isra's a tracker. Perhaps he can find where he went."

"He thinks a devourer got him. I heard him tell Bayron."

"Isn't that superstition?" Elaine said. "There's nothing out here that big."

"Something got Laury Bishop."

A shiver went up her spine and she had the image of millions of tiny beetles ganging up on them. "I don't want to think about that," she said, taking her breakfast and heading over to the edge of the pit.

Bayron had already attached ropes to the fallen Land Rover and Isra was steadily hauling the vehicle up the slope. Naheela came to watch.

Elaine asked, "Any sign of Jamie?"

"There are faint trails around the older pit but nothing specific. Koichas says we have to go check it out."

"We're not going back?"

"We have until mid-afternoon. Get your hat and sunscreen. We are heading out as soon as this vehicle is up."

It wasn't far to the next pit. Bayron reckoned Jamie could have easily walked it and since he wanted to look there, Naheela agreed to start the search there. Once Laury's Land Rover was raised she sent Bayron and Isra to take a look. Elaine asked to go too. She didn't see any point just hanging around while Matias tried to fix the wreck – it was either that or tow it back. Naheela wanted to stay near the radio in case further instructions came through.

~~~

Elaine stared down into the bowl. The sides were shallower, the hollow partly filled with blown sand which looked darker as if it had been exposed to the air for longer. If she wanted a word to describe it, she would have said *tarnished*. She thought that if she fell into this one she would be able to climb out.

"Why should this depression be different from the other one?" she asked.

Bayron pointed to the dune behind them. "Wind direction. To get the effect the wind has to be in the right direction."

"You still think it's like a kettle hole?"

"Why not?"

"Then what about the hole at the bottom?"

"Underground water course."

"That just happened to dump all those bones there?"

"Devourers," Isra said.

"Huh." Bayron didn't argue but he clearly didn't believe in them.

"We need to go down and look," Elaine said.

"Jamie's not here and no there's no sign that he was."

"I'm going down." Elaine stepped over the lip and allowed the sand to carry her to the bottom. Behind her she heard Bayron mutter "Stupid". It didn't worry her. She was sure she could get out, which meant Jamie could if he'd fallen in.

Reaching the bottom she stood and turned. Bayron had fixed the rope to the Jeep's bumper and was about to come after her. She took a step backwards and squealed as the ground gave way beneath her.

She landed with a thump on her back, all the air knocked out of her. As she stared at the circle of sky above the light was suddenly occluded. Her heart rate increased rapidly until she realised it was Bayron.

"You okay," he asked.

"Yeah." Her voice came out croakily. "Winded."

He swung down into the cavity, sweeping a torch beam around. She glimpsed bones and smelt the same mustiness. "Just like the other one," she said.

"Not quite," Bayron stepped across to a dark sand-encrusted shape. "This is hollow," he said.

It was like that soft, fungal mass they'd found in the other one but ripped open. There was nothing inside. Elaine touched the substance. Like the other, the outside was sticky to the touch, inside it felt like smooth plastic.

"It's like a cocoon," Bayron said.

"You think something was inside it?"

"If there was, it's gone now."

Elaine shivered, thinking about the shadow she'd seen over the moon. She turned slowly, hoping nothing was lurking in the darkness at the edges of the cavity. "Let's go," she said. "Jamie isn't here."

Bayron had to help her out of the cavity and it wasn't as easy scaling the sides of the pit as she had imagined. She wouldn't admit it but she was glad of the rope. Reaching the top, she heard the radio crackle to life. She followed Bayron over to the Jeep in time to hear Naheela say, "We've found Jamie." She sounded grim.

"We return," Isra said.

~~~

When Matias had brushed the sand out of the working parts of the Land Rover's engine, he'd put some of their spare fuel in the tank and taken it on a short drive to check that it was working properly. He'd found Jamie's body on the other side of a dune.

"How do you know it's Jamie?" Elaine asked. She suppressed the squeamishness she felt at the sight of the leathery skeleton. The skin was stretched over the bones as if all the soft tissues had been sucked out. Nothing, she thought, could work that fast.

"The remnants of his clothes, and his rifle," Naheela said.

It wasn't just the mummified condition of the remains that was disturbing. Several of his bones were broken as if he had fallen from a height, and his skull was crushed, the inside of which was empty.

"We go back to Koichas now," Naheela said. "Matias, can you drive the Land Rover?"

~~~

Bayron led with Isra taking shotgun. Naheela drove the second Jeep with the trailer while Matias coaxed the Land Rover in their wake. Elaine rode with Naheela as they threaded their way back through the dunes. In the dips there were still traces of the tyre tracks they had made on the way out. Mostly they relied on Isra's local knowledge and a compass. Naheela's GPS signal was fleeting and unreliable.

Elaine tried to relax, not easy when the vehicle was being jolted about by the uneven surface. Naheela hung back from the lead vehicle, keeping out of the dust kicked up by the wheels. Isra dropped out of sight over the crest of a dune. Naheela gunned the engine to give them the momentum to take them over the top. The nose tipped steeply downwards and Naheela slammed on the brakes. The Jeep skidded sideways, the trailer jack-knifing and throwing Elaine heavily against the dashboard, and slid to a halt. Before them was a deep pit.

Shakily, Naheela said, "That wasn't there before."

"Where's Isra?" Elaine said.

Naheela scrambled out of the vehicle and stood on the lip. "Down there."

The other Jeep lay on its side near the bottom of the depression in a very similar position to how they had found Laury's Land Rover. Elaine couldn't see any movement. She cupped her hands to her mouth and shouted, "Are you okay?"

No response.

"Get the rope from the trailer," Naheela said. "I'm going down there."

"Is that a good idea? We should wait for Matias."

"Just do it."

Naheela attached the rope to the front bumper and started walking backwards down the slope. Elaine watched, switching her attention between Naheela and the fallen vehicle. Naheela was almost at the Jeep when Elaine noticed a movement in the sand. First, she thought, hoped, it was Bayron or Isra. It was more at the centre, sand trickling down like water into a plughole. Before she could call out, something erupted from below. Elaine screamed. Naheela looked up, sensed the movement and half-turned. Huge serrated pincers fastened around her waist and pulled her under.

Elaine covered her face with her hands, her breathing fast and erratic, seeing the image of the massive head and jaws imprinted on the insides of her eyelids.

"What is it? Where are the others?" Matias grasped her wrist roughly, pulling her hand away from her eyes. She hadn't heard his vehicle arrive. She pointed.

"What happened?"

"It … it ate her."

"What did?"

"A thing, a monster. Isra's devourer." She could hear the hysteria in her voice but couldn't do anything about it. She began to cry.

When she finally calmed down, Matias handed her a mug of hot sweet tea. He'd unloaded the stove from the trailer and heated the water. She took it and stared at the surface of the liquid. She was tempted to laugh but bit back the sound. If she started she'd never stop. It seemed such an English thing to do, to make tea, and incongruous in the situation.

"What do we do now?" she asked, her voice a whisper in case she disturbed the creature.

"I don't know. Go back to Koichas."

"We won't get back there before dark. Not now."

"We can try. Unhitch the trailer and just drive. Fast as we dare."

Elaine nodded and sipped at the tea, hearing Matias working in the background.

"Ready to go?" he asked.

She stood up then and brushed the sand off her clothes, trying to make the motions ordinary. She looked up as a shadow skimmed over her. Rising over the dune was a huge winged creature. She screamed as it fastened its jaws around Matias's head. She took an involuntary step backwards, overbalanced and began to slide. She scrabbled at the surface in a futile effort to slow her descent.

Below, she heard the susurration of dry sand grains running over each other.

A Tournament of Shadows

1914

We watched them march away,
The young men of our village
Fifteen, sixteen, seventeen,
They lied about their age,
Eager to join the conflict to
Show the Hun the ways of civilised men,
To send the enemy back behind their borders
Brothers, fathers, lovers in their bright new uniforms
Ill-prepared and barely trained.
We'll be back by Christmas they cried
As they vanished beyond sight
Into the muddy fields of France.
The stories filtered back,
Of cold and rain and carnage,
Of screams and stinks and shrapnel
Like killing children, a postcard said.
They died on both sides, in thousands
And they called them heroes.

But what of us left at home.
Wives, daughters, sweethearts.
No-one talks of our pain, the loss,
The headless families.
They told us in school
That only one in ten would ever marry
A nation of spinsters
To raise the next generation
We fed the nation and the next war

We sacrificed our happiness
In the fields of Passchendaele,
The unremembered heroes.

1944

Conscripts, leaving love behind,
Exchanging pitchfork for rifle,
Spanner for tank, home for fear
In darkness, landing on a beach
Of shifting sands, Pinned down by fire,
The hidden sniper, the strafing Fokker
Take their toll of comrades barely met
In hasty training. Hundreds washed by the rising tide,
Led by officers tired from years of attrition,
Plotting strategies out-thought by others like themselves
Until Jack and Stripes together find the higher ground.
Villagers welcome with flowers
The liberators so long awaited,
With their lipsticks and stockings and tins of bully beef.
They praised a job well done, sent them home
And called them heroes.

But what of us left behind.
We took their places
In factories, and farmed the land
Kept the railways running
Delivered aircraft from Birmingham to Kent
And kept their families fed and clothed.
But returning they took back their jobs
Revoked our independence,
Consigned us to kitchen and hearth

And forgot that without us
There would be no heroes.

2004

Recruits, volunteers, they swagger
In their bright camouflage,
The latest guns, grenades and tanks
At their disposal. And overhead Lynx, Puma, Tornado
Give them covering friendly fire.
Cocooned in armoured Jeeps
Following the dust wakes of comrades
Embarked upon the same adventure.
They joined to learn a trade, to look good in a uniform
Impress their mates and pull the girls.
Death was not part of the deal,
The roadside bomb, the shattered limbs
They return home inside a wooden box.
Every one paraded, remembered
Reminding us, war is not a game.
The media calls them heroes.

But what of those they left behind.
The wives, parents, sweethearts
Who watched them fly away,
Who were told, see you in six months.
We hide our tears, our fear
And let our soldiers go, not knowing
If they would return, ever waiting
The knock on the door, primed to tell the children,
Daddy's never coming home.
Who are the real heroes?

Now

Somewhere the world is on fire
With the rages of conflict
We remember the dead, the dying,
But what of the damaged, the mutilated
The ones whose scars do not show
And the ones they return to
Those who take the parts war spits out
And love what remains.
Ask, who are the real heroes?

STORY CREDITS

"Angelo's Bar" first published in *Phantoms of Venice* edited by David A Sutton, Shadow Publishing 2001

"A Mother's Love" first published as "Lucy" in *Birmingham Noir* edited by Joel Lane and Steve Bishop, Tindal Street Press, 2002

"A Tournament of Shadows" – previously unpublished

"Away With the Fairies" – previously unpublished

"Beneath Namibian Sands" first published in *The Alchemy Press Book of Horrors 2* edited by Peter Coleborn and Jan Edwards, Alchemy Press 2020

"Birmingham Mythic" first published in the *Fantasycon Programme Book* 2015

"Chan Chan" first published in *Mummy Knows Best* edited by Theresa Derwin, Terror Tree Books 2017

"Closed Borders" first published in *Killer Bees From Outer Space* edited by Theresa Derwin, KnightWatch Press 2015
"Demon Hunter" first published in *Warrior Fantastic* edited by Martin H Greenberg and John Helfers, Daw 2000

"Devolution" – previously unpublished

"Dreaming of Dragons" first published in *Salvo 5* edited by Lynn M Cochrane 1998

"In The Tunnels" first published in *Beneath the Ground* edited by Joel Lane, Alchemy Press 2002 (reprinted in *Mammoth Book of Best New Horror 15* edited by Stephen Jones 2004)

"Leaving" runner-up in the Winchester Writer's Conference competition 1999: published in *Salvo 6* edited by Lynn M Cochrane and Jan Edwards 2001

"Life Marks" first published in *Salvo 7* edited by Lynn M Cochrane and Jan Edwards 2003 (runner-up in Birmingham Libraries Competition 2002)

"Lost" first published in *Something Remains* edited by Peter Coleborn and Pauline E Dungate

"Night Hunter" first published in *The Alchemy Press Book of Pulp Heroes 2* edited by Mike Chinn, Alchemy Press 2013

"Nina" first published in *Villains Victorious* edited by Martin H Greenberg and John Helfers, Daw 2001

"Plant Hunter" first published in *Under the Rose* edited by Dave Hutchinson, Norilana Books 2009

"Red Slave"– previously unpublished

"Skylight" – previously unpublished

"The Magic Roundabout" first published in *Merlin* edited by Martin H Greenberg, Daw, 1999

"The Scent of Elder Flowers" first published in *Narrow Houses* edited by Peter Crowther, Warner Books 1992

"Underrated" – previously unpublished

SHORT STORY COLLECTIONS PUBLISHED BY THE ALCHEMY PRESS

Compromising the Truth – Bryn Fortey

Dead Water – David Sutton

Evocations – James Brogen

Give Me These Moments Back – Mike Chinn

Leinster Gardens – Jan Edwards

Let Your Hinged Jaw Do the Talking – Tom Johnstone

Monsters – Paul Kane

Music From the Fifth Planet – Anne Nicholls

Music in the Bone – Marion Pitman

Nick Nightmare Investigates – Adrian Cole

Rumours of the Marvellous – Peter Atkins

Talking to Strangers – Tina Rath

Tell No Lies – John Grant

Where the Bodies Are Buried – Kim Newman